VITAL SINS

T.J. McCandless

HB

HELLA BOOKS

New York London Sydney

ISBN 978-0-9863957-3-4

Rev. 1.15

Acknowledgments

C.C., for her unfailing percipience

M.B.B., for his encouragement

J.D.M., for showing the way

"You must trust and believe in people, or life becomes impossible."

—*Anton Chekhov*

VITAL SINS

1

Andie McInnes knew she was in trouble. Bad trouble. And it was her own fault. She knew better than to walk alone after dark in certain areas of town. Yet there she was, on West Burnside bordering Portland's Chinatown district, with a trio of rowdy guys following her like wolves after a rabbit. She recognized one of them, the one with the shaved head, as a former classmate at David Douglas High. A total asshole.

"Hey, baby," he called out. "Don't be unfriendly. We just wanna talk to you a minute."

Yeah, right.

She walked faster, trying to widen the half-block distance between her and her pursuers. Maybe they'd lose interest.

But no, they kept pace with her, hooting and catcalling. One had a falsetto laugh that sounded like a hyena.

The .22 automatic in her shoulder bag gave her no comfort. The little pistol belonged to her friend Kayla. "I want you to take it," Kayla had said. "Just in case. And if you have to use it, just point it and squeeze the trigger." Andie put it in her bag to humor her, but guns scared her and always had.

She had an escape plan that didn't involve a gun: running. Her pursuers kept their distance, so she maintained walking speed. But once she was around the corner and out of sight on 4th Avenue, she took off like an Olympic sprinter. New Pumas gave her plenty of traction.

She made it a block and a half before they caught her.

They shoved her into an unpaved alleyway between the Shanghai Trading Company and Chinatown Kites & Fireworks, both closed. Then two of the creeps held her down while Shaved Head unfastened her jeans—cursing when he jammed the zipper's brass tag under his thumbnail—and slid them down over her hips, followed by her underwear. She lay there exposed, humiliated, and shaking.

"Holy Christ," one of them said, pointing. "That's a wang. We got us a friggin' he-she here." His hyena laugh echoed off the alley's brick walls.

The one holding her left arm let go as if she were a leper. "Jesus. To think I wanted to tap *that*. I'm gonna puke."

"Tell you what . . ." Shaved Head picked up a discarded two-foot length of rebar laying on the ground. "This is one he-she who won't be tricking anybody else." He smacked the rebar into his palm and grinned at his buddies.

She saw it on his face, a grim determination to bludgeon her to death. Needles of icy fear lacerated every pore. Her breath came in rapid, shallow gulps. The two who'd pinned her down moved away, giving Shaved Head plenty of room.

"C'mon, do it," Hyena Laugh said, his eyes glittering.

The gun . . . in the bag.

She snaked her hand into her shoulder bag and burrowed under clothes and makeup until her fingers closed around the little pistol. It felt cold in her hand.

Shaved Head started toward her, iron club raised to strike.

Just point it and squeeze the trigger.

She would just scare him and make a break for it, run for her life, literally. She pointed the gun over his head, closed her eyes, and squeezed the trigger. It made a loud pop that sounded like the firecrackers her dad used to set off on the Fourth of July.

Shaved Head dropped the rebar and clutched the left side of his neck, just under the corner of his jaw. He staggered back and sat heavily on the ground. Blood seeped out between his fingers. A lot of it.

His two cohorts looked from their fallen leader to her and then to the gun pointed at them. They backed away, toward the street. When they reached the sidewalk they ran.

She stuffed the gun back in the bag, pulled up her jeans, and scrambled to her feet.

Shaved Head's eyes were fixed on a spot on the ground about six feet in front of him. It took her a moment to realize he wasn't seeing much of anything. His hand, the one that had clutched at his neck, had fallen to his lap. The hand was covered with blood, as was his neck and half his chest. The wound on his neck pulsed wetly one last time and then was still.

She doubled over and vomited so violently it felt like the lining of her throat was being expelled along with the burrito she'd eaten earlier.

Shaved Head didn't seem to notice.

It was irony, cubed. She valued life—all life. So much so, she'd been thinking seriously about becoming a vegetarian. The thought of animals being hunted or slaughtered for their meat sickened her. She couldn't hurt a fly, literally. When she caught insects inside the house she released them outside unharmed. But now, without meaning to, she had killed a human being.

A despairing cry escaped her throat and merged with the approaching sirens.

2

Detective Sergeant Karen Wojanowski found fellow homicide detective Chuck Brown waiting for her outside the interview room. They exchanged nods.

"What's the story, Brownie?"

He gestured toward the one-way window. "Couldn't pull a thing out of her. I figured a woman might have more luck."

"Sometimes it works that way, sometimes not." Karen walked over to the window. A girl who looked to be in her late teens sat at the table. Tears had washed away most of her makeup, her blue eyes were rimmed with red, and her blond hair was a mess. She was probably pretty, although it was hard to tell. Karen opened the door.

"Hi, Andie. I'm Detective Wojanowski." Karen sat down across from her. "You've had better days, I'm sure."

Andie's chuckle had a bitter edge.

"Can I get you anything? Maybe a Coke?"

"Sure, thanks."

"Be right back." Karen made a quick trip to the break room next door and returned with a glass full of ice and a can of Coke from the vending machine. She set them in front of the girl and sat down again.

Andie poured Coke over the ice. "Am I under arrest?"

"No. We're just trying to find out what happened."

Andie looked down at the table.

"We've already heard Mr. Pfaff's and Mr. Burleson's side of the story. We'd like to hear yours."

Andie looked up. "What did they tell you?"

"They said you attacked them and shot their associate—" Karen consulted her notes. "Howard Hinshaw, age nineteen. They said you shot him in cold blood."

"*I* attacked *them*? That's a total lie!" The pitch of her voice rose as she unleashed a torrent of words: "They were following me, and I tried to run from them, but they caught me, and they pushed me into that alley, and they pulled down my pants, and they were going to rape me, and one of them was going to beat me to death with a rusty piece of rebar, and then I remembered I had the gun, and I meant to shoot over his head to scare him, but—"

Karen held up her hand. "Hold on." She checked to make sure the light on the handheld digital recorder indicated green. "Let's try it again. Calm down, take your time. Don't leave anything out, try to recall every little thing. The more detail, the better. Okay, now—from the beginning."

It took Andie about ten minutes to go through the incident. Calmly and articulately she told the story. And unlike the tale Pfaff and Burleson had cooked up between them, it was obviously the truth. However, she left out one significant detail. Like most who transition early, Andie blended so perfectly she couldn't be detected as trans. She probably never disclosed unless she had to. *Stealth*, they called it. Karen let it slide for the time being.

"I remember puking after I realized he wasn't alive. Then the police arrived and brought me here."

"I have a few questions. Let's start with the pistol you had with you. Where did you get it?"

"It belongs to a friend. Her boyfriend gave it to her. Look, I don't want to get her in trouble. She insisted I borrow it just in case, since I was on foot at night alone."

"Which brings me to my next question. Why were you walking by yourself in that area at night? It's a pretty rough part of Portland."

"I know, but I thought I could make it to the MAX station at Fifth and Couch. It was only five blocks away."

"From where?"

"From where I'd been staying on Ash. I . . . wore out my welcome there. I was going to take the bus to another friend's house. She said I could stay with her a few days."

"Where are your parents, Andie?"

"They were killed in an auto accident when I was fifteen. I've been on my own since then."

"Relatives?"

"An aunt in Baltimore. She's super religious. She didn't want to have anything to do with me."

"What about school?"

"I . . . dropped out in my sophomore year."

"And then eluded Children's Services for three years, until you turned eighteen. Where did you live?"

"I stayed with friends, mostly. Sofa-surfed."

Karen shifted gears. "Your three attackers were going to rape you. What made them decide to kill you instead?"

"You'll have to ask them."

Without the slightest doubt, Andie's being transgender played a major role in the confrontation. It was time to get down to business. "Why do you think Mr. Pfaff and Mr. Burleson referred to you as a 'crazy tranny'?"

Andie stiffened but said nothing.

"They pulled down your pants, you said. I have to ask—are you preoperative?"

After a slow five-count Andie nodded.

"And that's why Hinshaw was going to beat you to death?"

She nodded again.

It must have been a shock to the Neanderthals with rape on their minds. Their intended victim had beautiful hair and skin and delicate features. Everything about her was unmistakably female. Almost everything.

"I didn't mean to kill him. I swear to God I didn't."

A knock at the door. Karen switched off the recorder and pushed her chair back. "I believe you."

Lieutenant Lawrence Eichler was waiting out in the hall. "Kellenberger's on his way."

Karen snorted. "Does he know there won't be a photo op?"

"Let's try to get along with him, Woj."

"No worries, L.T.—I wouldn't dream of upsetting the D.A.'s wunderkind."

Eichler grunted and nodded toward the interview room. "I was upstairs while you were in there interviewing her. What's your read on how it went down?"

"Three skells shove her into an alley, planning to rape her, but it turns out she's preop trans. So they get pissed and decide to kill her instead, beat her to death with a piece of rebar. But she remembers she has a friend's gun with her and tries to scare the one with the rebar by shooting over his head. She accidentally hits him in the throat. The small-caliber slug does a number on his carotid and he bleeds out in a matter of seconds. His cohorts rabbit."

"Hate crime that broke bad for the perps."

"Thing is, even if she had meant to kill him, it's obviously a case of self-defense ."

"I wouldn't bet any money on it, Detective." Assistant D.A. Breton Kellenberger strode up to them, impeccably dressed in a pinstriped suit. "We're charging her with murder."

"You've got to be kidding," Karen said.

"I'm serious as a heart attack. Charge her, read her her rights, and book her."

"Murder? C'mon, Kellenberger, that's insane. She shot him in self-defense."

"Then she can plead not guilty at her arraignment and we'll let a jury decide." Kellenberger walked over to the one-way window and stared a minute. Then he turned away, shaking his head. "If I didn't know better," he said, "I'd swear that was a real girl."

Karen opened her mouth to object, but Eichler put his hand on her arm.

"Now that we're all on the same page," Kellenberger said, "I'll leave so you can do your job."

Karen watched him walk away, strutting as though for a fawning audience. She turned to Eichler. "It doesn't make sense, charging her with murder."

"It does if you understand that every move Kellenberger makes is calculated to advance his career. Word is, he's about to make a bid for the Republican nomination for the third district's House seat in Congress."

"I don't see how railroading this girl would benefit him one iota."

"Beats the hell out of me, Woj. Pfaff is the son of a county commissioner. Maybe that has something to do with it."

"Whatever his motive, charging her with murder is bat-shit crazy."

"Maybe a judge will agree and throw it out."

"We're going to miss you around here, L.T. When's your last day?"

"End of September. Two and a half months from now."

They stood watching the girl through the window as she sat at the table, her expression glum. She couldn't see them, of course. The window was one-way, mirrored on her side.

"I hate to leave Portland," Eichler said. "I'm taking the job in San Francisco for Bonnie. The doctors think it will be good for her to be near her family. If she feels better it'll be well worth it."

"San Francisco is a beautiful city. SFPD's lucky to get you." But the thought of Eichler leaving was a cold stone in her gut. He was the best boss she'd ever had.

He turned away from the window shaking his head. "A damn shame."

"Amen. Now I have to go in there and tell her how bad she's jammed up." Karen took one more look at her through the window. Andie was slumped over the table, her head resting on crossed arms. Maybe she was taking a quick nap.

It was going to be the rudest of awakenings, learning she was under arrest for murder and facing twenty-five to life in Salem. An all-male penitentiary.

Karen took a deep breath and reached for the doorknob.

3

Representative Dale Boonstra of Slapout, Oklahoma tossed the issue of *Vanity Fair* in a desk drawer when the phone on his desk buzzed.

"Sir," his office manager said, "a call for you from a Mr. Kellenberger on line two."

"Thanks, Ronette." He punched a button. "Hope you got good news for me, Bret. I could surely use some."

"I don't think you'll be disappointed, Dale. The little matter you were concerned about has been taken care of."

"So the pervert who shot and killed my nephew is behind bars?"

"Not only behind bars, but charged with murder. Twenty-five to life if found guilty."

"And the chances of a guilty verdict?"

"Seeing as how I'll be handling the prosecution personally, I'd say they're pretty damn good."

"Son, that's the best news I've heard all month."

"You can count on me, Dale."

"I know that, I know that. And in return, I'm loaning you the best goddamn campaign manager in the business. That's the way it works here in D.C.—you scratch my back, I scratch yours."

"Dale, I foresee a long, mutually beneficial relationship."

"I'm banking on it, son. You take care now, hear?"

Boonstra replaced the handset in the cradle and removed a cigar from the humidor on his desk. Using special scissors, he expertly trimmed the end and reached for his gold lighter, a gift from a lobbyist. He lit the cigar with great care, puffing gently while rotating it near the flame—but not in it—until the tip had an even burn. Then he leaned back in his chair and blew smoke rings at the ceiling.

The matter of his nephew's killing seemed to be getting resolved quickly. That would give some comfort to his sister Joylene. Her boy Howard always was a shiftless bastard. But he was family, and you don't mess with family. More to the point, you don't *kill* family.

The cigar had burned down to the paper band when the office door opened and Ennis Judson, his chief of staff, walked in. Boonstra stubbed out the cigar in a cut-crystal ashtray. Then he got the *Vanity Fair* from the drawer and tossed it on the desktop. "You seen this?"

Judson curled his lip. "Unfortunately. As if that wasn't bad enough, now that . . . *that* has a goddamn TV show."

"Surely that's not disapproval I detect?"

"Makes me want to vomit."

"You need to open your mind a little, old son. Otherwise, the sophisticated, enlightened, highly advanced liberals will accuse you of being a close-minded bigot."

"Let 'em."

Boonstra pointed at the magazine cover. "Hey, you got to admit, that's a looker right there."

Judson's face was a study in consternation.

Boonstra slapped his knee and guffawed. Ennis was a good ol' boy, but he sure-damn got shortchanged in the sense-of-humor department. Leaning back, fingers interlaced over his belly, Boonstra smiled at his chief of staff. "Ennis, gestating in my noggin is one hell of an idea. S'pose you set yourself down in that chair right there, and I'll tell you all about it."

4

The holding cell smelled of disinfectant and stale sweat. Institutional green windowless walls and slate-gray vinyl floor contributed to her bleak mood. Harsh florescent lights overhead gave everything, including Caucasian skin, a bluish starkness. Along one wall, a narrow bed. In the back corner, two stainless steel amenities: a small basin and a toilet with a built-in seat. No privacy screen. Occupants surrendered their modesty along with their freedom. But the cell had one saving grace: She had it all to herself.

At the Multnomah County Court Holding Facility, prisoners usually shared a dorm with a dozen others. But the jailers certainly couldn't risk putting her in with males, not the way she looked. Nor could they stick her in a dorm with women; it would violate regulations, since she wasn't *legally* female yet. And so she got a cell all to herself, and that was just fine with her.

Her introduction to jail began the night before, when they processed her into the system on the Assembly Line From Hell. They took her mug shot, fingerprinted her, itemized the contents of her bag, counted her cash (fifty-one dollars and nineteen cents), interviewed her about her medical condition (healthy) and criminal record (none), and issued her a set of jailhouse blues and a pair of flip-flops. All her possessions, including her clothes, were impounded.

Her debasement would have been complete if they'd given her men's blues to wear. But the large woman in charge of dispensing clothing looked at her and didn't hesitate; she reached for women's blues, tailored to accommodate a female body shape. She silently blessed the woman for sparing her that indignity.

She hadn't been in the facility for a full day yet, but already she knew the worst part about jail wasn't the constant noise, the scary people, or even the confinement. The worst part was the waiting. Jail was a Greyhound bus terminal with locked exits. An impersonal waiting room where everything happened on someone else's schedule, where the desires of the individual were irrelevant, and where order and routine were sacrosanct.

Ordinarily, she'd write an observation like that in her journal, but they'd taken it from her along with her other belongings. Recording her thoughts in the journal was one of the few things that gave her a sense of continuity. When she couldn't make regular entries her life felt fragmented and chaotic. If she asked them, maybe they would allow her to have the journal and something to write with. She had plenty to write about, that was for damn sure.

She sat cross-legged on the bed and reviewed the events of the past sixteen hours, concluding with her court hearing two hours earlier. She'd gone to the hearing expecting to be given a chance to explain to the judge what had happened, to make him understand that the shooting was an accident, and then of course he would let her go scot-free.

Talk about naive.

She got a dose of reality right off the bat. First, the judge made her speak her deadname (ugh), and then he asked her if she had the means to retain counsel.

"No," she told him. "I've got about fifty bucks to my name."

"You are entitled to representation nevertheless. Counsel will be provided for you at the state's expense." The judge turned to a man standing to Andie's right. "Mr. Kellenberger, does the State have a recommendation as to bail?"

"We do, Your Honor," Kellenberger said. "The defendant is a flight risk and a danger to the community, and therefore the State recommends that she—*he* be held without bail."

Living on the street had taught her how to size up people instantly, essential for self-preservation. She inspected Kellenberger. Early thirties, she guessed, and well groomed, like the rich guys she saw downtown in the financial district. Everything about him—his charcoal pinstriped suit, burgundy tie, expensive shoes, and salon haircut—added up to narcissistic asshole. Leaning on the wrong pronoun when he'd asked the judge to deny bail confirmed the asshole part.

The judge pulled on his mustache a moment and then said, "I'm going to set bail at five hundred thousand."

Might as well have been five hundred million.

Lying on the cot in her cell after the hearing—hanging on, trying not to lose it—her head felt like a 50,000-volt transformer. To quiet her thoughts she used a technique she'd learned from a book about Zen meditation: Visualize a serene lake with a surface as smooth as glass. Easy to describe, hard to do. It required one to stop thinking; thoughts created disturbances in the water. Minor concerns made ripples. More serious worries made waves. The lake's surface at present resembled a storm at sea.

After meditating for half an hour she managed to calm the waters but, try as she might, she couldn't maintain a glass-like surface for more than a few seconds at a time. A singular persistent thought formed waves that lapped at the shore. She waited. When the thought finally surfaced, she realized she was dead wrong about the endless waiting being the worst part about jail.

Because in all the confusion she'd completely forgotten about her 'mones. When she was processed into the jail system, they'd confiscated everything in her possession. That included the hormones she took every morning without fail. She'd been on them five years—since she was thirteen—and had never missed a single dose. Until now. She had to get them back as soon as possible.

The consequences of hormone deprivation were rapid and disastrous. Estrogen and progesterone were necessary to maintain normal female levels. But by far the most critical medication, spironolactone, was not a hormone, but a hormone blocker. Until she had surgery her body would continue to produce testosterone. If not blocked, the powerful male hormone would masculinize her. She would have body and facial hair growth, increased muscular development, and lowering of her voice. Most of the changes were irreversible. A fate worse than death—at least, to her.

She sprang to her feet and ran to the small window in the door. The corridor was empty. But it was a busy facility, so it wasn't long before a uniformed holding officer walked past her door.

"Excuse me," she called through the window.

The officer halted and turned around. His gut stretched the uniform's shirt snare-drum tight. "What do you need?"

"Please, I need to see a doctor right away."

"You're sick?"

"I—yes, I'm sick. I'm real sick." It wasn't far from the truth. The thought of what would happen to her if she didn't get at least some spiro in her system made her want to hurl.

The officer sighed. "Okay, sit tight for a minute or two." He set off down the corridor.

Five minutes later she heard the cell door being unlocked. The door swung open and Big Gut said, "All right, come with me."

He escorted her up the corridor, down a flight of stairs, and along another corridor until they came to a door marked "INFIRMARY." Big Gut opened the door and ushered her in.

The doctor's wispy gray hair and lined face put him on the far side of middle age. He motioned for her to sit down and peered at her through the middle lens of his trifocals. "What seems to be the problem?"

"They took away my medications last night when I got here. I really need them."

"What medications do you take?"

"Estrace, two milligrams. Provera, two-point-five milli-grams. Spironolactone, one hundred milligrams. That's what I take daily."

He raised his eyebrows. "Why are you on hormone replacement therapy at your age? And why do you take spironolactone?"

Andie dug her nails into her palms. She hated disclosing her trans status to people who didn't know. Their reaction was always the same: initial surprise, then curious inspection. No way around it, though—she had to tell the doctor. "I'm transgender. Preoperative."

"You don't say," he said (*initial surprise, check*), and then he looked her up and down (*curious inspection, check*). "Are you under a doctor's care at this time?"

"No, I . . . not now."

"Then you don't have prescriptions for the medications?"

"I bought them from a friend."

"Undocumented prescription medications are confiscated as illegal drugs. I have no authority to override that policy. "

"Could you write the necessary prescriptions for me?"

He smiled sadly, shaking his head. "I'm afraid Multnomah County Corrections would take a dim view of that."

She swallowed. A shred of hope remained. "I can get along for a while without the hormones, but if I don't take the spironolactone, I'll have physical changes I absolutely do not want. Couldn't you at least get me the spiro?"

"I'm sorry," he said. "It's out of my hands."

And that was that.

She only dimly remembered trudging back to her cell, escorted by a different holding officer. She didn't know how long she'd been sitting cross-legged on the bed, her back against the wall, staring at the opposite wall. Hours or min-utes, it didn't matter.

Nothing mattered anymore.

5

The story made the front page of the City/Region section of *The Oregonian*, above the fold:

Transgender Woman Arrested For Murder

PORTLAND – Andrea McInnes, 18, of Portland was arrested and charged with murder Thursday in connection with the shooting death of Portland resident Howard Hinshaw, 19, on July 14.

Assistant District Attorney Bret Kellenberger said Hinshaw and two friends, Norman Pfaff, 20, and Gary Burleson, 19, both of Gresham, were walking west on Burnside around 10 p.m. when McInnes accosted them and forced them into an alley at gunpoint, whereupon McInnes shot and killed Hinshaw. Pfaff and Burleson fled and called 911. When police arrived, they found Hinshaw dead from a single gunshot wound to his throat. McInnes was taken into custody for questioning and formally placed under arrest later Thursday.

In an initial hearing Friday, McInnes' bail was set at $500,000. Arraignment is set for July 21.

McInnes, who is transgender, has no previous arrest record and no permanent address. A public defender has been assigned to her.

Karen set the paper aside and reached for her phone and punched in Sarah Soong's number.

It rang three times before Sarah answered. After they exchanged pleasantries, Karen asked her, "Did you happen to see the article in today's *Oregonian* about a young trans girl arrested for murder?"

"No. I haven't had a chance to read the paper yet. I'm not looking forward to it now. Hate reading depressing articles."

"I had the sorry task of arresting that girl, at the behest of Assistant D.A. Kellenberger. She's only eighteen."

"She killed someone? What were the circumstances?"

"Well," Karen said, "according to Andie—that's her name —three guys were going to rape her, but they discovered she was preop. So they were going to kill her instead, beat her to death with a piece of rebar. But they didn't know she had a borrowed pistol with her. She tried to shoot over the head of one of the attackers, the one with the rebar, to scare him, and then she was going to run like hell. Unfortunately, her aim was a bit off, and she shot him in the neck instead. Hit the carotid, and he bled to death. So that's her side of the story."

"Let me guess—the accounts the two accomplices gave you differed from hers?"

"That's right. They claimed she jumped the three of them and shot their pal for no reason. They said she threatened to kill them as well, but they ran away before she could."

"Her story sounds more convincing."

"No question. It's a classic case of self defense. Nevertheless, Kellenberger charged her with first-degree murder. She's being held on a half-million-dollar bond. No family or friends to put up bail. She's being railroaded, big time. If she's found guilty, she will do twenty-five to life in the men's penitentiary in Salem."

"God. What are the chances of a not guilty verdict?"

"Slim. They assigned her a public defender, a real yo-yo. Keeps using the wrong pronouns."

"Oh no. Really?"

"And as if she didn't have enough trouble, they took away her hormones, because she didn't have prescriptions for them. She's more upset about that than anything else."

"I imagine so."

"I wish you could meet this girl, Sare. She's been on her own since she was fifteen, living here and there, working odd jobs for cash. She's extremely bright and articulate. Spends all her free time in the library. You would never know she dropped out of high school in tenth grade."

Sarah was quiet for a slow five-count, and then she said, "I trust your instincts, Karen. I'll talk to the director and see if we can give this girl some help."

"Thanks, Sare. I was hoping you'd say that."

6

Andie lay on the narrow bed, trying to get into a dog-eared paperback of Leon Uris' *Topaz* a holding officer had given her, when the door to her cell opened. It was Big Gut, the officer who'd escorted her to the doctor earlier.

"Let's go, blondie" he said. "Your bail's been posted."

It must be an administrative error, a mix-up of some kind. Certainly no one she knew could scrape together $5000, let alone $50,000, the fee a bail bondsman would charge for a $500,000 bond. She shrugged and went with Big Gut. At least it would be a break in the soul-crushing monotony.

Her escort led her through various corridors until they came to the area where she'd been processed into jail the night before. Mistake or not, they went through the motions of processing her release, including giving her back her jeans, top, underwear, shoes, and socks. She gladly shucked the jailhouse blues and dressed in her own clothes.

Except they weren't all her own clothes. The jeans and underwear were new and had Nordstrom tags attached. They were both size 6, her size. As for style, close enough. She came out way ahead on the trade, no question. Not just set free— set free wearing new clothes. *Booyah!*

If it was a snafu, she wasn't about to point it out to them. She'd hit the pavement running and never look back. *Gone with the wind.*

A holding officer directed her to an anteroom. A black man in a dark suit and thick horn-rimmed glasses rose to his feet when she walked in. He was maybe thirty, medium height, slim. She'd never seen him before. Whatever his reason for bailing her out, she wasn't about to object.

"Miss McInnes?"

"Yes. Who are you?"

He produced a small case, covered in black leather, that opened with a touch. It contained business cards. He removed one and handed it to her.

LONGCYPHER, CANNADY & MOORE
Attorneys
(555) 903-5768

Elias J. Ritter

"You bailed me out of jail. Why?"

"I'll fill you in once we're out of here. Do the new clothes fit okay?"

"Yes, but what happened to my old clothes?"

"The clothes you were wearing when you were arrested are evidence."

That stopped her cold.

"Ready to leave?"

She nodded. Anything to get away from there.

He escorted her out of the building, to a lot where a white Range Rover SUV was parked. He opened the door for her and she climbed in.

When they were underway she asked him, "Where are we going?"

"My instructions are to take you to the Transcend Foundation."

"And what is the Transcend Foundation?"

"My client and your benefactor. They posted bond to bail you out."

"Why?"

"You can ask them. We'll be there shortly."

She pawed through her shoulder bag, taking inventory. Money, makeup, photos, journal, clothes—all there. No gun, not that she'd expected to see it. But she had hoped to find her hormones among the contents. Wishful thinking. Her first order of business, even before finding a place to crash for the night, was scoring enough to get by until she could replace the nearly full vials she'd lost.

The vehicle slowed and turned into a private driveway. They stopped before a heavy iron gate with gray brick pillars on each side. Andie noted video cameras atop each pillar. The gate opened inward and they proceeded through.

The asphalt driveway wound through well-tended landscaping, emerging within sight of what looked much like a community college campus, with buildings of metal, glass, and polished granite.

So this was the Transcend Foundation.

They pulled up in front of a tall building's entrance. An Asian woman in a white coat, the kind doctors wear, was standing outside the glass doors.

"This is as far as I go, Miss McInnes" Ritter said. "But I'll be back. I'm going to be representing you in your upcoming trial. We have lots of preparation to do."

So he was her attorney for real. Yet more generosity from the mysterious Transcend Foundation. What did they expect from her in return? No such thing as a free lunch, as they say.

She stepped out and closed the door behind her. With a final nod from Ritter, the vehicle pulled away, leaving her standing there on the concrete.

"Hi, Andie." The woman in the white coat stuck out out her hand. "I'm Dr. Soong."

Andie shook her hand. "You work here?" She indicated the buildings and campus with a sweeping gesture.

"I'm the medical director. Welcome to the Transcend Foundation. Shall we go inside?"

Andie accompanied her through the glass doors and then stopped, transfixed by a twelve-foot-tall iron sculpture of a swan, its wings spread, in the middle of the lobby. Thin strips of rainbow-hued metal feathered the great bird, somehow creating the impression of softness.

Dr. Soong touched Andie's elbow. "Let's drop by the cafeteria first and get us some refreshments."

The "cafeteria" was more like an upscale restaurant, with indirect lighting and elegant decor. It lacked only waiters.

Dr. Soong pointed to a table. "What can I get you? Are you hungry?"

"Just a Coke, please." She pulled out a chair and sat down.

"Coming right up." The doctor set off toward what looked to be the kitchen and returned a few minutes later with two Cokes with ice. "Here you go."

"Thanks." Andie took a drink of her Coke while looking at the doctor over the rim. She looked a little like Lucy Liu.

"I'm sure you have plenty of questions. Most people do. They'll all be answered in the orientation video. But let's get you settled in first."

Andie blinked. Orientation video? Settled in? What kind of setup *was* this? It'd be just her luck to have fallen into the clutches of a cult. Out of the frying pan . . .

"By the way, Mr. Ritter told me the jailers confiscated your hormones. So you've done without for twenty-four hours? No need to worry. That's not long enough to cause problems. All the same, after we're finished with our Cokes we'll head over to my office. I'll do a quick exam and requisition a blood workup. Our lab will have the results in an hour."

"Wait a minute—blood workup?"

"To check your hormone levels, among other things. If everything looks good I'll let you have some samples to tide you over until you can fill the prescriptions I'll write for you."

"That would be awesome." The epitome of awesome.

"After that little matter's taken care of I'll show you to your apartment. It's small, but it's comfortable and private."

Andie couldn't hold back any longer. "I don't understand. You get a lawyer for me, bail me out of jail, replace my 'mones, and now you give me a place to stay—so what's your angle? Why are you being so kind to me?"

The doctor laughed for the first time. "All our candidates ask that same question. They might phrase it differently, but it's essentially the same one—what's our motive?"

"Candidates? For what? And what *is* your motive?"

"Candidates for sponsorship by the foundation. The orientation video explains everything. You can watch it tomorrow."

Sponsorship—a code word masking something sinister? The Transcend Foundation's benevolence hadn't tranquilized her street-smart wariness. Kindness might well be part of their *modus operandi*—lull the "candidate" into dropping her guard, and later they'd serve her cyanide-laced Kool-Aid.

On the other hand, if Dr. Soong came through with the 'mones and spiro, it would go a long way toward allaying her suspicion. Not all the way, though. She'd reserve judgment until she had more info. And the orientation video supposedly answered all questions.

The doctor set her empty glass down. "Ready to go?"

"Sure." Andie popped a cube of ice into her mouth, slid her chair back, and stood. "Lead the way."

The doctor escorted her across a park-like courtyard to another building, inside of which was the doctor's office.

And there Dr. Soong made good on her promise.

Awesomeness.

7

Doodling on a yellow legal pad, Boonstra listened to the phone ring on the other end. He counted six rings and was about to hang up when an out-of-breath female voice answered. "Assistant District Attorney Kellenberger's office. May I help you?"

"Congressman Boonstra, returning Mr. Kellenberger's call." Placing it himself, since Ronette was still at lunch.

"One moment, Congressman."

Click. "Dale, thanks for calling back. I thought you'd want to know—McInnes is out on bail. As of last night."

"Didn't you tell me the judge set bail at half a mil?"

"Right. Somebody posted bond."

"Who?"

"Unknown, but a lawyer from Longcypher, Cannady, and Moore. Portland's top law firm, took delivery of McInnes."

"A lawyer like that would be expensive. That means some serious money's behind this. But it's well-insulated by lawyer-client confidentiality. We got us a big problem, Bret."

"I'm going to make an end-run around it. By coincidence, my secretary's sister works in his firm's accounting department. I'll have a friendly chat with her."

"My boy, that kind of thinking will take you far in D.C."

"I'll check back in with you soon as I know something."

"You do that, son. Take care now, hear?"

The phone buzzed ten seconds later. He snatched it up. "Yes?"

"Sir," his office manager said, "your sister's on line one."

"Thanks, Ronette."

He punched the button. "Joylene?"

"Dale, I wanted to tell you again how much I appreciate you personally seeing to it that the ... *thing* that murdered my poor Howie was brung to justice."

"Baby sister, it's still early in the process, but Howard will be avenged, trust me." No point in mentioning that McInnes was out on bail.

"I knew it was a mistake to let Howie go stay with his dad way the hell and gone out there in Oregon."

"Not your fault, Joylene. He was old enough to make his own decisions."

"You're right, but that doesn't make it any easier. I was just thinking ... you haven't been back to Slapout since I can't recall when. When you coming home again?"

"Got a load of work to attend to here in D.C., but I'll try to make it home for the Nye Festival in June."

"I'm going to hold you to it. Listen, you're probably busy, so I'll let you go. Love you."

"You, too, Sis." He replaced the phone in its cradle and took a fresh cigar from the humidor. After trimming and lighting it he sat back and blew a plume of smoke toward the phone. Hopefully, it would stay silent for a while, give him time to think.

Next time he talked to Kellenberger he needed to drive home the importance of getting that murder conviction. If her son's killer got off, Joylene would probably have a stroke.

He took a thoughtful puff. Someone had hired a high-powered lawyer and posted a sizable bond for the tranny's release. According to Kellenberger, McInnes had no money, no family, no permanent address, and had made no phone calls from the county jail.

Something mighty strange was going on.

8

Andie woke up with a start and blinked hard at the daylight streaming through the blinds. Her thin T-shirt was damp with sweat. All four walls of the holding cell had been moving inward, inch by inexorable inch. Like an Escher illusion, they defied geometry and the physics of solid matter, but they were going to crush her to death nevertheless.

Her new bedroom's walls were reassuringly motionless. She turned her head to look at the bedside clock. 11:47. She'd crashed for nearly ten hours. She had needed the sleep, after tossing and turning on the holding cell's hard, narrow bed night before last. Then she'd compounded the sleep deficit by staying up late last night writing in her journal, getting it all down while the memories were fresh. It took her two and a half hours to bring it current.

She yawned and tossed back the covers and swung her legs off the bed. She padded into the bathroom and caught her breath when she sat down on the icy toilet seat to pee. The bathroom had two sets of towels and washcloths, soap, and even hand lotion. They'd thought of everything.

Well, almost. She rummaged in her shoulder bag and found the travel-size bottles of shampoo and conditioner and a compact hairdryer. She opened the shower door. After adjusting the water temperature she peeled off her underwear and stepped into the warm spray, determined to scrub the jail off.

It was 12:30 by the time she finished drying her hair and taming a couple of unruly waves with a travel-size flat iron. A clean top from her bag, the new jeans, a light application of makeup and she was ready to rock, with no visible indication she'd spent a night and most of a day in the slam.

Dr. Soong expected her at one. At ten minutes before the hour she slipped her bag's strap over her shoulder. Hand on the doorknob, she paused to admire the bungalow again. It had everything a person would need: bedroom with queen-size bed, bathroom with tub and shower, kitchenette. Totally nice. Nicer than most of the places she'd stayed at. Nice enough to sucker the unwary into joining a sinister cult.

She closed the door behind her and set off for the doctor's office.

Two hours later she unlocked the apartment and tossed her bag on a chair. After a trip to the bathroom she got a ginger ale from the refrigerator, picked up the journal and a fine-point Pilot, her writing instrument of choice, and flopped down on the sofa.

Saturday, July 16, 2016 3:05 p.m.

I swear to God, I don't know how I get into these situations. I'm a freakin' trouble magnet. Like the time that guy offered me a job as an "executive assistant," but it turned out he was a straight-up pimp. Or the time Bristol's friend Lester "generously" let me stay in his place while he went back east, only it wasn't his place, and the actual owner was pissed off to find me there. Or the time . . .

I could go on, but what's the point?

So I met with Dr. Soong and watched the orientation video on a 65-inch flat-screen TV. It was slick. Big-time slick, like an Apple commercial.

According to the video, the Transcend Foundation's primary goal is to provide support to transgender individuals through a broad spectrum of support services: counseling, medical care, legal services, employment, living accommodations, education, and financial aid. And by the way, financial aid includes footing the bill for gender confirmation surgery.

Now, if I were going to devise a pitch to suck in trans people, that's exactly what I'd come up with.

So . . . after the video was over I hit Dr. Soong between the eyes with it, told her I thought the Transcend Foundation was a big-ass cult, like Scientology. She laughed and flat-out denied it, but of course she would deny it. I mean, she's not about to say, "Yeah, Andie, you clocked us."

One thing's for sure, they've got money up the wazoo. This setup, the land and buildings, not including the personnel to keep everything running, cost a fortune. And they put up half a million for my bond and hired an uptown lawyer to defend me against the murder charge.

They must really want me.

And for now I'm in their clutches—living under their roof, eating their food, even using their hormones. I'm waiting for the mask to come off. It will eventually, I'm sure of that.

Just remembered—my new bracelet. The sky fell in on me before I had a chance to write about it. Sterling silver. Retailed for two hundred, but I got it for ninety. Engraved on it is a Latin inscription: *Non credere*. It means trust no one.

I can dig it. It's a philosophy that kept me alive on the street, and it's going to help me survive this bizarro cult.

I hope.

9

Foundation Director Laura Gannon was on the phone when Sarah walked into her office. Gannon put her hand over the mouthpiece. "I'll just be a minute."

Sarah nodded and sat down in one of the wingbacks in front of the director's desk. The huge mahogany desk had seen over a century of service, during which time it collected a multitude of superficial dents, nicks, and scratches, giving it a battle-scarred nobility.

"Sounds like you have everything under control," Gannon said. "Keep me posted." She put the handset in its cradle and looked up at Sarah. "Mr. Ritter, with a progress report. He believes Kellenberger has a weak case against our newest guest. He's going to move for dismissal of charges before her arraignment hearing."

"That's encouraging."

"You've had a chance to spend some time with Andie. Still think she's a good candidate for us?"

Sarah smiled. "I think she's a *perfect* candidate."

"Brief me on her, if you would."

"She transitioned at age twelve. Her parents were very enlightened, she said. She started seventh grade as a girl. The parents died when she was fifteen. An aunt in Baltimore didn't want anything to do with her transgender niece, for religious reasons."

"How did her parents die?"

"Killed in a car wreck. She didn't want to go into foster care, so she dropped out of high school and struck out on her own. She was fifteen, trans, and on the street. Many girls in those circumstances fall into sex work. Not Andie. She found work cleaning houses, babysitting, walking dogs, mowing lawns—anything that paid her under the table in cash. Later on she bought a fake Social Security card, one with a female gender designation, and worked at fast food joints. If they wised up to the bogus card, she'd get another and get a new job."

"Can't fault her work ethic."

"She's a high school dropout, but bright and articulate. Reads a lot. Hemingway, Faulkner, Proust. When she wasn't working or sleeping she was at the public library. Keeps a daily journal, wants to be a writer."

"Maybe she can help me with my memoir. Go on."

"I haven't broken through her veneer yet. She's suspicious of our intentions. Keeps looking for a catch, certain there is one. The only explanation that makes sense to her is that we're a cult."

"A cult?" Gannon laughed at that.

"I know, right? But I can see how the foundation might seem like a cult to someone used to a dog-eat-dog life, where almost everyone has an ulterior motive."

"She'll come around. Give her time."

Sarah took out her phone, found the photo she'd snapped of Andie, and handed the phone to the other woman.

Gannon studied the photo. "The advantage of early transition," she said, wistfulness in her voice. "Andie McInnes, you don't know it yet, but you've won the damn lottery."

Hard to say what Andie's reaction would be, though.

Her phone displayed an alert: "Missed call from Karen Wojancwski." Sarah tapped *Call Back*. Two rings. "Hey, Karen. Missed your call."

"Thanks for calling back. First, how's Andie doing?"

"Better. She's glad to be out of jail. Prefers the apartment we gave her to a cell."

"No accounting for taste."

"And she thinks we have an ulterior motive."

"What could that be?"

"She suspects we're a cult, out to brainwash her. Or something equally nefarious. She didn't go into specifics. I told Gannon about it. She thought it was funny but sad."

"You can't really blame Andie. In her world everybody's got an angle. Suspicion kept her alive."

"That's what I told Gannon. So what's on your mind?"

"A little matter that concerns the Transcend Foundation. I thought you should be aware of it."

"Is this something Gannon should hear?"

"Judge for yourself. First, according to an unnamed source, Kellenberger spoke at a luncheon for local Republican power brokers. At said luncheon he boasted that he was going to 'rid the town of undesirables,' as he put it, and he pointed to his impending prosecution of Andie for murder as a step toward that goal."

"Rat bastard," Sarah said.

"Here's what you should be aware of—after lunch he was asking around about the Transcend Foundation. My source didn't think he had any luck, but the point is, he was asking. And that should concern you. Kellenberger is up to something. I'm worried that he could cause you folks a lot of trouble."

"Thanks, Karen. I'll relay it to Gannon right away. Let me know if you hear anything else, please."

"I will. In the meantime, stay on your toes."

After the call, Sarah nibbled at a cuticle. How did Kellenberger learn the Transcend Foundation even existed?

10

Thirty seconds into the call from Kellenberger, Boonstra stifled an impulse to crush the phone under his heel. "Goddamn it, Bret, you assured me this case would be a slam dunk. You're wimping out before it even goes to trial."

"Dale, I—"

"Did you or did you not tell me you were going to get a murder conviction?"

"I know, I know. But there have been ... developments. Did you see *The Rachel Maddow Show* today?"

"Not hardly. It'll be a cold day in hell before I watch that bitch. She made me out to be a racist last year."

"She had a segment that portrayed McInnes as a victim of discrimination. One of her guests was a lawyer from GLAAD, who said the murder charge is flaky."

"How the hell did this get on Maddow's radar? "

"No idea, but fifteen minutes after the show aired, my office received a request for information from the Southern Poverty Law Center."

"I had a run-in with those assholes, around the time Maddow did the hatchet job on me."

"The SPLC, GLAAD, and the liberal media will do their damnedest to whip up public sentiment against us, paint us as bullies picking on a poor little transgender girl who was only trying to protect herself from three thugs."

"Goddamn meddling polecats."

"We've got a more immediate concern. My boss asked me this morning if I was sure I could prove intent, necessary for a murder charge. He wouldn't ask if he didn't have grave doubts."

Boonstra's exasperated sigh sounded like the air brakes on a Mack truck. "So what's our next move?"

"I think it'd be prudent to offer her a plea deal. Second-degree manslaughter. She'll do six years, three months."

"Okay, I can live with that. But that has to be our line in the sand."

"Check. Nothing less than man two."

"Have you found out who's picking up the tab for her bail and that fancy lawyer?"

"Yes, for all the good it does. My inside gal at Longcypher, Cannady, and Moore said the retainer was paid with a check drawn on an account owned by the Transcend Foundation, a fairly new nonprofit located here in Portland. I asked around, but I couldn't find anyone who knew anything. I looked up their articles of incorporation, but all the officers listed are lawyers and accountants at Atlantic Trust in Boston. I made a phone call to them, but they wouldn't tell me squat, not that I expected them to. They won't discuss their clients without a signed court order, and no judge will accept curiosity as a compelling reason to sign one."

"Another veil of secrecy."

"An impenetrable one, I'm afraid. Impasse."

"Son, you just concentrate on getting a conviction. I'll see if I can pry something out of Atlantic Trust. We'll unmask the mysterious Transcend Foundation yet."

11

The law offices of Longcypher, Cannady & Moore held dominion over the top three floors of the venerable Talbot Building, a sacrarium built by Old Money, old as Portland itself. The Talbot's bottom three floors hosted two financial advisers, an investment bank, and a company that measured pension fund growth. The common denominator: money. The smell of it saturated the Talbot like grease in a diner.

Eli Ritter had a corner office on the fourth floor. Small and sparsely appointed compared to any of the partners' offices, it suited him just fine. With its century-old burnished wood paneling, thick carpet, and a view overlooking Pioneer Square, it made the cramped office he'd shared when he was a public defender seem primitive. But he hadn't left there for a better office. He'd done the public defender gig for four years. It was time to move on. When Douglas Longcypher invited him to join his firm, it didn't take much persuading.

But Longcypher's unilateral action caused resentment in the other partners, in particular Easton Cannady, who had huge control issues. As did his son-in-law, Vernon Trollinger, whose job it was to assign cases to the firm's lawyers. In the two and a half years Ritter had been with the firm, he'd had to contend with Trollinger's not-so-carefully concealed antipathy. The feeling had become mutual.

And now Trollinger wanted to see him. What about, Ritter had no idea, but the Troll's secretary had delivered the summons. He'd been sent for.

Climbing the stairs to the fifth floor, he recalled a line from *Donnie Brasco*, one of his favorite movies: "In our thing," Al Pacino's character said, "you get sent for, you go in alive, you come out dead." Not that he was worried about being whacked, but he had a gnawing sense of foreboding just the same. Outside Trollinger's office, he took a deep breath and opened the door.

Trollinger covered his phone's mouthpiece with a meaty paw when he walked in. "Be with you in a minute, Eli. Have a seat."

Instead, he wandered over to some photographs on the wall, most of them of Trollinger with various people who looked like they might be important. Three featured Trollinger in hunting regalia posing with his hapless kills—a deer, an elk, a moose—and looking quite pleased with himself. Trollinger, fearless hunter, Papa Hemingway's pudgy heir.

Trollinger hung up the phone and indicated a chair.

Ritter sat down and waited.

Trollinger sorted papers on his desk for over half a minute before he said, "Eli, I have a case for you."

"Already got a case."

"Yeah, I know. McInnes. But it wasn't assigned to you, it just fell into your lap by default. As it happens, Dillard wants it. And he has seniority."

"Dillard can find another case. This one's mine."

"Eli, be reasonable. He has more trial experience than you."

"Doesn't matter. It's my case and I'm going to win it."

Trollinger's fleshy face reddened. "Some words of advice. One, being a team player is just as important as winning cases. Two, making enemies in this firm will be to your great disadvantage, guaranteed."

Ritter got to his feet. "Thanks for the advice, Vernon."

Meeting room 103 was located on the far side of the five-acre campus, next to Administration. Andie took a shortcut through a causeway between two buildings and across a courtyard. After almost a week of exploring she knew the layout cold. She arrived at her destination five minutes early.

The lawyer had phoned her earlier, said he had something important to discuss with her. He'd sounded fairly upbeat. Was he going to tell her the judge had granted his motion for dismissal? Too much to hope for.

Still, her luck seemed to be on an upward slope, thanks to the Transcend Foundation. For a cult, it was going to incredible lengths to ensnare her.

"Andie." It was the lawyer, hailing her from thirty feet away. He transferred a leather attaché case to his other hand and glanced at his watch.

She nodded hello. "Mr. Ritter."

"Call me Eli." He opened the door for her. "Shall we?"

The meeting room wasn't what she'd expected. No long table surrounded by chairs. Instead, two velour sofas faced each other, with a coffee table between them. The walls were paneled, the floor carpeted. Several plants, and a large flat-screen TV recessed into one wall. They sat down across from each other. Eli set the attaché case on the coffee table, opened it, and removed a document.

"Well," he said, "it seems Mr. Kellenberger is offering you a deal, a plea bargain. He'll reduce the charge to second-degree manslaughter. Man two carries a mandatory minimum sentence of six years, three months."

She swallowed. "Six years is still a long time." Even six days in a men's prison sounded to her like an eternity.

"Not as long as twenty-five to life, which is what a murder conviction would get you. But there's more to the deal. In return for a guilty plea, instead of serving your sentence at Oregon State Penitentiary in Salem, Kellenberger will guarantee you'll serve it at Coffee Creek Correctional Facility in Wilsonville. It's a women's facility. No idea how he can swing it, but that's what he's offering."

"What do you think I should do?"

"Kellenberger is a devious character. I think he'll reduce the charge even if you reject the deal. Murder is a drastic overreach and he knows it. Coffee Creek is the actual deal. He's dangling it in front of you, hoping you'll jump at it to avoid going to a men's prison."

"If I turn down the deal, what are the chances of a not-guilty verdict?"

"In my opinion, excellent. This is as clear a case of self-defense as I've ever seen. I think the evidence will back that up. What's more, the prosecution's key witnesses, Pfaff and Burleson, are about as credible as a couple of crackheads on a street corner. I think the odds of a guilty verdict are slim. Nevertheless, you need to realize that it is a possibility."

"Mr. Ritter—Eli—do you think I should take the deal or turn it down?"

"That's a decision only you can make, Andie. If I advised you to reject the deal and you were found guilty, you would have a legitimate grievance."

Andie chewed on her lower lip. Taking the deal would be the safe choice, the lesser of two evils. She would do six years and three months, until she was almost twenty-five, but at least she'd be among other women. And safe.

Rejecting the plea deal would be a risk. If found guilty, she'd have to serve the sentence in a men's penitentiary, where she'd probably be raped repeatedly and abused. That is, if they didn't confine her to 24/7 solitary to prevent it, which would be its own kind of hell.

But she shouldn't have to choose between two evils.

Because, like Eli said, it was self-defense. She hadn't meant to kill Hinshaw; it was an accident. If she hadn't defended herself she would be dead, beaten to a bloody pulp.

And yet, one fact was undeniable—she was the only one carrying a gun that night. That alone seemed incriminating, as if she'd been looking for trouble.

Play it safe or roll the dice? The choice she made would affect the rest of her life.

Eli slipped the document back into his attaché case. "Don't feel like you have to make a decision right now. It's a doorway of no return, so think about it."

"I've decided," she said. "I'm going to reject the deal."

Back in her apartment, now and then she'd groan. More of a whimper, actually. She dropped into a chair and grabbed the journal.

Wednesday, July 20, 2016 4:15 p.m.

Oh God, have I made a horrible mistake, turning down that offer? I hadn't expected to have a blue-pill-or-red-pill choice foisted on me. If I'd thought about it a bit more I might not have chosen the blue pill. Eli even told me I didn't have to make an instant decision, but it went in one ear and out the other, never encountering brain matter. Now I have post-decision remorse. But what's done is done.

Call me Neo. I am the One.

If I'd gone for the offer and served six years in that women's prison, I'd be only 24 when I got out, still young. Well, fairly young. On the other hand, I'd be a convicted felon, unable to vote or own a firearm—not that I want anything more to do with firearms. The point is, a criminal record would hound me for the rest of my life, in all sorts of ways.

Eli said the chances of a not-guilty verdict were excellent, and he's from a primo law firm—best in the city, Dr. Soong said. So I guess I'll go with the flow and hope for the best at tomorrow's arraignment.

I just hope it doesn't bite me in the butt.

12

The arraignment hearing commenced at 9 a.m., when a portly bailiff with jowls like a bloodhound entered the courtroom from a side door and in a sonorous monotone said, "All rise. Court is now in session, the Honorable Judge Thomas Bondurant presiding. All those having business before this court draw nigh and they shall be heard."

A door behind the bench opened and a black-robed man with iron-gray hair and matching Teddy Roosevelt mustache took his place at the bench.

Eli touched her elbow. Her legs felt shaky as they stepped forward to stand in front of the judge. Kellenberger stood six feet to their right. Out of the corner of her eye Andie could see the spectators in the gallery behind them. Around a dozen, she estimated, several of whom were writing in notebooks. To stop her hands from trembling she clasped them in front of her stomach. Which felt like it was inside-out.

"Relax, " Eli whispered, leaning in close. "It'll be over in no time."

Not soon enough to suit her.

The judge tilted his head back and peered through the bottom half of his rimless bifocals at the document in front of him and said, "In the matter of The People of the State of Oregon v. Andrew—" He grunted and looked up at Andie. "State your full, true name."

Andie froze, unable speak her deadname. A name that no longer applied to her.

"Elias Ritter, attorney for the defense, Your Honor. I beg the court's indulgence. Ms. McInnes is a transgender woman, but she hasn't yet legally changed her name. However, from the age of twelve the name she has used and is known by is Andrea Lynne McInnes."

The judge regarded Andie. "Very well. In deference to your situation, in oral matters before this court all parties shall refer to you as Ms. McInnes. However, court documents and your signature shall use Andrew Lee McInnes, until such time as your name has been legally changed. Will that be acceptable, Ms. McInnes?"

Eli nudged her. "Yes, Your Honor," she said. "I thank the court for its indulgence." Out of the corner of her eye she saw Eli's head snap around to look at her, a sign she'd better rein in the courtroom lingo she'd picked up watching *Law & Order*.

"Objection, Your Honor," Kellenberger said.

The judge stared at him for a moment. "On what basis?"

"The defendant's legal name should take precedence."

"Overruled," the judge said with a note of finality and then turned back to Andie. "Ms. McInnes, before you enter your plea, have you understood the proceedings thus far?"

"Yes, Your Honor."

"Andrea Lynne McInnes, in the complaint before this court you are charged with a felony violation of Oregon Revised Statute one six three dot one two five, manslaughter in the second degree, in which it is alleged that you displayed reckless disregard, resulting in the death of Howard H. Hinshaw of Portland. Do you understand the charge against you?"

"Yes, Your Honor."

"To that charge, what is your plea?"

Eli leaned close and whispered, "Kellenberger assumes that you're going to accept his plea deal, I'd bet money on it. Answer the judge."

"I plead not guilty."

Sure enough, a surprised grunt came from Kellenberger.

The judge said, "The court finds that the defendant's plea was voluntarily made with an understanding of the nature of the charges pending, as well as the consequences of the plea. The court finds there is a factual basis for the plea. The court accepts the defendant's plea of not guilty. A preliminary hearing shall be scheduled within the next ten days."

After the judge rapped his gavel, Ritter gathered up his stuff and then ushered Andie up the aisle and out of the courtroom. Kellenberger had beaten them out and was already holding forth in the hall, surrounded by a scrum of reporters and video cameras.

"Look at that guy," Eli said, shaking his head. "Never misses a chance to grandstand."

Kellenberger was speaking, gilding his words with oratorical flourish: ". . . prove beyond a shadow of a doubt that the defendant demonstrated reckless disregard in shooting and killing Mr. Hinshaw."

"One good thing about it," Eli said, "it will give us a chance to slip past unnoticed."

It was not to be. One of the reporters spotted them and called out, "Miss McInnes . . . Miss McInnes . . . would you answer a few questions?" And then all the reporters deserted Kellenberger and began shouting questions at her: Are you sorry you killed him? Do you always carry a gun? Is it true you're a cold-blooded killer?

Eli interposed his body between her and the reporters. "Miss McInnes justifiably defended herself against three young hooligans who were threatening to kill her. She has no further statement at this time." He put a protective arm around her shoulder and steered her toward the exit.

A die-hard reporter trailed after them and called out, "Have you had sex-change surgery?"

They left the building. The reporter didn't follow them out.

Back in the little apartment, she made her favorite quick-fix casserole: Rice-A-Roni (Broccoli and Cheese flavor), cooked ground beef, chopped black olives, French cut green beans, garnished with garlic salt. Twenty minutes in the microwave and dinner would be ready to serve. She washed and dried her hands and then picked up the journal.

Thursday, July 21, 2016 5:16 p.m.

I didn't feel like eating in the cafeteria tonight. Eli was kind enough to stop at Safeway on the way home so I could pick up some casserole makings. It's cooking in the microwave now. My first dinner in this apartment.

God, I freaked out in that courtroom today, trembling like a chihuahua. And it was only my arraignment. What am I going to be like in the trial?

That Kellenberger creep—he had the gall to object when the judge ordered that I be referred to as Ms. McInnes. What a jerk. He looks at me like I'm a pile of dog shit on the sidewalk.

And those reporters, barraging me with rude questions as we were leaving, that shook me up again. I wish I had an invisibility cloak.

In cheerier matters, the foundation has a library! Discovered it last night. It has all the classics, plus many contemporary works, all hard cover. Pure heaven. I borrowed *Heart of Darkness* by Joseph Conrad. I've always wanted to read it. Coppola's *Apocalypse Now* was supposedly based on it. I'm starting it tonight.

I could get used to staying here. In fact, I already have. The apartment is perfect for me in every way. I'll hate to leave it when the time comes.

Hey, the microwave just beeped. Has it been twenty minutes already? Guess so.

Later.

13

Boonstra stubbed out his cigar, picked up his desk phone, and stabbed a button. When his office manager answered he said, "Ronette, call Ennis Judson and ask him what's the goddamn holdup. He was supposed to pick up someone at the airport and be here forty minutes ago."

"Mr. Judson and another gentleman just now walked in, Congressman."

Boonstra's office door opened. His chief of staff and another man filed in. Judson closed the door and said, "Congressman, this is Richard Ronson, from the Family Morality Council."

"Pleasure, Mr. Ronson." Boonstra shook the man's hand and looked him over. Thin, humorless face; rimless glasses; colorless hair neatly parted on the side. Tight-lipped and probably tightassed.

"Likewise, Congressman." He had a thin, reedy voice.

Boonstra indicated an overstuffed love seat and two club chairs that formed a conversation area in front of the desk. Ronson chose one of the club chairs, Boonstra and Judson the love seat.

Boonstra treated the visitor to a warm and friendly smile. "Thank you kindly for coming on such short notice."

"Always happy to accommodate one of our country's most esteemed lawmakers."

"Mr. Ronson, I was sorry to hear that you lost your appeal on the civil judgment. A shame."

"The appeals court judge was an Obama appointee, so I didn't have a snowball's chance. My lawyers have petitioned the Supreme Court to hear my case, but it's a long shot."

"What was the final amount of the judgment?"

"The first proceeding cut the plaintiffs' award in half, twenty-five million. Five to each of them."

"That ain't chickenfeed by anybody's measure. Listen, I know a congressman from New Jersey who's good friends with Alito, and he owes me a favor. Maybe he can put in a good word."

"That would be much appreciated."

"In the meantime, how would you like to even up the score a little?"

"Very much. What would I have to do?"

"Give me your support and expertise on some legislation I'm putting together."

"What sort of legislation?"

"The kind I'm sure you'll approve of." Boonstra leaned forward and handed his visitor a folded newspaper with an article circled in red. "First, I'd like your take on this."

Ronson's lips were a thin line as he read the article. He handed it back to the congressman. "Quite disturbing. I'm sure the parents of other children who attend that elementary school hate the thought of their daughters sharing a restroom with a confused boy who thinks he's a girl. The LGBT Nazis are determined to force this perversion down the throats of parents all over the country in the guise of 'modern school administration.' Congress needs to pass a strict law against such travesties, for the sake of the children."

Boonstra smiled. "Funny you should say that. I'm calling my legislation the Protect Our Children Act."

"Good name. Difficult to oppose without looking like you don't care about kids."

Boonstra leaned forward and held out a draft of the bill. "Have a look at what we've got so far."

Ronson took the draft and read it, grunting from time to time. After he finished he looked up. "Pretty good first cut. Mind if I make a couple suggestions?"

"Please do."

"First, I think you should expand the section dealing with school restrooms to include gym classes, shower facilities, locker rooms, sports teams, and any other activities that are separated by gender."

"Good point." Boonstra turned to his chief of staff. "Make a note of that, Ennis."

"Second, you might add a section allowing Christian schools and other faith-based institutions to expel students who have gender identity issues. That will sew up evangelical support for your bill."

"Done. And perhaps you could give us a hand mobilizing those folks?"

"I will indeed."

Boonstra chuckled. "Liberals are sure-God going to shit their pants when this makes the news."

"Undoubtedly. But then, they're not the people you're trying to convince."

"I'm counting on getting a passel of conservative-leaning Democrats on board, so the bill will have bipartisan support." Boonstra took out a handkerchief and blew his nose. "We'll incorporate your suggestions and send you the revision to look over. After you approve it I'll take it to committee."

"Which one?"

"The House Education Subcommittee on Early Childhood, Elementary and Secondary Education."

"Do you anticipate any problem getting it through?"

Boonstra laughed. "Not hardly. The bill will sail through without a hitch, since I happen to chair that committee."

"Ah."

"Once the bill's out of committee I'm confident it will pass the House. Getting it though the Senate without a Democrat filibuster and with a veto-proof majority will be a challenge, but I'm working on that. I'm going to call in some gold chips."

"I wish you good luck."

"Mr. Ronson, this bill is just a stepping stone. I want to follow up with another bill that will have a broader focus."

"By that you mean it won't focus only on children?"

"Bingo. I also chair the House Energy Subcommittee On Health, which has broad jurisdiction over matters of public health policy. See the connection? When the time comes I'll likely call on your expertise again."

"It will be a pleasure, Congressman."

"Do you live here in D.C.?"

"No, I live in Eugene, Oregon, a hot-bed of liberalism in a blue state. But I've been spending more and more time here."

"Well, I surely do thank you for your input, Mr. Ronson, and for your help with the evangelicals. We'll be in touch."

They shook hands and Boonstra escorted Ronson out. Ordinarily, he'd have his arm around a departing visitor's shoulder, but something told him the man would resent the familiarity.

"Odd little guy," Boonstra said after he shut the door. "But he'll do us some good with the bible thumpers." He took out a handkerchief, blew into it with a resonant honk, and stuffed it back in a pocket.

"He had a couple of good suggestions,."

"Ennis, this piss-ant education bill is going to get me some front-page publicity, perhaps even get me on one or two of those Sunday shows. And it's just the beginning, old son. I got a feeling this transgender crap is going to be a gold mine."

14

Eli returned to the table with two Cokes; he set one in front of her. "I'll tell you one thing," he said, "this is the poshest cafeteria I've ever seen."

"Yeah, it's pimp."

"Pimp?"

"Nice."

It was 3:30 in the afternoon, so they had the place all to themselves, other than occasional in-and-out coffee seeker.

"Okay, progress report," Eli said after he sat down. "We're in the discovery phase of the case."

"What's that?"

"Discovery is the process by which Kellenberger and I learn about each other's case. It includes requests for physical evidence, which in this case is the piece of rebar and your jeans and underwear. The lab that's processing the DNA on those items has a big backlog, so the results aren't back yet. That proved to be to our advantage."

"How so?"

"Depositions. In a criminal case the defendant cannot be deposed without her consent—which of course you've with-held—but the plaintiff's witnesses do not have that privilege. I deposed the prosecution's two star witnesses, Pfaff and Burleson, in separate sessions. Both stuck to their story that you attacked them and shot Hinshaw for no reason."

"A total crock."

"I know. Their answers were too pat. They used exactly the same words and phrases, a clear sign they'd rehearsed them. But I threw them a curve ball. I asked them whether they or Hinshaw had any physical contact with you, and both said absolutely not, they never came near you."

"That's a damn lie."

"And they're on the record now. Depositions are pretrial testimony, given under oath in the presence of a court reporter, who prepares written transcripts of the sessions. Kellenberger stood by while his witnesses perjured themselves. Because the results aren't back yet, he had no idea the DNA evidence on your clothes will, hopefully, impeach those well-rehearsed depositions in a most embarrassing fashion."

"And then what?"

"Then the judge will probably dismiss the case."

"That would be beyond awesome." Her street-hardened cynicism hadn't let her dare hope for a dismissal.

"It hinges on the DNA."

"Thank God for modern science."

Eli snapped his fingers and opened his attaché case. "You told me that you regret procrastinating about changing your name." He placed a document in front of her. "This is the application form for a legal name change. After it's submitted a public notice will be posted for two weeks. Then you'll have a hearing and a judge will sign the order. If we get the ball rolling right away it will be all done by the time the trial commences." He held out a pen. "Sign here."

"With my deadname, I suppose."

"It will be the last time you'll ever have to sign it."

She took the pen and, eyes closed, signed the form.

"After your name has been legally changed, you need to get a drivers license, Social Security card, voter registration —documentation that will attest to Andrea Lynne McInnes' standing as a solid citizen. Okay?"

A solid citizen. Getting her mind around the concept would take some time. "Anything you say, Eli."

Back in the apartment, journal open on her lap and a cup of Earl Grey within easy reach, she took a sip and then picked up the pen.

Friday, July 22, 2016 4:20 p.m.

Arraignments, depositions, prelims—I'm becoming a freakin' legal expert! But I had a solid foundation: hundreds of episodes of *Law & Order*. Looks like they weren't a total waste of time after all.

I met with Eli in the cafeteria and discussed the depositions, and about how Pfaff and Burleson lied their asses off. He's sure the DNA evidence will contradict their story, so there's a strong possibility the case will be dismissed. When he told me that, I wanted to hug him. By the way, without those coke-bottle glasses he'd look a lot like Denzel Washington. It's his smile. If I were, like, ten years older . . .

Hey, my name change is underway! In just over two weeks my legal, kosher, USDA-inspected name will be Andrea Lynne McInnes. Eli also wants me to get a driver's license, a Social Security card, and a voter registration card. All before the trial starts. A credibility thing. Andrea Lynne McInnes, solid citizen. My crew on the street, no way they're gonna believe it.

Eli's optimism must be catching. I'm starting to think I might get out of this mess yet.

15

They ambushed him as he emerged from the Congressional building's main floor restroom, a young woman reporter and a cameraman with a scraggly beard. He recognized the reporter as one of MSNBC's "fresh, new faces," Kasie Something-or-other, a pretty brunette and liberal as they come.

"Congressman Boonstra, could I ask you a few questions about the bill you just introduced in the House, HB1010?" She aimed the handheld mic at his face.

He cursed his prostate. Whenever the urge hit him he had to find the closest restroom available. So the background for the interview, rather than the Capitol Building's stately exterior, was a door marked "MEN"—not exactly ideal optics. After subtly checking his fly, he switched on the down-home charm. "Ma'am, nothing would please me more."

"Thank you. Congressman, you named your bill the Protect Our Children Act. Given the fact that it discriminates against transgender children, isn't that a rather ironic title?"

He gave her a measured smile. "Depends on your point of view. Parents who object to their daughter being forced to share a restroom with a classmate who is biologically a boy would fail to see the irony. Those folks want their children protected. This bill does that."

"According to Representative Jeffers it violates Title IX, which prohibits discrimination against transgender students."

"My dear friend and colleague from across the aisle is badly mistaken. Title IX makes no mention of transgender students or gender identity in any way, shape, or form."

"Nevertheless, on the basis of Title IX, courts have ruled that transgender students have the right to use restrooms and other facilities consistent with their gender identity and cannot be forced to use separate facilities."

"Sadly, the Department of Educations' Title IX has been wrongfully interpreted by activist judges, trampling on the rights of nontransgender students. The Protect Our Children Act will correct that state of affairs."

"Representative Jeffers also said the bill will likely face serious opposition from Democrats in the House and Senate as well as from LGBT organizations."

"Probably, but it has the support of millions of Americans across this great country who have children in public schools funded by their tax money. It also has the support of several Christian organizations, such as the Family Morality Council. The concept of 'gender fluidity,' as it has been called, violates deeply held religious convictions of people of faith."

"Can you count on your caucus for support?"

Boonstra smiled. "When this bill comes up for a vote next month I'm confident it will pass with unanimous Republican support. And I'm counting on a few Democrat votes."

"However, if it makes it onto President Obama's desk he'll likely veto it, and overriding his veto will require a two-thirds majority in both chambers."

"I believe the support's there."

"So why are you picking this particular fight?"

"Kasie, I was elected to represent the people of my district and in a broader sense the good people of Louisiana and this country. I take my responsibility seriously. This is an issue that has my constituents very concerned, and so I'm acting on their behalf. I would be derelict in my duty to refuse."

"Congressman, thank you for your time."

"My pleasure, ma'am." He touched the brim of an imaginary hat and headed for the exit.

Outside, he took out a lighter and a cigar he'd pretrimmed. After the cigar was burning evenly he set off for his office in the Rayburn Building, swearing under his breath about Title IX. He launched a wad of spit at a sapling as he went by and hit it dead center.

So . . . MSNBC had gotten wind of his Protect Our Children Act legislation and sent Kasie to pitch him rude questions about it. Did they think they were dealing with a chimp? He swatted every pitch over the outfield fence. Not that the coverage wasn't welcome—a little publicity never hurt—but it was chicken feed. Not to mention, chickenshit.

After the bill was signed into law, he'd be giving interviews on *FOX and Friends*, *Hannity*, *The O'Reilly Factor*, and *Megan Kelly*. (At their studios—full of leggy, stacked honeys. Where he maybe could cadge himself a smooch. Even a feel. Hooray for "fair and balanced.")

As for CNN and MSNBC, they could kiss his ass.

"Representative Boonstra."

He turned to see who'd hailed him. "Mr. Ronson," he said, "An unexpected pleasure."

"Your office told me you were on the House floor, but I missed you. Someone said you gave an interview in the hall before you left."

"To MSNBC. Seems the liberal media's in a tizzy about my bill. And it was just introduced. They'll work themselves into a lather when the House passes it. You wanted to see me about something?"

"Do you know who Omar Mullen is, Congressman?"

"The jillionaire?"

Ronson's lips formed a thin smile. "And a man of faith who lends his financial support to godly causes. I told him about you and about your legislation. He wants to meet you."

"I'll be delighted to have a sit-down with Mr. Mullen." In fact, he'd crawl over broken glass if need be. "When?"

"He's off the coast of Buenos Aires on his yacht currently, but he's on his way up here. I'll set up a meeting."

"I greatly appreciate your efforts, Mr. Ronson."

"Fellow soldiers, fighting the good fight."

"Right you are, old son."

Ronson looked at his watch. "I'm supposed be somewhere in twenty minutes." He extended his hand. "I'll be in touch."

Back in his office ten minutes later, Boonstra dropped into his chair, stubbed out his cigar, and lit a fresh one. He had cause to celebrate. He took a few puffs and watched tendrils of smoke drift lazily toward the ceiling.

Ronson had come through like a champ. Billionaires did not pop out of the woodwork every day. With Mullen's bankroll, his legislation would surely slide through the House and Senate like a greased pig.

And name recognition—the Holy Grail in politics—would follow, propelling him from House obscurity to national prominence, right up there with Louie Gohmert, Marsha Blackburn, Steve King, and Virginia Fox.

Rising political star Dale Boonstra felt an urgent need to take another leak.

16

Andie eased the door open and slipped out into the dusk. Not a soul in sight. She'd been waiting for a chance to explore the foundation's grounds and look for escape routes, in case she had to leave in a hurry. She probably wouldn't get a better opportunity.

Using shadows for cover, she made her way across the grounds to the stone wall that surrounded the foundation. Near it, not a single tree or structure of any kind, on either side. Eight feet high, with shards of broken glass set into the top, the wall was designed to prevent unauthorized entry. Or exit.

Spaced along the top of the wall every hundred feet or so, surveillance cameras.

Ominous.

In the fading light she almost didn't see the figure following her, about a hundred yards back. A man, judging by the gait. Up ahead the path branched. She took the left one.

So did he.

No fear this time, only irritation. She rounded a bend and ducked behind a camellia bush in a well-lit area and waited, arms crossed.

Whoever he was, he was out of shape. He came steaming up the path, puffing like a locomotive. When he drew near, she stepped out.

He yelled and leaped back. "Miss McInnes," he said, gasping for breath, "I tried to . . . catch you . . . at your apartment."

"Why?"

"The director . . . wants to see you. Now, if possible."

She recognized him then. He worked in administration, in the office. "Okay," she said, "I'm on my way."

The admin offices were dark, except for the director's office. She knocked and opened the door without waiting for an invitation. The director was sitting at her desk, Dr. Soong in a chair in front. She nodded at them.

"Andie," the director said. "Thank you for coming." She gestured at the chair beside Dr. Soong.

Andie sat down and waited. Whatever it was they wanted to talk to her about so late in the day, it wasn't likely to be good news. The wall-mounted displays of military ribbons and crossed swords added to her apprehension.

The director smiled at her. "So how are you doing, Andie?"

"Fine, thanks. So far."

"You've been here, what, ten days now?"

"That's right."

"Have you given any thought to what you're going to do after this court case is behind you?"

"If I don't have to go to prison, you mean? Not really. I hadn't planned that far ahead. Why?"

"We'd like to offer you a job."

Warning bells. "Doing what?"

"We need someone to assist us with younger prospects—locating them, interviewing them, evaluating them, that sort of thing. Interested?"

"A job? On the square?"

"Yes, a staff position. With salary and benefits."

"But . . . why? I didn't even graduate from high school."

"Don't sell yourself short," Dr. Soong said. "I'd bet you could hold your own with college students. I think you'd be ideal for the position."

Andie chuckled. "The last time someone told me that that was when I applied for a job at KFC. Only worked there a week. The manager was a douchebag."

"I think you'll find the foundation a more agreeable employer," the director said. "And if you want to continue your education the foundation will underwrite the cost of tuition and books. You can live and work here and attend classes at Portland State."

Andie blinked. She'd given up on college long ago.

"Maybe you need some time to think about it?"

"No need. I'm in." Might as well play along.

The director held out her hand. "Welcome aboard."

"Thanks."

"I understand your name-change process is underway," Dr. Soong said. "Have you thought about surgery?"

"Excuse me?"

"Do you want to have gender confirmation surgery?"

"Sure, but it's been way out of my reach."

"Until now. When the time comes I'll help you make the necessary arrangements."

"Unless this job pays a whole lot, it's going to take me a long time to save up that kind of money."

"The foundation will pay for everything—the surgeon's fee, hospital fees, post-surgical accommodations, travel expenses, and meals."

"Sounds too good to be true." Like most scams.

"It's true. And you can have the surgeon of your choice. Do you have one in mind?"

"A girlfriend of mine went to Suporn in Thailand. She's ecstatic with her result."

"I can recommend Suporn. He did my surgery."

"You mean—are you . . .?"

Dr. Soong laughed. "Not just me. Everyone at the Foundation is trans, from the groundskeeper to the director."

Andie stared at her, mouth open. The surprises just kept coming. "I'm the world's worst at clocking trans people," she finally said. "My friends tease me about it."

"School and surgery are important, but they'll have to be put on a back burner for a while," the director said. "Your highest priority is to get this ridiculous murder charge off your back."

Andie nodded. "Eli seems pretty sure I'll get off."

"Mr. Ritter has our full confidence. Douglas Longcypher, founder of Longcypher, Cannady and Moore, said he's the best defense lawyer in Portland."

"Hope he's right." Or she'd be toast.

The director stood. "Glad we had this little talk, Andie." Apparently, the little talk was over.

Andie shook hands and left. The walk to her apartment was a total blank, as though she'd been teleported from the director's office to her door. Inside, she kicked off her shoes and reached for the journal.

Monday, July 25, 2016 8:55 p.m.

Tonight I scoped out the perimeter wall and—surprise!—it would be impossible to climb over it without special equipment. A damn ladder, for example. I couldn't find any weak points, not a single one. And surveillance cameras were everywhere. I'm S.O.L. if I need to leave without being seen.

As I was checking out the wall I realized that some guy was following me. I jumped out from behind a bush and scared the bejeezus out of him. It turned out he was only delivering a message from the director that she wanted to see me. So I went from there to the director's office.

Right away she and Dr. Soong laid a hella-huge rap on me. They offered me a salaried position with benefits, college tuition and books, and confirmation surgery. In Thailand, no less. In short, everything I've always wanted. It was straight out of the Big-Ass Cult Handbook, "How To Gain a Target's Trust."

They want me to think they've got my back. But no one's had my back since Mom and Dad died. Since then nobody's given a final damn if I lived or died, so why would total strangers?

The thing is, I really wanted to believe it, all of it. I ached for it to be true. But I'm back on planet Earth now and this I know for sure: They're totally full of shit.

I need to decide how to play it. I know I won't get anywhere by confronting them. I already tried that, with Dr. Soong. They won't admit a thing. The smart thing to do would be to pretend I've been totally taken in—act as though I believe whatever they tell me, no matter how fantastic.

I don't see a better alternative.

"Come with me, Andie" the director said. "It's time you learned the truth about the Transcend Foundation."

She led her down a dank, dimly lit passageway, lined with the same type of stone as the perimeter wall, until they reached a massive door. Iron hinges moaned in protest when the director pushed it open. "After you," she said.

Standing inside a cavernous laboratory, Andie could only stare. An antiseptic smell and an electrical hum, as from a transformer, inundated her senses. Rows of individually lighted cylindrical glass containers provided the only illumination. There must have been thousands of them.

She read the label on the nearest container: "CPU1939J." Suspended in a bluish liquid was a human brain, attached to which were a pair of eyeballs and a serpentine spinal cord connected to a wiring harness. Convolutions on the brain's surface pulsated obscenely. The eyeballs goggled at her.

She whirled to face the director.

"Yes, Andie?"

"Don't tell me it's alive?"

"They're all alive, all conscious and aware. More than two thousand of them. All trans, by the way."

The door creaked open and a white-coated figure entered.

"Ah, Dr. Soong," the director said. "Glad you can join us."

The doctor smiled at Andie. "What do you think?"

"I think it's monstrous."

"You don't understand how wondrous it is. It's an organic computer, the first of its kind. Two thousand forty-eight human brains connected in parallel. Powerful enough to solve problems that have vexed mathematicians for centuries."

"But . . . why? Why have you done this?"

"Because we can. What can be done will be done. That's been the case throughout history, without exception."

"Why only trans brains?"

"Our research indicates that transgender subjects are least likely to be missed."

"You're stealing people's lives."

"Look at it this way—they're making a valuable contribution to humankind."

"This is just smothered in wrong sauce."

A look passed between Dr. Soong and the director. "Told you," Dr. Soong said.

The director moved closer. "Andie, we're disappointed in you. We had such high hopes. Perhaps a decade or two in a glass jar will adjust your attitude." She clutched Andie's upper arms in a vice-like grip. "Our brain-extraction facility is a marvel to behold. You'll see."

She tried to shuck off the director's hands. They morphed into a bedsheet and blanket that encircled her. She kicked them off and lay there panting.

Another damn nightmare.

The night air felt chilly against her damp T-shirt. Waking up in a cold sweat seemed to be the default lately. It was getting old fast.

17

The white Lincoln limousine docked in the space marked "R.H.L." The chauffeur got out and opened the door for his passenger.

"Thank you, Lonnie." With a grunt of effort Rafe Lambeaux extricated his bulk from the vehicle and looked at his watch. On time, as usual. He prided himself on punctuality. Not that anyone would say squat to him if he were late.

Dana, his assistant, fell into step beside him as soon as he walked into the building. "You've got a substitute engineer today," she said. "Ryan's having a root canal."

Lambeaux groaned. "Hope it's not the idiot that subbed for Ryan last time. If you'll recall, we had four minutes of very expensive dead air right in the middle of the second hour, until Captain Cerebral finally realized he'd accidentally toggled the wrong switch."

"How could I forget? Affiliates were foaming at the mouth, and your sponsors weren't exactly thrilled."

Lambeaux paused a moment to admire the wall-mounted, stylized version of his signature rendered in two-foot-tall gold letters, and then he set off down the corridor. The studio was at the end. Before he took his seat at the mic he poked his head into the control booth. The guy at the console adjusting knobs and sliders looked familiar. He'd subbed before and knew what he was doing. One less thing to worry about.

The studio door opened and Hal Terry, production director and call screener, walked into the studio. "You've got a new sponsor, Rafe. Bainberry Precious Metals. I plugged them into the number three slot."

"Fine." Lambeaux dropped into his cushy chair, put on his headphones, and looked over some handwritten notes he'd made for the show.

"Two minutes." The engineer's disembodied voice had a nasal twang. "Check your mic level?"

Lambeaux spoke his customary test phrase: "Socialists suck serious swamp water."

"Okay, good to go. One minute to air."

Lambeaux inhaled and exhaled deeply several times, to oxygenate his brain and turbocharge the neurons, sharpen the synapses.

The ON AIR sign lit up, the theme music swelled, and the voice-over announced: "And now, the man who strikes fear into the hearts of liberals everywhere . . . Rafe Lambeaux."

"Hello, America. As if we need more proof that liberals are out to destroy this country from within, the Department of Education's Office For Civil Rights found that a Wisconsin suburban high school discriminated against a transgender student. The DOE gave Townsend High School District One-Nineteen a month to force the school to grant the transgender full access to girls' restrooms and other school facilities or lose federal funding. Last year the district received six million dollars in federal money that was contingent on compliance with anti-discrimination rules.

"The transgender student and the ALCU, which brought the complaint on the student's behalf, of course applauded the finding, while the school district called it 'serious overreach.' Which it is.

"The school district, which includes six high schools west of Madison, defied the DOE and continues to deny access to the transgender student. Good for them.

"Assistant Secretary for Civil Rights Catherine Lawson said, 'All students deserve the opportunity to participate equally in school programs and activities, and have access to school facilities. Those are basic civil rights.'

"The student's parents issued the following statement: 'Our daughter has been living full time as a girl since she transitioned three years ago. She is totally female in appearance. If a school administrator hadn't stumbled across her transgender status in some old records, this would not have erupted into a controversy. After four months of meeting with the administration, the district left us no other remedy but to file a complaint with the Department of Education, with the help of the ACLU of Wisconsin. Despite the district's best efforts to frame the DOE's findings as big government's attempt to regulate at the local level, it is the district that has trampled on the rights of our daughter. The fact that Super-intendent Bates has the nerve to claim he's being "bullied" into complying with the law indicates he has absolutely no sensitivity or compassion for what my daughter or any other transgender youth in the district has suffered under his policies. His is the lowest form of political posturing and utterly reprehensible.'"

Lambeaux stuck out his tongue and made a rude sound. "Well, there you have it folks. And this is by no means an isolated case. It's happening in schools all over the country.

"So what qualifies someone as transgender? If a boy goes to school one day wearing a dress and says he feels like a girl, does he automatically get to use the girls' restroom? The DOE says he does, otherwise his precious rights will be violated. But the real victims here are the girls who are forced to share their restroom with a schoolmate who's physically male.

"Folks, the liberals are actively promoting the destruction of our society's moral fiber. They don't care one whit what psychological or emotional harm they cause. Their actions are designed to disarm our children, belittle their feelings of modesty or shame, strip them of their right to privacy, and stigmatize anyone who objects.

"Unless you've been in a state of suspended animation, you've noticed that transgender incursions into society are becoming more and more frequent. Everywhere you turn these days it's transgender this and transgender that.

"They're Hollywood's latest darlings, featured in movies and television programs in which they're portrayed as normal citizens. Yeah . . . right—the she-male next door.

"Transgenders will soon be allowed in the military, believe it or not. The defense of our country entrusted to men in skirts. That's a reassuring thought, folks. I feel safer already.

"Here's a stunner—Girl Scouts now welcome transgenders. Their website states that 'if the child is recognized by the family, school, and community as a girl and lives culturally as a girl, then Girl Scouts can serve her, in a setting that is both emotionally and physically safe.' I'll bet the other girls in the troop and their parents are delighted about that.

"And now self-proclaimed transgender children have the right to use school restrooms consistent with their 'gender identity.' If it makes their schoolmates uncomfortable—well, that's just bigotry they learned from their parents.

"It's all very disturbing. However, there's a ray of sunshine. Representative Dale Boonstra of Oklahoma has introduced a bill in the House of Representatives, the Protect Our Children Act, which restricts use of public school restrooms, showers, and locker rooms to children whose birth gender corresponds to the facilities' gender designation. In other words, no whizzywhackers allowed in the girls' bathroom. So we should all commend Representative Boonstra for standing up to the liberals, who are dead set on shoving the transgender agenda down everybody's throat.

"Our first caller is Mike Shepherd from Chicago. Mike, what do you want to say to our listeners?"

"Hey, Rafe. I just have to say this. That school district is flat wrong. And that congressman is just grandstanding for the bigots, politicizing hate. It's fear mongering. Targeting transgender children like that is disgraceful."

"Well, folks, sounds like we have a liberal caller. Never let it be said that Rafe Lambeaux doesn't let liberals have their say. Go ahead, Mike."

"I have a friend whose twelve-year-old daughter is trans-gender. She's unquestionably a girl. No one could look at her and believe otherwise. You're portraying kids like her as confused boys, but you couldn't be more wrong. I'm not—"

"Here's a newsflash, Mike. They *are* confused boys, and I blame their parents for indulging a childish fantasy. It's reprehensible. Okay, that's enough out of you. Our next caller is Naff Birdwell from Gaffney, South Carolina. Go ahead, Naff."

"Hi, Rafe. Tell you one thing, the schools around here, if one of them he-shes pokes his head into the girls' bathroom, he's liable to get his ass beat clear off. We don't take kindly to that type of stuff in these parts. It's . . . *pre*version, no matter what the gov'ment says."

"Can't argue with that, Naff. Thanks for calling. Our next caller is Nancy Quackenbush from Branson, Missouri. Go ahead, Nancy."

"Rafe, I teach home economics and I'm extremely upset about this situation. It's social engineering run amok, a total usurpation of school and parental control. It should be left to the discretion of each individual school district instead of imposing a government mandate that affects every class-room in the country, from kindergarten through twelfth grade. It's an outrageous invasion of privacy. With a failing educational system like ours, the government unilaterally decides *this* is a priority? I don't get it."

"Me neither, Nancy, but thanks for the call." Lambeaux caught Hal Terry's signal. "Folks, we're going to pause at this juncture to learn how Aegis Sentry, the ultimate in identity theft protection, can make your life more secure. We have a whole lot more to talk about, so stick around for the fun."

A breathy female voice-over purred, "You're listening to the Rafe Lambeaux Show on the CIB—the Conservatism In Broadcasting network."

18

Judge Thomas Bondurant's chambers could have been a *Law & Order* set: dark wood paneling, forest green carpet and drapes, an imposing desk, and a bookcase filled with leather-bound law books.

The judge sat behind the desk, his fingers steepled in front of him. "Mr. Ritter, I do understand your dilemma and I sympathize, but postponing Ms. McInnes' preliminary hearing is impossible. The court has a full docket."

Ritter groaned. "My defense depends almost entirely on the DNA evidence. LOIS has only one item on file under the case number. There should be three."

"Lois?"

"An acronym for Laboratory Online Information System, used by the Forensic Services Division."

"Oh—right. I thought you were referring to Lois Kranz, head of the records division at the courthouse and a stickler for exactitude. Anyway, now that we're on the same page, what evidence is missing?"

"The jeans and underwear the defendant was wearing. The DNA testing of the two items will likely be most important evidence to my case. Crucial, in fact."

"The item that LOIS had on file, have you gotten back the test results on that?"

"The rebar. Yes, I did."

"So you have something to go on?"

"Yes, but it's not enough."

"Well," Bondurant said, "the prelim isn't until Friday, three days away. Perhaps you can track down the missing evidence before then. I wish I could give you more time, but as I said . . ." He spread his arms wide.

"I understand. Thank you for your time, Judge."

He left Bondurant's chambers with a chunk of ice in his gut. He'd counted on a postponement. His slam-dunk case was fast becoming a head-first dunk in the toilet.

The lab had found Hinshaw's DNA on one end of the rebar, but so what? Pfaff and Burleson could always claim that Hinshaw had picked up the rebar to defend against an armed assailant. The case needed those missing items, needed them badly.

He had to find out what happened. Which would require some detective work. Probably the best place to start was to talk to the policewoman who'd bagged and tagged Andie's clothing at the holding facility. Cheney, Chafley . . . Chaffee, that was it.

He'd parked on the parking garage's top level. Spiraling down to street level, the screeching of the tires gave voice to his frustration over the missing evidence. At the bottom of the ramp he aimed the SUV toward the Portland Police Bureau on 2nd Avenue.

When he walked into the station house the desk sergeant was speaking to a woman in a placating tone: ". . . could be hard to catch in the act, ma'am. Most likely it's someone in your neighborhood. Some kid, probably. Here's what you do . . . next time you spot the drone hovering outside your bedroom window, take a photo of it with your phone and give us a call. Okay?"

The woman didn't seem the least bit placated. She glared, tight-lipped, at the desk sergeant for several seconds and then stomped off

As he watched her go out the door, the desk sergeant said, "Or you could close your curtains, lady." He looked at Ritter. "What do you need?"

"I'm looking for Officer Chaffee. Is she around?"

The desk sergeant consulted a schedule. "You lucked out. Her shift starts in fifteen minutes. If you want to wait, you can catch her before she goes on duty."

"Thanks, I'll do that." Ritter picked a bench against the wall, a ringside seat, and sat back to watch the show.

First to walk on stage: a patrol officer escorting a skeletal woman. She had stringy blond hair, bad teeth, and skin with a greenish cast. Obviously a meth devotee, she looked to be in her late thirties.

"Nineteen," she told the desk sergeant when he asked her age.

Next to be booked, a man in baggie jeans and wife-beater shirt. Badly drawn tattoos festooned his bare arms from his shoulders to his handcuffed wrists. He favored beer-scented cologne.

"DUII," the arresting officer said to the desk sergeant. "Another one."

The desk sergeant shook his head slowly, looking sad. "What is this, Mr. Snell—your third?"

"Fourth."

"In that case, we'll let you have the Presidential Suite. The bed has Magic Fingers."

"Funny."

As he was being led off, the desk sergeant called after him, "Ring the desk if you need room service, sir."

"Kiss my ass," the guy said over his shoulder.

Ritter was so caught up in the entertainment he almost missed Chaffee, who walked in with another officer. She was a stocky brunette who couldn't have been older than thirty. He hopped to his feet and intercepted her. "Officer Chaffee, Eli Ritter. We met week before last at the Multnomah County Court Holding Facility."

Her face lit up with recognition. "Sure, I remember."

"Could I have a few minutes of your time?" He nodded toward the bench.

She sat down and turned to Ritter. "How can I help you, Counselor?"

"I've got a problem you might be able to help me solve. It seems the evidence you collected at the holding facility on the fifteenth has turned up missing. It's not in the LOIS database, and the lab can't find it in their LIMS."

"Wait a minute ... the main purpose of LIMS is to keep track of evidence, right?"

"I asked the head of the DNA lab the same question when I talked to him on the phone. He assured me their LIMS software was next to infallible. I'm driving over to the lab to have a look around and ask some more questions in person. Would you mind going over your bag-and-tag procedure step by step, so I can rule out a pre-lab slip-up?"

"No problem. I followed the protocol in the Oregon State Police Physical Evidence Manual, used by all law enforcement agencies in the state. Wearing latex gloves, I packaged the items separately in paper evidence bags, which I sealed securely with tape. Then I used a Sharpie to label each bag with the case identifier, a brief description of the contents, my initials, and the date. The writing overlapped the seal, to prevent tampering."

"By the book. What did you do with the bags?"

"I gave them to the property officer when I got back to the station house. He sent them to the lab in Clackamas. Had an officer run them over, since you requested an expedited process."

"What's the property officer's name? I need to talk to him next."

"Ask for Sergeant Malone."

"Officer Chaffee, you've been a big help."

"No problem."

19

The police forensics lab in Clackamas, also known as the Portland crime lab, shared a modern facility on several acres next to a creek. The other tenants were the state police and medical examiner. Ritter parked and walked to the entrance. Inside, a mezzanine overlooked the lobby. The woman behind the help desk had a very pleasant smile and a bosom that seemed larger than her diminutive frame could easily carry.

"I'm here to see Dr. Hunsaker," he told her. "Eli Ritter."

"One moment, Mr. Ritter." She got up and disappeared down a corridor. When she returned she said, "Dr. Hunsaker will be right out."

Ritter thanked her and glanced around at the building's interior. The wall clock indicated 4:07. He was *almost* on time. Damn traffic.

"Mr. Ritter." A man in a white lab coat strode toward him, hand outstretched. "Don Hunsaker." Even wearing the lab coat, Hunsaker didn't look much like a scientist. With his toothy smile and affable manner, he could be a State Farm agent or the manager of a department store.

Ritter shook his hand. "I appreciate your taking the time to meet with me."

"Glad to," he said. "Let's head on down to the lab so we can talk. This way."

The Forensic Services lab complex occupied a significant portion of the building. In the vestibule, Ritter saw a dozen white coats hanging in a rolling rack and a freestanding, life-size cutout of Princess Leia pointing a blaster at him.

Nerd alert.

Gun-toting Star Wars characters in the lab were probably *de rigueur.*

"How about a quick tour, Mr. Ritter?"

"Sure, if you've got time."

They walked past a display that showed the various methods of retrieving fingerprints. Another displayed bullets of different calibers. A corner of a lab was devoted to breathalyzers used by law enforcement over the years. With names like "Drunkometer" and "Intoxilyzer," they'd be serious contenders in a Silliest Moniker contest.

Laboratory workbenches and tables were crammed with computer terminals, high-powered binocular microscopes, centrifuges, and instruments of every size and description. Hunsaker pointed out an expensive-looking device. "That's our liquid chromatograph, used to analyze drugs and bodily fluids such as blood and semen." He'd said it with the pride of a kid showing off a new Schwinn.

Ritter counted twelve white lab coats, their wearers all immersed in their work, paying no attention to Ritter and Hunsaker. Seven men, five women. A ponytailed fellow let out a whoop as he peered through a microscope.

Hunsaker walked over to him. "That sounded to me like a cry of triumph, Brian. You were examining evidence from a suspected arson, right?"

The man looked up from the microscope. "It was arson, no doubt about it. I found accelerant." He held out his fist and Hunsaker obliged him with a fist bump.

Hunsaker turned to Ritter. "Shall we continue our tour?"

They passed by shelves crammed with small envelopes, hundreds of them. "Confiscated street drugs," Hunsaker said. "Heroin, cocaine, opium, methamphetamine, and synthetic designer drugs. All awaiting analysis."

In the firearms lab they watched a technician position two bullets side by side under a microscope and examine them. He looked up at Ritter and Hunsaker. "No match," he said. "Care to have a look?"

Through the powerful instrument the striations on the bullets were clearly different, even to Ritter's untrained eye. "Fascinating. Thanks for the peek."

The DNA extraction lab was the tour's final attraction. Ritter asked Hunsaker where they kept evidence they tested for DNA. Hunsaker showed him a room filled with shelves and cabinets and said they currently contained around three thousand items, many of them yet to be processed. It was clear to Ritter that locating any missing evidence among all that stuff would be a difficult and time-consuming task. Like finding a proverbial needle in a haystack.

"Check this out," Hunsaker said, and swung open a heavy door. Ritter felt a blast of cold air. It was a walk-in freezer that contained hundreds of sealed and labeled vials. "DNA samples are stored in here," Hunsaker said.

Another haystack. But then, Ritter hadn't expected the missing evidence to jump into his arms. "The identifiers on the vials correspond to records in the LIMS database?"

"Correct." Hunsaker removed one of the vials from a rack and sat down at a computer terminal. After he logged in, a *JusticeTrax LIMS-plus* logo filled the screen; he entered the vial's identifier. The record was displayed almost before his finger left the enter key. "Let's see . . . it's a semen sample, obtained with a rape kit. Analysis done January third. And LIMS' sample tracking indicates the sample's location in storage. Makes it easy for us to locate."

Ritter pointed. "That's a description of the evidence you tested for DNA, right? Do me a favor and search for 'jeans' in that field."

Results: 1713 records.

"Okay, now add a date range. The evidence was sent over here on the fifteenth. Make it from then to today."

Results: No records found.

Ritter took a Post-it from his shirt pocket and put it in front of Hunsaker. "Here's the case number. Search on that."

Results: 1 record found.

"That's the rebar," Ritter said. "So at what point in the process is a record created in LIMS?"

"When the evidence is received by the lab."

"And in LOIS?"

"After the DNA analysis has been completed."

"Here's what I don't under—"

A sullen-faced young guy walked in carrying a computer keyboard. He didn't look like a lab worker. "Keys stick on one of your terminals, right? Got a replacement for you."

"That one over there," Hunsaker said, pointing.

The guy went to the terminal, unplugged the existing keyboard, and plugged in the replacement. The old keyboard under his arm, he nodded to them and left.

"Sorry about the interruption," Hunsaker said. "The IT Division takes good care of us."

"No problem. Here's what I don't understand. According to the police property officer, a Forensic Services Request Form was submitted with the evidence. Because time was of the essence, a police officer delivered the evidence here in person and obtained a receipt signed with a squiggle instead of a signature. The evidence was received by the lab on the fifteenth. Why isn't it in your LIMS' database?"

Hunsaker shook his head, his brow furrowed. "I don't know. This has never happened before. I won't be able to rest until I figure out how it happened."

Ritter handed him a business card. "Here's my number. Please give me a call if you come up with anything."

"I will."

"Thank you for the tour."

On the twelve-mile drive back to his office in downtown Portland it began to sink in that, sure as hell, he was going to have to go into the prelim with only the rebar as evidence that his client was innocent.

Unless Hunsaker found the missing evidence in time.

But considering how much evidence was waiting to be processed, it would take a small army to find the two bags. He'd gladly hire a whole battalion, if it weren't for one small problem: Handling by non-lab personnel would break the chain of evidence.

Three days to the prelim.

20

Boonstra selected a cigar from the humidor and pre-pared it, his movements automatic, no motion wasted. After the cigar glowed evenly he buzzed his office manager.

Fortunately, she was back from lunch. "Yes, Congressman?"

"Ronette, get Atlantic Trust in Boston on the horn for me. Ask for Harv Driscoll."

"Yes, sir."

He leaned back and blew smoke rings at the ceiling until the black desk phone buzzed. He snatched up the handset. "Harv? How are things, kid?"

"Been a while, Dale. I'm doing fine, just fine. Marjorie and I have a beautiful new granddaughter, as of last week. How's D.C. treating you?"

"Can't complain, can't complain. Say, old son, what can you tell me about the Transcend Foundation?"

Five seconds of silence went by before Harv answered. "I know that it's one of our clients and that Harold Cavenaugh handles the account, but that's about all I know. Why?"

"The name popped up in a matter I'm involved with and I was curious who they were, what they were about."

"Well, as I said, my knowledge is pretty limited. Tell you what—give me an hour to nose around and I'll get back to you."

"I would surely appreciate that, Harv."

"My pleasure. I figure I owe you a huge favor for getting my youngest son, Jim, an internship with one of your House colleagues. He's only been there six months, but Jim's setting his sights high. Has his eye on the chief-of-staff position."

"I wouldn't bet against it."

"Talk to you in an hour or so."

It took ol' Harv longer than that; almost three hours ticked by before he called back, apologetic for the delay.

"No worries, Harv."

"Getting any information whatsoever on this foundation was like pulling teeth. Security is very tight. It's the gosh-damnedest thing, Dale. You'd think it was a black ops outfit."

"Have any luck at all?"

"Well, I couldn't suss out any financials or information about the foundation's principals. Only Cavenaugh's inner circle has access, on a need-to-know basis. But I did manage to prise out one thing: what the Transcend Foundation does, its stated purpose."

Boonstra spat a piece of tobacco into the crystal ashtray. A ten-dollar cigar should have better quality control. "Well?"

"Philanthropy."

"And the beneficiary of their philanthropy?"

"Are you ready for this? The transgender community. Didn't know they had a community."

"Interesting." It explained why the Transcend Foundation hired a high-priced lawyer and posted a half-million-dollar bond for the transgender who shot his nephew.

"And that's all I could find out."

"You done good, Harv. Far as I'm concerned, we're square. You take care now."

He leaned back in his chair and watched the smoke drift toward the ceiling.

As part of their philanthropy the Transcend Foundation were trying to toss a monkey wrench in Kellenberger's sure-thing prosecution.

An outfit like that, with more money than God, could do pret' near anything it took a notion to, and that made it a formidable enemy. But how to stop something so clandestine when information about it was near impossible to come by?

He sat up straight, cigar halfway to his mouth. The Transcend Foundation was in Oregon. Ronson lived in Oregon. He could drop it in Ronson's lap and let Mr. Morality run it to ground. Brilliant.

He snatched up the remote, switched on his television, and watched the Nationals lose to the Red Sox.

21

Ritter glanced at Andie, picking at the edge of the defense table with her fingernail. He leaned over and whispered, "This is only a preliminary hearing, remember. You won't have to testify, so relax."

She folded her hands in her lap. "Guess I'm a little freaked. You think there's a chance the case will be dismissed?"

"Yes, there's a chance." But he had no illusions; it was a long shot. He'd need to convince the judge that the case against Andie had no merit. In prelims usually only the prosecution presented evidence. Nevertheless, he planned to do whatever he could, including presenting the evidence he had, to nip the case in the bud. Because if Andie had to stand trial, it would turn into a carnival sideshow with her as the main exhibit.

"All rise. The Honorable Judge Thomas Bondurant."

They stood while the judge entered the courtroom and took his place at the bench. He wasn't one to waste time on preliminaries. He recited the charge and the ORS law it violated and had Kellenberger and Ritter introduce themselves. Then he looked out over the courtroom. "This proceeding has but one purpose—to determine whether there's probable cause to proceed to trial. If the prosecution fails to establish probable cause, the case will be dismissed."

Out of the corner of his eye Ritter saw Andie cross her fingers. He'd take all the help he could get, even supernatural.

"Mr. Kellenberger," Bondurant said, "is the prosecution ready to proceed?"

"Yes, Your Honor. First, I would like to submit People's Exhibit A into evidence." He held up a small black automatic pistol with a tag attached. "This pistol, used to kill Howard Hinshaw, was in the defendant's possession. The crime lab found the defendant's fingerprints on it. Here is a copy of the forensic report, which I will submit as People's Exhibit B. People's Exhibit C is a copy of an FICS report that determined the pistol was stolen during a home burglary last year." Kellenberger handed the three items to the court clerk.

Ritter winced. He hadn't seen that coming.

Andie leaned over. "My friend Kayla told me her boyfriend gave her the gun. No way would I have let her talk me into taking it if I'd known it was stolen, no way."

For a moment Ritter considered putting her on the stand to explain how a stolen gun came to be in her possession. But it wouldn't gain them much, and besides, he had promised her she wouldn't have to testify. Not that he'd let it go unchallenged, but he would have to wait until it was his turn at bat.

"Your Honor," Kellenberger said, "at this time I would like to call Norman Pfaff to the stand."

Pfaff came forward. Andie had described him as a thug, but with his fresh haircut, close shave, white polo shirt, tan slacks, and shoes polished to a high luster he looked like a college student, president of Tau Kappa Epsilon. Kellenberger had cleaned him up to bolster his credibility. But Kellenberger couldn't do anything about the surly look on Pfaff's face or the way he smirked at Andie as he was being sworn in. Ritter saw Bondurant's eyes narrow as he regarded Pfaff. It was a hopeful sign, in a case that had a serious shortage of hopeful signs.

Kellenberger stood in front of the witness box. "Mr. Pfaff, please describe the events that occurred on the evening of July fourteenth, beginning with what you and your companions were doing in Chinatown."

"Okay. Me and Gary and Howie were headed over to the Greyhound depot on Fifth and Glisan. We walked west on Burnside and turned north at the Chinatown sign on Fourth. We were walking along, just minding our own business, when *he*—" Pfaff pointed at Andie. "—when *he* jumped out of an alley, screaming crazy stuff and acting really pissed off."

"Objection," Ritter said. "The defendant's gender identity is obviously female. Masculine pronouns are inappropriate."

Bondurant turned to the witness. "Mr. Pfaff, you will use feminine pronouns when referring to the defendant. Please continue."

Pfaff shrugged. "When *she* pulled out a gun we were, like, 'whoa!' She forced us into the alley with the gun. Our first thought was we were being robbed, but she didn't ask for any money. We were scared shi—real scared. Howie, he bent down and picked up a rusty iron rod laying in the alley, but she shot him before he could even straighten up."

Kellenberger nodded. "And then what did you and Mr. Burleson do?"

"We took off before she shot us, too. Gary called nine one one on his phone after we were a safe distance away. When the police came we told them what happened. They hand-cuffed her and put her in the back seat of their police car."

"Thank you. No more questions."

Andie leaned over to Ritter. "Now you get to cross-examine him, right? Tear him a new one."

Ritter stood and walked over to stand in front of the witness. The smirk on Pfaff's face was a dare. Ritter took it.

"Mr. Pfaff, you testified the defendant forced you and your companions into the alley at gunpoint. Once you were in the alley, what would you estimate the distance was between her and the three of you?"

Pfaff looked away. "About eight feet."

"Did you or Mr. Burleson or Mr. Hinshaw come any closer to Ms. McInnes than that or make physical contact with her at any time?"

"No way. She was pointing a gun at us."

"Help me visualize the scene in the alley. Were the three of you standing, sitting, or lying down?"

"We were standing."

"Was the defendant standing, sitting, or lying down?"

"Standing. And pointing a gun at us, as I said."

"How far were you from the entrance to the alley?"

"About ten feet or so, I guess."

"Where in the alley did Mr. Hinshaw find the rebar?"

"On the ground in front of him, almost between his feet."

"So Mr. Hinshaw bent over and picked it up, correct?"

"Yeah. I think he planned to throw it at her."

"Why didn't he?"

"She shot him before he could."

"Before he straightened up, you said in your deposition."

"Exactly right."

Ritter walked over to the court clerk and got the rebar. "The police recovered this in the alley. The lab found Mr. Hinshaw's DNA on one end. With the court's permission, I submit Defense Exhibit A." He handed the rebar back to the clerk and looked at Pfaff. "Now . . . did Mr. Hinshaw bend over forward, backward, or sideways to pick up the rebar?"

"Huh? Forward, of course."

"So Mr. Hinshaw bent over forward to pick up the rebar. Was he facing the defendant or away from her?"

"Facing her. Howie totally didn't take his eyes off the gun. Neither did me or Gary."

Ritter produced a document. "I submit Defense Exhibit B, Your Honor, a report from the Multnomah County coroner." He handed it to the judge and turned back to Pfaff. "The coroner's report indicates the bullet entered Mr. Hinshaw's neck at an upward angle of approximately forty degrees. How could that be possible when, according to you, Mr. Hinshaw was bent over forward?"

"Objection," Kellenberger said. "Calls for a conclusion."

"Withdrawn," Ritter said. Feint with a left, follow with a right cross. "Mr. Pfaff, what would you say if I told you Ms. McInnes claims you raped her?"

Pfaff laughed, a shrill falsetto. "Impossible."

"Why?"

"*She* doesn't have a—doesn't have the right equipment."

"And you know this how?"

"Call it an educated guess."

"In your statement to police you referred to the defendant as 'that crazy tranny' three times. Tell me, how did you know that Ms. McInnes is transgender?"

Pfaff smirked, as though enjoying a private joke. "We could just tell, that's all."

"Mr. Hinshaw and Mr. Burleson—they knew as well?"

"Yeah. We all clocked her as a tranny."

"Interesting. By the way, the term *tranny* is considered a slur. Are you aware of that?"

Shrug. "Guess I'm not all that politically correct."

"So you three were certain she was transgender." Ritter gestured toward Andie. "Look at the defendant, Mr. Pfaff. How could you or *anyone* possibly 'clock her,' as you put it?"

"Four chan," Pfaff said, the smirk back on his face. "Four chan dot org, a very cool site. It hipped us to traps."

"Traps? Explain, please."

"A trap is a dude who looks so much like a real girl that by the time you realize you made a mistake it's too late. That's the trap part."

"I gather you believe transgender girls like to trick unwary males. Ever been tricked?"

"No, but I know guys who have."

"Is it possible that you and your pals learned Ms. McInnes was transgender—a 'trap'—only after pushing her to the ground on her back and pulling down her pants, with the intention of raping her?"

"No," Pfaff said. "No frickin' way."

Ritter gave him a cold stare. "Are you sure? It would explain your certainty that she was transgender, as well as the upward angle of the bullet."

"Objection," Kellenberger said. "Asked and answered."

"Sustained," Bondurant said.

"No more questions." Ritter took his seat next to Andie.

"Redirect, Mr. Kellenberger?"

"No, Your Honor. The prosecution rests."

Bondurant excused Pfaff, who left the stand with a smirk.

Ritter stood. "Your Honor, I submit Defense Exhibit C, the defendant's statement to police, in which she indicates that the gun was lent to her by a friend who had gotten it from her boyfriend." He handed the document to the judge. "Ms. McInnes told me a few minutes ago she had no idea it was a stolen firearm."

"Objection, hearsay," Kellenberger said. "Let the defendant take the stand and tell the court herself she didn't know the gun was stolen."

Bondurant closed his eyes for several seconds and then said, "Mr. Kellenberger, I remind you, this is not a trial. In a preliminary hearing the defendant is not obligated to testify, and hearsay may be considered, including the defendant's statements to her attorney. Please proceed, Mr. Ritter."

"Your Honor, I move to dismiss, in light of evidence that the shooting was in self-defense, to prevent a deadly assault."

"Motion to dismiss is denied, due to insufficient evidence."

"Then the defense rests."

The judge looked out over the courtroom. "I hereby order Andrea Lynne McInnes bound over for trial for manslaughter in the second degree. Ms. McInnes may remain free on bond. This proceeding is adjourned." He rapped his gavel once.

Ritter laid a hand on Andie's shoulder. "It was a long shot. Motions to dismiss are almost never granted unless overwhelming evidence is produced. Without the DNA test results we came up short."

"You blew big holes in Pfaff's testimony. Doesn't that count for anything?"

"It will when we get to trial. Right now let's try to sneak out before the reporters are all over us, yes?"

No point informing her that the judicial deck was stacked against transgender individuals, and particularly trans girls. She was already more aware of that than he'd ever be.

Poker. An apt metaphor for the situation.

Ordinarily he'd have an ace or two up his sleeve, but not this time. If he couldn't find a way to shuffle the damn deck, "destack" it, Kellenberger would hold all the cards and win the big pot. Ritter grimaced at the thought.

A high-stakes game, for him as well as Andie. Her freedom and his reputation were riding on it.

22

The Cessna Citation knifed through thin air above the scattered clouds, following the Atlantic coastline south. The sleek craft carried a single passenger, a congressman. Through a portside window, Boonstra spotted a tanker ten miles off the coast, headed north.

He'd planned to have a steam bath, massage, and a thick sirloin at the Capitol Hill Club. A phone call from Richard Ronson necessitated a change in plans.

"A private jet is waiting for you at Dulles," Ronson had said. "It will take you to Miami."

And now he found himself jetting south at 450 knots, according to the pilot, who despite his uniform looked to be barely out of high school. (Boonstra couldn't resist asking him how old he was. Turned out he was 33.)

He looked over the briefing his chief of staff had prepared for him. As usual, Ennis had been concise:

"Omar Mullen, 74, is the founder and principal stockholder of PharmaLogic, currently the second-largest pharmaceutical company in the world. *Forbes* estimates his net worth to be 54 billion. Mullen is a devoutly religious man known to support socially conservative causes. He reputedly donated twenty-five million to the failed effort to defeat gay marriage."

Mullen sounded like an ideal candidate for what he had in mind.

An hour and forty-five minutes after their departure from Dulles the Citation descended, preparing to land at Miami International. "Please fasten your seat belt, sir," the pilot said via an overhead speaker.

After a sweeping right turn over Miami Beach, its miles-long ribbon of bone-white sand speckled with sun worshipers, the aircraft lined up for a straight-in approach at Miami International. Boonstra, who hated landings, kept a white-knuckled grip on the armrests.

He needn't have worried. The transition from flying to touchdown was almost imperceptible. The jet braked hard and turned off the runway. They negotiated labyrinthine taxiways and came to a full stop in front of a huge hangar. A resounding silence replaced the sibilant whine of the engines.

The pilot came back to the cabin and opened the door, which was hinged at the bottom so it could swing down and become stairs. After a nod to the pilot, Boonstra started down. He was met at the bottom by a man wearing a white short-sleeve shirt with tie, navy baseball cap, and sunglasses.

"Please come with me, Congressman," the man said.

Boonstra accompanied him a short distance, to where a white helicopter squatted on the tarmac. On its side was the same *PL* logo as on the Citation. He helped Boonstra into a seat in the rear of the craft and then climbed into the right-front seat and donned a headset. After the pilot received takeoff clearance they were airborne, headed south southwest. Forty-five minutes later they were over Key West.

Ten miles due south of Key West the pilot pointed and said, "That's the *Pharma Queen*, one of the largest luxury yachts in the world. Five hundred seventy-four feet in length, built in twenty-twelve by Lurssen Yachts in Germany. Crew of eighty-nine."

"Lordy, that's not a yacht," Boonstra said. "That's a ship."

The futuristic-looking vessel sliced through the sea below, its wake evincing high speed. With a superstructure that rose six levels above the main deck, the *Pharma Queen* looked like it could belong to a cruise line instead of one very rich man.

"Last year," the pilot said, "pirates intercepted the *Queen* off the coast of Somalia, intending to seize her. Big mistake. Half the *Queen*'s crew are ex-military and extremely well armed. They killed all the pirates and sank their vessel."

Boonstra laughed. "I think I read about that. Just desserts."

The chopper landed squarely on the helipad on the aft deck. Boonstra got out and stood blinking at the sun's glare.

An Asian crewman in a crisp white uniform appeared. "Please follow me, sir," he said.

The crewman escorted him to the ship's salon, located amidships on one of the upper levels. "Mr. Mullen will be right with you, sir," he said and disappeared.

Boonstra stood rooted to the spot, gawking at the salon's appointments—burnished teak bulkheads and cabinets; thick Persian rugs on a deck of green marble; sofas and chairs covered in leather, its grain invisible to the eye; and a score of paintings and vases that were probably worth more than many smaller yachts. It was by no means a small space, but it felt remarkably intimate, thanks to the furnishings and the recessed lighting.

No ashtrays in sight, not a one. Boonstra had been jonesing for a cigar since he left Dulles and wanted one badly now. He heard a sound behind him and turned around. And forgot all about cigars.

Omar Mullen, titan of industry, stood only five foot two. Wiry rather than frail. Thick white hair. Dark eyes below bushy white brows. Hawk-like nose. When he spoke, his voice was deep and resonant. "Congressman, welcome to my home." He extended his hand.

Boonstra shook it. "A pleasure."

"I trust your flight was pleasant."

"Very pleasant, thank you."

Mullen gestured at a pair of soft chairs in an L-shaped arrangement with a low cabinet in the space between them. "Might as well be comfortable." After they were seated, he said, "Can I offer you a cigar, Congressman?"

Boonstra grinned. "You're playing my song, Mr. Mullen."

Mullen reached over and pressed a hidden button on the cabinet. The top folded back and a humidor rose from the interior, accompanied by two ashtrays, each with its own lighter and cutter. He selected two cigars and passed one to his guest.

Boonstra inspected the band. It was a Louixs, reputed to be the finest cigar in the world. He had never even seen a Louixs, let alone smoked one. After trimming the end and lighting it with care, he took a first puff. Pure bliss. He smiled at his host. "Now that's a cigar. Exceptional."

"A Saudi prince once presented me with a box of Gurkha Black Dragons, which cost eleven hundred fifty dollars apiece, but I'll take a fifty-dollar Louixs over a Black Dragon any day of the week."

Boonstra nodded. "Hard to improve on perfection."

"I agree. But you're not here to discuss cigars, Congressman." He flicked his cigar's ash into the ashtray. "First, I want to express my admiration for your Protect Our Children Act. Do you anticipate much trouble getting it though the House?"

"I'm not worried. Some conservative Democrats are on board, so I'm confident it will pass with a supermajority."

"And the Senate?"

Boonstra took a puff of his cigar and blew the smoke at the overhead. "The Senate is a bit more uncertain. Democrats have threatened to filibuster, and an Obama veto is a certainty if we can't get a two-thirds majority. It'll be tough."

"What's it going to take?"

"Persuasion."

"Persuasion can be expensive."

"It can, depending on how persuasive you want to be."

"So what's the big picture? Beyond this bill, I mean."

Cue the pitch. "I want to stop the transgender movement dead in its tracks. It's a threat to our family values and to religious liberty. It could destroy our way of life. It must be stopped."

"How do you propose to do that?"

"With legislation. The Protect Our Children Act is just the beginning. I'm working with Richard Ronson and his Family Morality Council on future legislation to rid society of this demonic scourge at every level."

"An ambitious undertaking."

"But worthwhile."

"Mr. Ronson is a godly man. Given his involvement, I'm optimistic about your chances of success."

Boonstra knocked the ash off his cigar. "But we've run up against . . . an unforeseen obstacle. One that poses a serious threat to our plans."

"What sort of obstacle?"

"An outfit that calls itself the Transcend Foundation, a nonprofit based in Portland, Oregon. According to their mission statement, they exist to further the goals of the transgender community and provide support and assistance to individual transgenders, or words to that effect. And they have deep pockets. Real deep."

"Support and assistance, huh?"

"I'll give you a personal example. They furnished bail and high-powered legal counsel for a transgender who shot and killed my nephew, who lived in Portland. There's a chance the transgender will beat the manslaughter charge."

"Only in a godless country could that happen."

Now for the wrap-up. "Mr. Mullen, up against an organization like that, stopping the transgenders is likely to be an uphill slog, with a high probability of failure." He held his breath.

Mullen stubbed out his cigar. "Congressman, I'm going to give you a shove up that hill. You and Mr. Ronson will have the funding you need."

"Mr. Mullen, you are the answer to our prayers."

"I consider it an investment on behalf of the Almighty."

"God willing, we shall prevail." He felt like dancing a jig. With Mullen bankrolling him, he'd surely prevail at anything he wanted to do, including bringing the Transcend Foundation to its knees.

He couldn't wait to get back and set things in motion. Right off the bat, though, he'd need to funnel some of that loot into his reelection campaign, currently running on fumes. Everything depended on him keeping his seat.

"Now that we've got that settled, I'll give you a tour of the *Queen*. She's my primary residence these days."

"I'm champing at the bit to see it," he said, hoping he'd get another crack at a Louixs before he had to go.

23

The name-change hearing took all of ten minutes. After they left the courtroom, Ritter patted Andie on the back. "Congratulations, Andrea Lynne McInnes."

"Thanks." Andie looked again at the judge's signature on the court order. "Legal and official. For me that's a first."

"Still want to get your driver's license today?"

"Sure, why not? I've been studying the manual all week. Got it down cold." She reached into her bag and took out two documents folded in thirds. "I have my birth certificate and a DMV Change of Gender Designation form filled out and signed by Dr. Soong. Together with the name-change order, that should satisfy them."

"All right, then. Next stop, the DMV."

As luck would have it, the Department of Motor Vehicles on Southeast Powell was having a midmorning rush, its huge parking lot jam-packed with vehicles. Ritter suggested they try the office in Gresham and Andie agreed.

Twenty minutes later they walked into the Gresham DMV, which had two people standing at the counter, eight others waiting to be served. Andie took a number from the machine and sat down beside Ritter.

"I just hope I don't flub the actual driving test," she said.

"You shouldn't have a problem if you drive as well as you did yesterday. You're a natural."

"Thank you again for the lessons."

"You're welcome. Here . . . you're going to need this." He handed her a printout. "Proof of insurance. The foundation added you to their policy."

"Thanks." She looked it over.

"Since you'll be taking the test in my vehicle they'll also check it out, make sure it has brakes, turn signals, etcetera."

"I can't believe all the hoops they make you jump through to get a driver's—"

"Excuse me, but they just called forty-seven. Isn't that your number?"

"Already?" She stood and walked to the front.

The heavyset woman behind the counter gave her a friendly smile. "And what can we do for you today, young lady?"

Andie returned the smile. "Hi. I'm here to get a driver's license."

"Okay. First, we'll need some identification."

"Right here." Andie handed her the stack of papers.

As the woman looked over the documents, her smile vanished, replaced by a stony expression. She looked Andie up and down and then shoved the stack back across the counter. "I can't help you."

"Excuse me?"

"I can't help you."

"Is there a problem with my documentation?"

"I can't help you, I'm sorry." She didn't look sorry.

Andie turned around and beckoned to Ritter. He got up and walked over, eyebrows raised in inquiry.

"She says she can't help me."

He slid his card across the counter. "I'm Miss McInnes' attorney. What seems to be the problem?"

"I can't help . . . this person."

"Why not?"

"It would be a violation of my faith."

Andie noticed the woman's pendant, a silver fish symbol with a cross in the center.

"Ma'am," Ritter said, "you're a public servant. Are you re-fusing to perform your job?"

"The First Amendment to the Constitution protects my sincerely held religious beliefs." She thrust her jaw forward.

"Let me talk to your supervisor."

"I'm the senior clerk in this office."

Ritter locked eyes with the woman for five long seconds. "What is your name, ma'am?"

"Madeleine Sanger."

"Ms. Sanger, Miss McInnes is here to get a driver's license, not a marriage license. And this is Oregon, not Kentucky."

By that time, the squabble had attracted a half-dozen in-terested onlookers.

A flush crept up the woman's neck and across her cheeks. "I don't have to put up with rudeness. If you have no further business you have to leave."

"Is the State of Oregon aware of your refusal to perform your duties?"

"I will call the police if I have to."

"We'll leave, Ms. Sanger. And I hope you relish publicity, because you're about to get a ton of it."

The woman glared at him, her lips thin white lines.

"C'mon, Andie, let's go. We're due back in the twenty-first century."

After they climbed into the Range Rover, Ritter turned to her. "Can you believe that woman?"

Her laugh had a bitter edge. "When you're transgender you get used to that kind of treatment."

"If her religious beliefs won't allow her to fulfill the duties of the job, she shouldn't be a public servant."

"You're preaching to the choir."

"Feel like trying another DMV?"

She considered it for a moment and then shook her head. "If you don't mind, let's do it another day. I think I'd like to just go home now."

"Can't blame you there," Ritter said and started the engine.

Tuesday, August 2, 2016 5:38 p.m.

Bit of a rant follows.

Today I encountered a religious hypocrite. This one worked behind the counter at the DMV in Gresham. In fact, she was the supervisor, called the shots in that office. Her name was Madeleine Sanger. She was sweet as pie to me until I handed her my documentation. As she read it, her face turned to granite. No dice, she said, her eyes twin lasers of hate. Her "sincerely held religious convictions" would not allow her to process my application for a driver's license.

It always catches me off guard. It shouldn't, but it does. It's such an anachronism (I almost never get a chance to use that word) in the twenty-first century. I don't expect it. Especially from a public employee in a state government office.

Wearing a fish symbol as a pendant and using her faith as a cudgel (another word I hardly ever get to use) the woman looked at me like I was a dog turd on an ermine rug.

I didn't want to argue, I just sicced Eli on her. But the fact that he was a lawyer didn't cut any ice with Madeleine. She dug in even harder. Then she informed us we had to leave the premises.

Observation: When Eli gets pissed he wields words like a Hattori Hanzo sword, eviscerating opponents with surgical precision. I sure wish I could do that.

Anyway, she made us leave, threatening to call the cops if we didn't. I was glad to put as much distance between her and me as possible.

Eli and I agreed that we've had it with so-called Christians who cloak bigotry in religious faith while trumpeting their piety to everyone within earshot.

Somewhere I read that, in the mid-twentieth century, people calling themselves Christians used religion to justify segregation and persecute black people. I guess trans is the new black.

What would Jesus do?

My guess—He'd smack Madeleine across the chops with a flounder, since she's so fond of fish.

24

Hunsaker was eating lunch, his feet propped up on his desk, when Forensic Technician Cindy Barndollar walked into the DNA extraction lab. "Hi, Cindy," he said. "What's up?"

"Excuse me, Dr. Hunsaker. That memo you emailed everybody—you know, about the missing DNA evidence?"

"Yes, what about it?"

"I was on duty on the fifteenth—that's when you said the evidence was sent over—and I think I logged it in."

"No kidding." He set down the half-eaten sandwich and gave her his undivided attention. "Tell me more."

"Well, it's kind of unusual when a police officer personally delivers evidence to us, instead of sending it over by courier, so that's why I remembered it."

He stroked his chin. "You definitely remember receiving the evidence? Can you describe it?"

"Yes, two sealed and labeled bags, women's jeans in one and women's underwear in another, according to the labels. I left the bags sealed, of course, and put them with all the other evidence to be tested. Oh—and I also entered them into LIMS with their location in storage."

His pulse quickened. "Did you find them again?"

"Didn't look. We have several thousand items of evidence waiting to be tested, many of them in similar bags. It would be like looking for two needles in a very large haystack."

He was getting very tired of that simile. Finding those bags was a priority, even though the lab was far behind in its processing of evidence. His reputation, as well as the lab's, depended on it. "I owe you lunch, Cindy."

She started toward the door. "I'll hold you to that."

"Oh, before you go . . . this episode has driven home the necessity for legible signatures on receipts, yes?"

"Yes," she said. "You won't see any more squiggles from me or the rest of the team. We were in too much of a hurry. Led to bad habits."

After she left, he picked up the sandwich and pondered the problem as he chewed. Locating the two bags must be done efficiently, discreetly, and with utmost regard for preserving the chain of evidence.

They would be found. Even if he had to examine each and every bag in the lab personally.

But what had happened to the two LIMS records Cindy had entered for the evidence? Database records didn't just vanish spontaneously; LIMS had safeguards to prevent that. They must have been deleted intentionally.

Deleted by whom? And why?

25

The drone hovered five hundred feet above the Transcend Foundation's main building, transmitting the view from its high-resolution camera to a large, square utility van parked on a street bordering the foundation's south side. The faded "A-Z Plumbing" on the back and sides of the vehicle contributed to its streetside invisibility.

Hunched over a display screen inside the van, Neil Pomerenke flew the drone in a slow circle over the facility and then sent it a command to return automatically to its point of origin. "Proof of concept," he said to the man beside him. "Pomerenke Investigations has gone high-tech."

The other man whooped and then said, "I'll bring it in." He made his way to the door in back and climbed out.

Pomerenke had a drone's-eye view of him exiting the van and looking up as the drone descended to land on the grass strip between the street and sidewalk. After it touched down he set the transmitter on the workbench.

The back door opened and the other man climbed in and set the drone beside the transmitter. "Sounds like angry bees."

"Or wasps." Pomerenke connected the drone to a charger to replenish its battery.

The sleek craft had an X-shaped carbon-fiber fuselage with a propeller at the end of each arm. Slung underneath its middle section was a camera with a sizable lens.

"Expensive?"

"Twenty-nine hundred bucks, but it's one of the most sophisticated drones available under five grand. Top of the line, state of the art. We've got two of them."

"Two? Why do we need two?"

"So one can be charging while the other's flying, Einstein."

"Oh, right. What's the transmitter range?"

"A mile. Actually, a bit farther, because the transmitter uses an external antenna on the roof of the van."

"That explains how you can be inside the van and still—"

His cell phone trilled. "Hold on a sec." He tapped the "Answer" button. "Pomerenke."

"Status, please." The voice had a high, reedy quality, like a busted clarinet.

"Yes, sir. I'm in position, with a clear view of the entrance."

"I want photos of all persons and vehicles going in or out."

"You got it."

A click indicated the conversation was over. No goodbye, kiss my ass, or go to hell. But that was okay. $500 a day plus expenses—in cash, of course—made it plenty okay.

He pocketed the cell phone and turned to the other man. "Gordo, run down to Arby's and get me a couple of roast beef sandwiches and a coffee. Don't forget the Horsey Sauce. Get yourself whatever you want." He held out a twenty. "This ought to cover it."

For the umpteenth time that day, Pomerenke tried to fish a pack of smokes from his empty shirt pocket. Quitting cold turkey was a bitch, even three months down the road.

He unwrapped a stick of Juicy Fruit and popped it into his mouth. He'd bought a case of the stuff. The sugar rush dulled the tobacco craving. For a while, at least.

Drone One needed to be wiped down. He grabbed a micro-fiber cloth.

26

On a crisp, bright Monday morning Ritter strolled through Lownsdale Square, a small park near the courthouse, and then crossed Southwest Salmon, headed for City Coffee on 4th. Before entering the restaurant he fed four quarters into the newspaper vending machine on the corner and stuck a folded copy of *The Oregonian* under his arm.

Inside, he ordered a latte and worked his way to a table in the back corner. As usual for a weekday, the place was teeming with lawyers, court clerks, people on jury duty, even a judge or two, due to its proximity to the courthouse.

Still, he liked the unassuming atmosphere, the friendly servers, the smooth jazz from hidden speakers, and most of all the delicious aroma of freshly ground coffee beans. He inhaled deeply. Coffee's taste never fulfilled the promise of its aroma, it seemed to him.

In National/International news, the UN passed a resolution condemning Iran for seizing a Bahraini cargo ship in the Strait of Hormuz; Kim Jong-un announced that North Korea was "very close" to having a long-range missile capable of reaching the West Coast of the United States; televangelist Jimmy-Jeff Johnston denied hiring a prostitute, claiming he was only trying to save her immortal soul. Sure he was.

In the City/Region news, an article below the fold almost jumped off the page at him:

DMV Clerk Fired For Refusing To Assist Transgender Woman

A clerk at the Department of Motor Vehicles in Gresham has been suspended for refusing to assist a transgender woman who tried to apply for a driver's license. The clerk's suspension followed an investigation by the Oregon Department of Transportation in response to a complaint filed by the transgender woman's attorney, Elias Ritter.

The clerk, Madeleine Sanger, 47, explained that her religious beliefs prohibited her from assisting the applicant. "Transgenders are abominations," Sanger said. "I shouldn't be forced to deal with them."

ODOT spokesperson Lynn Rickman said that in this circumstance Sanger's religious beliefs were irrelevant to the performance of her job duties. "Ms. Sanger is a public servant," Rickman said. "Taxes pay her salary. The individual she refused to help is a taxpayer and entitled to service. Ms. Sanger's disapproval of a DMV customer, whether for religious reasons or otherwise, is totally irrelevant."

Not surprisingly, Sanger has a different point of view. "This is the United States of America," she said. "As a U.S. citizen, the First Amendment of the Constitution guarantees protection for my sincerely held religious beliefs. This suspension is an attack on religious liberty."

The Family Morality Council, an Oregon-based evangelical group, weighed in on Sanger's side. Director Richard Ronson said, "Ms. Sanger is right. This is a vicious attack on religious liberty and one more example how Christians are harassed." Ronson said his organization will provide legal counsel for Sanger.

Ritter laughed, one short bark, drawing curious looks from other customers. He covered his mouth and pretended to cough. ODOT had acted on the complaint only a week after he'd filed it. The news would brighten up Andie's day.

Scanning the editorial pages, he glanced over the top edge of the paper and spotted Kellenberger standing with a young man at the order counter. Ritter ducked behind the paper, hoping Kellenberger hadn't seen him. It had been a pleasant, relaxing morning and he didn't want to spoil it.

"Hey, Eli. That you hiding back there?"

Ritter winced and lowered the paper. "Hello, Bret."

Kellenberger gestured to his young companion. "Eli, this is my brother-in-law, Jason Sepers."

Ritter acknowledged him with a nod. He looked familiar, something about his posture and sullen expression. Ritter couldn't recall where he'd seen him before.

"Eli is one of Portland's top defense lawyers, Jason."

"What do you do, Jason?" Ritter asked. More information might jog his memory.

"I'm in IT."

"Jason's modest," Kellenberger said. "He's an information technology guru for the State of Oregon."

And then it clicked. The police crime lab in Clackamas—that's where he'd seen him before. The IT guy who replaced the keyboard in Hunsaker's lab was Kellenberger's brother-in-law. Small world.

"See you around," Kellenberger said.

After they left the shop, Ritter resumed reading the paper, but the articles might as well have been written in cuneiform. He folded the paper and got up. Lost in thought, he bumped into a table on the way out and apologized profusely to its occupants.

27

Senator Jim McCoy from Washington state finger-combed his hair and adjusted his tie. Camera crews from three local network affiliates jockeyed for position below McCoy on the Capitol Building's steps, all grimly determined to get the obligatory shot of the dome looming over his shoulder. A reporter from WJLA-TV with chin-length hair and more than her share of teeth said, "Whenever you're ready, Senator."

McCoy looked out over the crowd of kibitzers that always gathered whenever cameras were present. "Good afternoon. The deceptively titled Protect Our Children Act, which Republicans passed in the House yesterday, is a vile piece of legislation that discriminates against children who are members of a misunderstood and persecuted minority.

"If enacted into law, this bill would force transgender girls to use the boys' restroom and transgender boys to use the girls' restroom, which psychologists say is senseless, cruel, and liable to cause these children emotional damage as well as subject them to physical danger.

"What's more, it's in direct conflict with federal law, Title IX, which prohibits sex discrimination in schools. This foul legislation would *institutionalize* discrimination in schools.

"The bill will now be sent over to the Senate. I will do everything in my power to make sure the discriminatory Protect Our Children Act does not pass. Thank you."

Microphone in hand, the reporter from WJLA-TV climbed up three steps to stand beside McCoy. "Senator, the bill's supporters claim that it was written to protect the privacy of nontransgender children."

McCoy snorted. "It's the 'bathroom panic' meme, the ridiculous notion that boys are going to put on dresses as a lark so they can peek at girls using the restroom."

"You don't think it's a legitimate concern?"

"There is a world of difference between a boy in a dress and a transgender girl. For one thing, it's not a lark to the transgender girl. For another, the boy in the dress didn't have to be examined and vetted by experts in psychology and endocrinology like she did. In that never-gonna-happen scenario, the dress-wearing boy would deserve detention or suspension."

"They also claim that gender-nonconforming children are just going through a phase, as kids often do, and that all they really need is parental guidance."

"What they're really saying is there's no such thing as a transgender child. Or a transgender adult, for that matter. Despite the consensus of the medical and psychological communities, they refuse to accept the idea that human beings can be transgender. These are the same folks who reject evolution, climate change, and the need for vaccinations. It's an anti-science mindset."

"The evangelical Family Morality Council issued a statement today in support of the bill, declaring it was 'essential for the preservation of traditional moral values.'"

McCoy snorted again. "They've been fearmongering about a so-called 'transgender agenda' that brainwashes children into believing they're transgender and indoctrinates them into a 'godless transgender lifestyle.' The Southern Poverty Law Center lists the Family Morality Council as a hate group."

"Other evangelical groups are also supporting the bill."

"And here's the strange thing about that—not a single reference to transgender people can be found in scripture. You'd think that would discourage them from condemning transgender people as sinners and abominations. Not a chance. They're bound and determined to use religion to justify their bigotry any way they can. The bill should be renamed the Protect Our Bigots Act."

"Do you think you can stop the Senate bill?"

"I'm going to do my best, even if I have to filibuster until humans colonize Mars."

"When will the bill come to the floor?"

"Not until it goes through committee and they've lined up the votes. Unless decency prevails and they scrap it."

"Senator McCoy, thank you for talking with us." Her broad smile exposed her molars.

"My pleasure."

McCoy boarded the Metro and found a seat next to a window. Unlike his Senate colleagues, he used public transportation most of the time, consistent with his man-of-the-people style. The trip, from the center of D.C. to Spring Hill, where he resided in an apartment when Congress was in session, would take about half an hour.

As he sat down he noticed a man sitting across the aisle two rows back wearing mirrored aviator glasses. He'd been in the crowd of onlookers on the Capitol building's steps, McCoy was sure of it.

Ten years of practicing law, sizing up an unending procession of jurors and witnesses, had honed McCoy's powers of observation.

Mirrored Glasses Guy, for example. Mid-thirties. Upscale-casual duds: khakis, polo shirt, suede leather jacket with front zipper, Reboks. Short brown hair worn high and tight. Off-duty military, possibly. The set of his jaw and his impassive face gave the impression he'd be a tough witness to cross-examine.

After he entered politics McCoy found that his ability to quickly size up colleagues, lobbyists, and constituents was indispensable, enabling him to avoid perilous political shoals.

He switched on his tablet and tapped a blue icon. *The Washington Post*, online edition, filled the screen. He scanned the international, national, and local news and then checked out the opinion page. A piece by the *Post*'s editorial board about the Republican National Committee caught his eye. He was almost finished reading it when the Metro pulled up at the Spring Hill stop. He and three other passengers disembarked, including Mirrored Glasses Guy.

During the three-block walk from the Metro stop to his apartment McCoy had the unsettling feeling he was being followed. Several times he stopped to look back. Nothing, only a deserted street. He had to be imagining things. All the same, he was relieved when he reached the front steps of his apartment building.

His second-floor apartment faced the street. As he closed the front window's drapes, he took a look outside. A shadow moved on the sidewalk below. Or had he only imagined it? He watched for five minutes but saw no further movement.

The Colt .38 was in the desk drawer, where it had been since he bought it at Cabela's in Gainesville. He had never fired it. He picked up the new leather holster, clipped it to his belt in back, and holstered the Colt. The weight and pressure at the small of his back was noticeable, but his coat covered the gun completely. At a fellow senator's urging he had obtained a concealed-carry permit, even though the notion of carrying a gun around had struck him at the time as silly. It still did. But he had to admit, the walk home wouldn't have been quite as unnerving if he'd had the revolver with him.

He drew the gun and pointed it at an imaginary assailant. "Hold it right there, mister," he said aloud.

His phone's shrill ring almost made him drop the weapon. He returned it to the holster and answered the call. It was his appointments secretary, calling to remind him of an early morning meeting. After hanging up he went to the window and peered through the part in the drapes. No movement below, shadows or otherwise.

He put the gun back in the drawer, feeling foolish.

The paranoia had a logical source: his addiction to political thrillers. The previous night he'd finished reading a gripping thriller in which the governor of a blue state had been abducted and tortured by a right-wing fanatic—hard-core, edge-of-the-seat stuff.

In reality, he wasn't in any physical danger. The gun would stay in the drawer. He just needed to lay off the thrillers for a while.

28

Forest Lawn Cemetery in Gresham looked almost exactly the same as it had three years earlier. It had been August then, too. That day had seemed totally surreal. Summer and funerals seemed an unlikely combination.

Andie parked the Prius on the side of the road that ran east-west through the cemetery. The foundation had loaned her the car, even though her driver's license was only one day old. She'd gotten it the day before at the DMV on Sandy, where the clerk didn't bat an eye at her documentation. She missed only one question on the written exam, and she aced the driving test. In the photo on the license she looked demented, but in the section labeled "Sex" there was an "F," and that was all that mattered.

She grabbed her bag and the flowers she'd bought at Fred Meyer on 82nd and got out of the car. Her parents' graves were four rows from the road, in the shade of a young ash leaf maple tree. Like all the markers in the cemetery, her parents' headstones were flush with the ground. She knelt and used her hands to brush away the dried grass cuttings that had obscured the engraving:

Katherine Jean McInnes   Thomas Michael McInnes
May 8, 1977 – August 3, 2013 June 11, 1975 – August 3, 2013
Beloved Mother   Beloved Father

She placed the flowers in recesses in the headstones—pink roses for her mother, white carnations for her father. She opened a bottle of water and poured half into each recess to keep them fresh for a while, until a mower lopped them off level with the grass.

"Hi, you guys. I didn't make it here last month, as you probably noticed. I wanted to, but ... something came up." No point in going into it. "Good news—I have a job. Not only does it pay well, it provides health insurance and other benefits. I also have an apartment of my own. And look—" She took out her new license and held it up. "I got a driver's license. My employer promised to cosign a loan for a car. But that's on hold ... for a while. Once I get a car I'm going to enroll at Portland State and work toward a degree in English. I still want to be a writer. I started writing a mystery novel titled *Inside Game*, but it's on hold until after—anyway, I'm trying to make you proud of me."

She got some Kleenex from her bag and dabbed at her eyes and blew her nose.

"I miss you both so much. I sure hope all that stuff about God and heaven is true, I really do, so we can be together again. And I hope Buddy's there, too. I miss that little guy. Now that I have a place to live, I've been thinking about getting another dog. But that's also on hold."

A flash of light caught her eye. To her left, perhaps five hundred feet from where she sat, a silver car was stopped on the road that encircled the cemetery. It hadn't been there when she'd arrived. A man was sitting behind the wheel, but she couldn't see his face. He didn't make any move to get out but just sat there. As she watched, a glint of reflected sunlight flashed in the driver's open window. Eyeglasses? Unlikely—the flash was too bright. She realized he was looking at her though binoculars. Creeps—they were everywhere.

Sticking around to find out what he was up to seemed like an awesome idea—not. She told her parents she loved them and promised to return soon. Then she shouldered her bag and started for the car.

Thirty seconds later she was rolling silently toward the exit. After a right onto Powell Boulevard she accelerated away from cemeteries and creeps with binoculars.

Her friend Caitlin lived in a trailer court on Rene Avenue, just off Powell. Andie had sofa-surfed at her place for several weeks last year. She'd intended to call Caitlin before leaving the cemetery, see if she wanted to hang out a while, maybe catch a bite. She considered pulling over to make the call (because a conscientious driver doesn't use her phone while driving), but Caitlin's place was only a couple miles away.

She should have phoned first, as it turned out, because Caitlin wasn't home. No big deal, though, now that she had a driver's license.

As she exited the trailer court onto Rene Avenue she almost missed the commotion in the parking lot directly across from the trailer court's entrance. About a dozen people were carrying signs, and they looked pissed off. It took her a moment to realize they were picketing in front of the Gresham DMV. She parked along the street and joined a group of bystanders observing the fracas.

The picketers' signs were all hand-lettered. Spelling was not their long suit: "TRANIES ARE ABOMBNATIONS," "THE DMV IS TRAMPELING RELIGOUS LIBERTY," "MADELIENE GOT CRUSIFIED FOR HER FAITH," "SUPORT CHRISTIANS NOT TRANGENDERS," "THE DMV IS INTOLARENT OF RELIGON." And variations.

She took a couple of photos of the picketers with her phone's camera and then walked back to the car, thoroughly bummed. *Deliver me from religious nuts.*

She wanted to believe in God. She didn't believe in religion.

After driving west several miles on Powell, on impulse she made a right on Southeast 138th. A visit to her old neighborhood might counteract the depressing scene at the DMV.

Although she'd been away only three years, the street had changed considerably. Newer houses and apartment buildings lined the stretch of 138th closest to Powell, empty fields a few short years before.

In one of those fields there had been an excavation that she and her friends called "the Old Hole," which seemed immense when she was a kid, but which turned out to be a minor cavity in the ground when she was older. Apartments covered the Old Hole now.

As she proceeded up 138th things looked more familiar.

The Bursons' house was on the left, at the foot of the hill she and the neighborhood kids used to slide down on home-made sleds in winter. The hill had been unpaved back then.

Old Pop's house was at the top of the hill on the right. Pop was a cantankerous old guy who liked to stand sentry on his front porch so he could rail and shake his fist at neighborhood kids who ventured too close to his property. She didn't see anyone on the porch. Maybe old Pop had died.

The house she grew up in was on a panhandle lot behind Pop's place. It wasn't much—a white clapboard house built in the 1940s, with three bedrooms, one bathroom, and a one-car garage. Her parents were both teachers—her mother taught elementary school and her father junior high—and the house reflected their modest means. Still, they never wanted for anything.

After her parents were killed, the house went to her, as sole heir. Unfortunately, the bank informed her, it had a first and second mortgage and was "underwater"—more was owed on it than it was worth. She signed it over to the bank.

Her parents had no life insurance or burial policies. She sold their 14-year-old Toyota Camry to old Pop for $3500. Her parents' double-burial funeral—an economy plan—cost $2500, leaving her with $1000. She held a yard sale and picked up an additional $500. The money lasted her a year.

The Douglas fir in their front yard had grown considerably taller, she noted before continuing up 138th. She climbed it once and got pitch all over her hands, arms, and clothes.

The Matthews' house was at the end, on the right. She used to play tag among the filbert trees in their front yard with their son Dick and Sonny Couch, who lived across the street. She pulled into their driveway and turned around.

Driving back down 138th, she wondered what had happened to all the people she used to know. She hadn't seen one person she recognized; strangers resided in the neighborhood now. Like the old saying went, you can't go home again. Still, she felt better for having tried. Felt almost cheerful, in fact.

Until she got to Powell. While waiting at the stop sign for a break in traffic she noticed a familiar silver car in a parking lot directly across the street, not a hundred feet away. Behind the wheel, Binocular Guy. Following her? The car faced out, toward Powell, its license plate clearly visible. She grabbed her phone, switched to camera mode, and photographed the silver car through the windshield.

She turned right onto Powell and floored the go pedal. The car instantly obliged, silently accelerating in a manner that startled her a little. *Easy there, Leadfoot. You want to get a ticket on your first day driving?*

She slowed to thirty-five and checked in the rear-view mirror to see if the silver car had followed her, but intervening traffic obstructed her view. Maybe she should shrug it off as a coincidence. He could have been visiting a grave in the cemetery and then just happened to pull into the parking lot across from 138th for a perfectly innocent reason. As for the binoculars, perhaps he was a birdwatcher. Nevertheless, all the way back to the foundation she watched for silver cars in the rear-view mirror.

Safely inside the foundation's gates, she parked the car and got out, slung her bag over her shoulder, and slogged toward her apartment, feeling drained.

On the way, an angry buzzing caught her attention. It didn't sound like bees, exactly. More like hornets. Once, when she was seven, she disturbed a hornet nest and received several painful stings. They left red welts that lasted almost a week. It instilled in her a healthy respect for hornets. But the buzzing faded away, thank heaven.

Wednesday, August 10, 2016 4:55 p.m.

Had a full day. I visited Mom and Dad at the cemetery, discovered I was being followed, drove through the old neighborhood, saw some religious bigots, and nearly got stung by wasps.

Beats me why the guy was following me. I noticed him at the cemetery, and then again later on Powell. I took a pic of his car, and it shows the front license plate. Eli or Detective Wojanowski should be able to find out who he is and what he's up to.

Seeing the old neighborhood was bittersweet. The Old Hole is long gone, covered by ugly apartments. Lots of new development, especially near Powell. Hate that. But the further I drove up 138th, the more familiar things looked. In fact, on the north end of the street it's as though no time has gone by. Everything, including our house, looks exactly the same. It was comforting.

Some religious bigots were picketing in front of the Gresham DMV, protesting that woman's firing. They carried homemade, hate-filled anti-trans signs, all misspelled. The illiterati are everywhere.

Why does the evangelical Christian right seem to be behind every meanspirited social protest? The poor, the homeless, gay people, trans people—all marginalized groups, all targets of Christian hate. What about Jesus' teachings? You'd think the faithful would be leading the charge to help the downtrodden instead of harming them. It's the height of hypocrisy.

Spirituality and faith were important to my sweet mom. She made sure I was exposed to the gospel. I read the bible cover to cover. It's loaded with contradictions and portrays God as angry, cruel, jealous, and vindictive. Maybe that's why many Christians are so mean.

I'd dismiss it all as superstitious nonsense but for one thing: I want to see Mom and Dad again. And my dog, Buddy. If it's not true then they're all lost to me forever, and I can't stand the thought of that. So I'm in a quandary.

Maybe something will happen to make a believer out of me, some miracle. In the meantime, I guess I'm an agnostic, same as my dad.

29

The phone rang just as Ritter stepped into the shower. It never failed. He shut off the water, wrapped a towel around his middle, and caught it on the third ring.

"Mr. Ritter? Don Hunsaker. From the forensic lab."

"What can I do for you, Doc?" Good thing he hadn't ignored the phone.

"You asked me to give you a call if there were any developments. I still haven't located the missing evidence, but I've made some progress in that direction."

"Oh? What have you learned?"

"One of our technicians remembers a police officer delivering two bags containing women's jeans and underwear last month. She put them in storage and made entries for them in LIMS. She admitted to being careless when she initialed the receipt for the evidence. I read the riot act to all the lab staff about squiggles instead of initials."

"So she confirmed that the evidence was received, but she doesn't know where it is?"

"That's about the size of it, Counselor. You saw our evidence storage areas, so you understand the problem."

"All too well, Doc." The sinking feeling in his gut attested to his grasp of the situation. "Your technician remembers entering the evidence into LIMS. Any ideas about how those two records disappeared?"

"Only one way that could happen—someone deleted them from the database."

"Doesn't LIMS log all user activity?"

"Yes, but the user activity log has had no deletions since July fifteenth. Must've been done via the command line."

"Who's responsible for installing and maintaining the LIMS software for you?"

"That would be the IT division here in the building. They take care of the network, servers, computers, and software."

"Think I could talk to someone in the IT division?"

"I don't see why not. Face to face?"

"Yes. Think I'll take a run over there. See you in about an hour."

Forty-five minutes later Ritter, escorted by Hunsaker, walked into the Information and Technology Division's second-floor suite.

Hunsaker flagged down a man with a monitor under one arm and asked him, "Excuse me, is Nicole around?"

The man gestured over his shoulder with his free thumb. "Break room."

Ritter followed Hunsaker down a corridor to a room with the expected amenities: vending machines, tables, chairs, sink, fridge. Only one person using it, an attractive black woman in her mid-to-late twenties. Holding a precariously full cup of coffee, she inched toward a table, brow furrowed with concentration. She risked a glance at Ritter and Hunsaker, and a dollop of the liquid splashed on the floor. "*Merde*," she said and set the cup on the table.

"Nicole LeFleur, this is Eli Ritter. The information he needs is in your area of expertise. I'll leave you two to talk. I'm in the lab if you need me." With a nod to each of them, he left.

"Very nice to meet you, Ms. LeFleur," Ritter said.

"Likewise," she said, wiping up the spill with a paper towel. "I understand you have some questions about LIMS." She had a lovely French accent.

"I do," he said.

She disposed of the paper towel and washed her hands. "We can talk here. Would you like coffee?"

"Coffee would be nice, thanks."

She went over to the coffee pot and filled another cup.

"You're French, Ms. LeFleur?" *Brilliant question, Counselor. What's next—You're black, Ms. LeFleur?*

"French-Canadian," she said and set the coffee in front of him and then sat down. "I am from Montreal. Quebec."

"You're a long way from home. How did that happen?"

"I answered an ad at Monster dot com for an information systems specialist at this facility. I emailed them my résumé. They hired me after I flew out for an interview. Portland was a big change from Montreal, but it is a very beautiful city."

LeFleur. French for "the flower." How fitting. She wore minimal makeup. Her flawless *café au lait* skin, large dark eyes, and long lashes eliminated the need for it.

"How did you get into this line of work?"

Hint of a smile. "Just lucky, I guess."

He laughed. "Okay, I deserved that."

"To answer your question, I learned to program almost before I could write. And now I have a masters in computer science from Université de Montréal."

"A grand institution." *Grand? Pretentious much, Counselor?*

"Are you satisfied with my *bona fides*, Mr. Ritter?"

"I didn't have any doubts. So here's a question. Is it possible to delete records from LIMS without it being detected?"

"*Certainement*," she said. "If one has root access to the LIMS server's database and Unix operating system, the data trail can be erased completely."

"How many here have access and the skills to do it?"

"Thirteen, counting me. Do you suspect someone in our IT section?"

"I wouldn't go that far. I'm just exploring the possibility. The problem is, even if I knew for certain who it was, I'd have a tough time proving he was the culprit."

"He? You seem to have eliminated me as a suspect."

"You noticed that."

"Back to your problem—proving it would depend on how carefully he covered his tracks, yes? Even careful people can overlook things."

"Good point. So if you should happen across something a careful person overlooked when he deleted two records from July fifteenth, I'd appreciate a call." He held out his card.

She took it from him and smiled, teeth white and perfect, other than a lateral incisor that slightly overlapped its neighbor. It didn't diminish her attractiveness one iota.

The signs were all there: feeling off-balance, saying dumb things, being charmed by her accent and mesmerized by her smile. He'd better cut the session short before he dissolved into a gibbering pile of goo. He needed to focus on the serious work that lay ahead.

"Ms. LeFleur, you've been very helpful and I do appreciate it. I won't take up any more of your time. Thank you for the information and the coffee."

"Nice talking with you." She extended a slender hand.

He shook it. "The pleasure was mine, I assure you." *God help me, I sound like Adolphe Menjou.*

He got out of there like he was double-parked.

She hadn't been back at her cubicle even five minutes before she had a visitor—Jason Sepers, wearing a gray T-shirt with Einstein's face and E=mc² on the front. Nerd chic. "Hi, Nicole," he said, pitching his voice lower than his natural register.

She waited him out.

"What did the lawyer want?"

"Why?"

"Just curious."

Not for the first time, she pondered why she found Jason so repugnant. His arrogant manner, that was part of it. Worse, he was the type to claim credit he did not deserve. And most irksome of all, he was always staring at her chest. "He needed information," she said.

"About what?"

"About the LIMS software."

"Why?"

"He did not say." Which was not exactly true.

"What did he want to know about LIMS, specifically?"

"Why do you care?"

"Like I said, just curious."

"He wanted to know what safeguards LIMS has to prevent data loss. And about the user activity log." Another impulsive fabrication, but she did not feel even a twinge of guilt.

"That's all?"

"You expected more?"

Shrug. "Not really." After a lingering look at her chest he set off toward his cubicle.

Just curious, he had said. Total *merde*. His interest had been much too intense to be driven by idle curiosity. When she told him Ritter had inquired about LIMS, panic spread over his face. Then obvious relief replaced the panic when he learned, due to her misdirection, that Ritter's questions were only superficial. Jason would do well to *éviter les jeux de poker*— avoid the poker games.

A thought that had been tugging at the back of her mind shoved its way forward: *Jason was Ritter's suspect.* It was hard to believe that Jason would tamper with an evidence database, a criminal offense with possible jail time. He was loathsome, but he was not stupid.

She picked up the lawyer's card. Elias J. Ritter. He had seemed reserved, even shy. His horn-rimmed glasses gave him a bookish appearance, but he had a nice face. His sudden departure, like he had used starting blocks, intrigued her. Men usually ran *to* her, not from. Perhaps that was another difference between Portland and Montreal.

The blinking cursor on her terminal's monitor seemed to be waiting for her. She put on her headphones, adjusted the volume, and logged into the LIMS server, her percussive key-strokes accompanying Mozart.

30

Rafe Lambeaux liked to close his eyes during the show's opening sequence. The heroic theme never failed to stir his heart. Or what passed for a heart, some would say. The voice-over, in tone and delivery, created the impression that an event of great significance was about to occur. (Hiring the actor who did a slew of those "In a world . . ." voice-overs for movie trailers had been a stroke of genius.) "And now, the man who strikes fear into the hearts of liberals everywhere . . . Rafe Lambeaux."

Thus invigorated, Lambeaux opened his eyes and launched into the morning's topic (the diatribe *de jour*, he liked to call it): "Mississippi's governor signed into law legislation that defined gender as 'immutable biological sex as objectively determined by anatomy and genetics at time of birth.' North Carolina passed a similar law decreeing that a person's gender shall be determined by their birth certificate.

"Lawmakers encountered setbacks in Georgia, Tennessee, South Dakota, and other states, but the defeat is temporary. I believe the tide has turned and common sense is conquering liberal overreach. Need proof? A hundred similar bills are currently pending in state legislatures around the country.

"Women and girls in North Carolina and Mississippi don't have to worry now about being molested by transgenders in women's restrooms.

"Oh, by the way—I received an email that took issue with my terminology. Here, I'll read it to you. 'Mr. Lambeaux,' it says, 'I'm writing to point out that using transgender as a noun, as you've been doing, is incorrect. In point of fact, the word transgender should be used as an adjective only, as in transgender woman or man. Referring to someone as a transgender demeans and objectifies them. Thank you for your attention to this matter.' And it's signed, 'Sharlyn Woodruff, Corvallis, Oregon.'

"My reply: 'Well, Ms. Woodruff, here's the truth—I don't give a flip what the PC police think about my terminology. I call them transgenders. If you have a problem with that, I'll have to find a way to live with your disapproval. God bless America, Rafe Lambeaux.'

"Where was I? Oh right, I was talking about the backlash against—plug your ears, Ms. Woodruff—transgenders. It had to happen. Push society far enough and society starts pushing back. It's called the Law of Equilibrium."

Hal Terry signaled him from inside the booth. Lambeaux said, "Folks, we have a very special guest caller this morning —Representative Dale Boonstra of Oklahoma, one of the few lawmakers in D.C. who's fighting the good fight. Welcome, Congressman."

"Thank you, Rafe."

"I've been telling our listeners about North Carolina's and Mississippi's new laws explicitly defining gender, to keep men out of ladies' rooms. What's your take on that?"

"Seems state legislatures all over the country are jumping on the bandwagon. State laws are great stop-gap measures. However, it's well nigh impossible to pass those laws in left-leaning states, so you end up with a patchwork—states that care about the privacy and safety of their females and states that don't give a diddly damn. Only federal laws can provide the nationwide protection that's needed."

"True, Congressman, but you know our socialist president will veto any federal legislation that's not liberal. You need veto-proof majorities in both houses, no small feat."

"It's a heavy lift, even though Republicans control both houses. Many of my colleagues tend to avoid socially conservative issues. Regardless, it's worth the effort. It's imperative that we have laws that protect America's females."

"What about males' safety and privacy? You're don't seem concerned about women pretending to be men in the men's room."

"Because it's not a problem, Rafe. Most men wouldn't mind sharing a restroom with a woman. The big difference is this— a woman wouldn't pose much of a threat. Not like a man in the ladies' room would."

"I can see your point."

"Children are of course the primary concern. Accordingly, I created the Protect Our Children Act, which if—*when* enacted into law will have jurisdiction over every public school in the nation. It passed with a supermajority in the House, and now a Senate committee will look it over before sending it to the floor. We need your prayers, yours and all your listeners', that it'll have a repeat performance there."

"We've got your back, Congressman—*we* being everyone connected with the CIB network and my fourteen million listeners, a.k.a. Lambeauxians."

"That'd be a powerful lot of prayer. And it wouldn't hurt if they'd email or call their senators and urge them to vote yes on the Senate bill when it gets to the floor."

"Hear that, folks? Do it for the children."

"Protecting the children takes priority," Boonstra said, "but it's only the beginning. I will be introducing legislation in the House that's much more . . . comprehensive in scope."

"How so?"

"Rafe, religious liberty is also at stake here. So-called anti-discrimination laws, which in reality give transgenders special rights, are disenfranchising the faithful. Last week a woman named Madeleine Sanger was fired from her job at the Department of Motor Vehicles in Gresham, Oregon when her deeply held religious conviction wouldn't allow her to serve a transgender license applicant."

"Sickening. I'll bet the Oregon DMV's administration is just crawling with atheistic lefties. I mean, come on, it's Oregon. Liberals are always yapping about tolerance, but look at their intolerance toward a person of faith. Hypocrites."

"Ms. Sanger's firing was a blatant violation of her First Amendment right to freely exercise her religion. She's got a lawyer and she's going to sue the State of Oregon for wrongful termination."

"More power to her," Lambeaux said.

"It just goes to show how the transgender agenda is running roughshod over decent, God-fearing Americans. When someone like Ms. Sanger can get fired for following her religious conviction, and when a man can legally enter a woman's bathroom by putting on a dress and claiming he's a woman that day, things have gotten out of hand."

"Way, way out of hand."

"And that's exactly why I'm drafting new legislation. I'm naming it the Freedom and Decency Act."

"Which is comprehensive in scope, you said."

"You decide. First, the use of restrooms and other public facilities will be restricted to persons whose identification corresponds to the gender the facilities are designated for. Second, a marker will be required on transgenders' birth certificates if they're revised. Third, doctors shall not provide surgery or hormone therapy, including hormone blockers, to persons under the age of eighteen. And last, the sincere religious beliefs and moral convictions of individuals, organizations and private associations are fully protected from punishment or interference by local, state, or federal government."

"Excellent. And the law's jurisdiction will be nationwide."

"That's correct, and it should go a long ways toward setting things right again."

"You can count on me and fourteen million Lambeauxians. We'll put some pressure on our representatives and senators to pass your commonsense legislation."

"I do appreciate it."

Lambeaux scanned the call queue on his monitor. Sixteen callers waiting to talk. He chose the first one in the list, from Montana, a deep red state. "Let's take some calls. Our first caller is Sabrina Ivanski of Kalispell, Montana. What do you do there, Sabrina?"

"I teach economics at Flathead Valley Community College."

"Flathead Valley. I've known a few flatheads in my time." He played a rimshot sound effect. "What did you want to say?"

"I'd like to ask you and Congressman Boonstra a question. What's with your obsession about bathrooms? Do you actually think it's a big problem, women being assaulted in restrooms by men wearing dresses? Listen, men who assault women in bathrooms don't bother with dresses. They just walk in and do it. But you're conflating men in dresses with transgender women. Here's the difference—I wouldn't want to share a bathroom with a man in a dress, but I wouldn't mind sharing one with a transgender woman. I don't know any women who would. Tell me this—are all social conservatives weirdos with a bathroom fetish?"

Lambeaux clenched his jaw. One of the reddest states in the country, and he gets a damn liberal. "Oh, sure—it's the people who are who trying to protect women's privacy and safety who are the weirdos, not the twisted men who assault little girls in public bathrooms. If we simply define them as women then problem solved, right?"

"You can't be serious. I challenge you to produce a single documented case in which a transgender woman assaulted someone in a public bathroom. You won't be able to, because no such cases exist. But countless trans women have been beaten or murdered when forced to use men's facilities. Bathroom laws will only encourage more of these attacks."

"So you feel men in dresses deserve protected status?"

"You keep calling them men in dresses, but transgender women are not men."

"Their biology proves they are," Lambeaux said.

"Now we're getting to the heart of the matter. You view transgender women—*all* transgender women—as men, right?"

"Men badly in need of psychological help."

"According to psychologists and other experts on gender identity, transgender women are *women*, not men, based on decades of research."

"You produce your experts, we'll produce ours."

"Look, just admit you're bigots and quit trying to cloak your bigotry as protecting women and girls. Goodbye."

Lambeaux massaged the corners of his aching jaw. He'd let the bitch get away unscathed. He must be losing his touch. "Well, there you have it, folks. Liberals don't give a damn about religious freedom or women's privacy and safety." He gulped down a mouthful of lukewarm coffee. "Still with us, Congressman?"

"Still here, Rafe."

"I think Sabrina might be a commie. Did you catch her last name? Ivanski, a commie name if ever there was one."

Boonstra answered with a hearty laugh.

"Congressman, I've got a feeling our next caller is a true-blue American. Mitch Bluesworth in Kennewick, Washington, what would you like to say?"

"Just that, looking at it realistically, these bathroom laws will be impossible to enforce. I mean, will every public bathroom have a security guard who'll inspect under women's skirts? Or check their birth certificates? Or run on-the-spot DNA tests? Seems to me these laws create more privacy issues than they supposedly solve."

Lambeaux caught himself clenching his jaw again. Opening the show with two callers in a row intent on breaking his balls, that was an ominous sign. "Congressman?"

"Enforcement," Boonstra said, "will be deployed only after complaints about suspicious activity are received."

"I see," Bluesworth said. "So anybody can complain about a person they decide is suspicious? Who do they complain to? Are they expected to detain the suspect until the enforcer arrives? What about false alarms and lawsuits that result from unfounded complaints? Hate to break the news to you guys, but these bathroom laws are unworkable."

"Mitch, every new law will have a few implementation wrinkles, but they're always solved. The minor problems you identified will be smoothed out quickly, because there's a big incentive—public safety and religious freedom are at stake."

"So you say."

Lambeaux impaled Hal Terry with a dagger stare. It said, *Did you even screen these callers?* Terry only shrugged.

"Okay," Lambeaux said, "thanks for calling, Mitch."

"Zero for two, Rafe," Boonstra said.

"Third time, charm, etcetera. Our next caller is Fred White from Coeur d'Alene, Idaho. Go ahead, Fred."

"Rafe, I have a solution to the transgender threat, and it's a damn sight more efficient than legislation."

"That's a bold claim. What's your solution?"

"Execute 'em all. Sharpshooters with sniper rifles. Quick, clean, permanent. One well-placed shot behind the ear, like switching off a light. The way it would work, every county would have a squad of well-trained militiamen—"

"Hold it, Fred. Your plan has a few problems, not the least of which is the reality that killing people is a capital offense. But thanks for calling." A tap on the screen and the psycho's metadata disappeared, along with his connection.

"Well," Boonstra said, "if nothing else, Fred showed how passionate some Americans are about this issue."

Lambeaux scanned the call queue, hoping to find a normal, ordinary, commonsense conservative, emphasis on *normal*. Chances were good a caller from the Deep South would fill the bill. "Folks, our next caller is Tal Kohler from Wadley, Georgia. What's going on up there in Wadley, Tal?"

"Not a heck of a lot. Say, I just wanted to point out that Georgia's governor—a Republican, by the way—had the good sense to veto the anti-LGBT bill the state legislature passed. He said, 'We don't have to discriminate against anyone to protect Georgia's faith-based community.' He also might have been afraid that big companies would flee Georgia like they did North Carolina, costing it billions. Georgia's economy couldn't take the hit."

Lambeaux looked heavenward and exhaled in a long sigh. "Folks, here's a word from Bainberry Precious Metals." He took off his earphones and beckoned to Hal Terry, lurking in the engineering booth.

Terry entered the studio, eyebrows raised.

"I got a question for you, Hal," Lambeaux said. "You seem to have decided that it's no longer necessary to screen callers. May I ask why?"

"C'mon, Rafe—"

Lambeaux held up his hand. "A steady stream of bleeding-heart liberals, that's what you gave me. Except for the psycho who wanted to shoot trannies. Are you going to tell me you screened them?"

Terry's shoulders slumped. "Sorry, Rafe. I was preoccupied, scheduling sponsors' spots. I own it."

"If we have another hour like the last one, sponsors' ads won't matter, because there won't be any." Lambeaux took a deep, calming breath. "Might I prevail upon you to screen the next hour's callers so that my show doesn't slide completely into the shitter?"

"I'm on it, Rafe."

"We need some right-thinking Americans, Hal. Make it happen."

The remorse set in when he was standing at the urinal. Hal Terry had been with him for thirty-one years. A more loyal guy didn't exist, but his occasional lapses drove Lambeaux up the wall. So then he had to tune the guy up. And when he did, Terry always reacted with a hangdog expression that made Lambeaux feel guilty.

He got back to the studio with twenty-six seconds to spare, ready to resume the show.

With a vengeance.

31

When Ritter ran the license plate on the mysterious silver car Andie had photographed, it turned out to be a 2004 Nissan Sentry registered to Gordon Millican, 33, Tigard address. A background check turned up the fact that Millican was employed by Pomerenke Investigations LLC, Portland. His credit score, as reported by Equifax, was 487, deadbeat territory.

Until Millican's occupation came to light, Ritter had been prepared to dismiss the incident as mere coincidence. The chances of that were close to nil now. So why would a private investigator tail Andie? Or more to the point, who hired him to tail her? Kellenberger of course came to mind. But surely even Kellenberger wasn't *that* brazen. Besides, what could possibly be gained by it?

He sat down in front of his laptop and, using his index fingers, typed a URL into the browser's address field. His two-finger typing, people told him, looked like featherless birds pecking at bugs. They got the job done, though.

Pomerenke Investigations' website was clean and professional-looking. Which wasn't a guarantee of anything, including credibility. Any kitchen-table outfit could have a slick site. "Fast, affordable, confidential," the front page proclaimed. "Discreet surveillance our specialty." Arguable, considering Andie spotted their tail and even photographed his vehicle.

The minimally informative About Us page had one photo, of Neil Pomerenke, a swarthy man whose jowly cheeks bore the scars of severe acne in his youth. He had the look of a man who'd been crushed beneath life's boot.

Nothing on the site about Millican, though.

Ritter picked up his phone and punched in the number. Four rings before someone answered.

"Pomerenke."

"Yes, hello. My name is Logan. I'm calling to inquire about your services. I suspect my wife is cheating, but I need to be sure. Do you folks do that kind of surveillance?"

"All the time. No better way to clinch a divorce or child custody case. We can even do aerial surveillance if necessary."

"That's great. How many investigators do you have?"

"We're lean and mean at the present time, just me and an associate. But one person could handle your job, no sweat."

"I'd like to meet with you to discuss the matter. Any chance of getting together today?"

"Unfortunately, I'll be tied up on a case all this week."

"Oh." Ritter imbued his voice with disappointment. "That's too bad."

"Tell you what. My associate, Mr. Millican, will be available to meet with you today."

"That would be fine." More than fine. Perfect, in fact. "I can be at your office on Stark at two o'clock. That work for him?"

"Sounds good. He'll see you at two then."

"Looking forward to it."

Ritter sat there a moment. He'd caught a break. But prying information out of Millican might be a challenge.

Pomerenke Investigations LLC occupied a seedy-looking office between a barber shop and a janitorial supply, both closed. The sign in the window had been created with metal stick-on letters commonly seen on mailboxes. Their exterior didn't exactly instill confidence.

Inside, it was just as seedy: dingy gray vinyl tile floor; walls that must have been white before years of smoke stained them nicotine yellow; two florescent lights that produced a constant, ominous hum; a trio of wooden desks that looked as though they'd suffered decades of abuse. In short, not likely to be featured in a *Contemporary Office Design* article.

The gawky guy behind one of the desks had to be Gordon Millican. But Ritter hadn't expected he'd be wearing a one-size-too-big gray suit and have a matching fedora sitting on his desk next to a smoldering ashtray. Probably had a gun in a shoulder holster under the coat. Ritter had to bite the inside of his cheek to keep from laughing out loud.

Mr. Private Eye stood, hand extended. "Mr. Logan? The name's Millican."

"Mr. Millican." Ritter shook his baby-soft hand.

"Any trouble finding our office?" Millican gestured at a chair next to the desk.

Ritter sat down. "No, I printed out the map on your website. Nice site, by the way. Very impressive."

"Thanks. I built it."

"You don't say."

"I enjoy doing that kind of stuff. Used to, rather. Detective work keeps me pretty busy these days."

Getting Millican talking about his profession might be the best approach. "You know, it's reassuring that you actually *look* like a private investigator."

Millican's chest seemed to swell. "I was born to be a P.I.," he said. "I got a knack for it."

"Interesting work?"

"It's never boring. No two cases are alike."

"Which brings us to my case. Tell me, how are you at tailing people? The reason I ask, obtaining proof that my wife's been cheating on me will involve a lot of it, because they go to different motels for their trysts. I've tried to follow her, but she's lost me every time."

Millican's pale face looked smug. "As it so happens, Mr. Logan, tailing people is my specialty."

"Excellent. I must say, this is fascinating stuff. Say, just out of curiosity, tell me about the last time you tailed someone. Without violating client confidentiality, of course."

Millican's eyebrows knitted for a moment and then his face brightened. "As a matter of fact, I tailed a young woman to Gresham and back just the other day."

"Any problems?"

"Smooth as silk. See, the trick in tailing someone is not to hide but to blend in. That's why I drive a vehicle that's as nondescript as they come. It's practically invisible."

"Smart. Why was the young woman under surveillance?"

Millican paused so long Ritter was afraid he'd pushed his luck too far. But Millican said, "A client wants us to keep an eye on her. He also wants round-the-clock surveillance of her place of employment. She has an apartment there."

"It's an ongoing case?"

"An open-ended investigation. We like those."

"Gosh, won't that cost your client a fortune?"

"This guy's got money to burn."

Ritter rolled the dice one more time. "Where that young woman lives and works—it must be a small place, if a two-man operation can handle round-the-clock surveillance."

"Nope, it's a big place. We're very good at what we do."

Ritter took a business card from the holder on the desk. "I'm very impressed with your professionalism, Mr. Millican. I want to talk to a couple other agencies, just as a formality."

Millican looked crestfallen. "Oh. Well, keep in mind that we'll do whatever it takes to make sure the client's satisfied."

"I will." Ritter stood and held out his hand. "You've been most helpful, Mr. Millican."

Driving west on Stark, Ritter chuckled about Gordon Millican, caught up in his private eye fantasy. Getting him to talk had been like putting coins in a gumball machine. One with a big payoff. Andie and the Transcend Foundation were going to be stunned to hear that private investigators were spying on them. And a very rich guy was picking up the tab.

Which eliminated Kellenberger. That was disappointing.

Maybe the foundation should fight fire with fire—hire another P.I. to investigate Pomerenke Investigations. It might reveal who hired him. He'd suggest it to Gannon.

Or maybe he should just talk to Millican again and stick a few more coins in the gumball machine.

32

The prearranged knock—three, then one, then two—sounded at the big van's back door. Pomerenke popped a stick of Juicy Fruit into his mouth and then lumbered back and unlocked the door. Millican climbed in and swung it shut.

"Gordo," Pomerenke said, "what's with the getup?"

Millican removed the fedora and tossed it on a counter. "I figured maybe I should dress more professional."

"Professional . . . *that*? Think you're Sam-frickin'-Spade?"

Millican looked like he was about to cry. "Neil, I—"

A suspicious bulge drew Pomerenke's eye. "You packing?"

Millican opened his coat's lapel to reveal a Colt 1911, a hard-boiled detective's gat of choice, in a shoulder rig.

"Gordo, have you lost your friggin' mind?"

"C'mon, Neil. I got a concealed-carry permit."

"So what? You don't need a gun. You're not Mike Hammer. Now put that thing away. Stick it in a drawer."

Sighing, Millican did as he was told.

"How'd it go with Logan?"

Gordo dropped into a chair. "You didn't tell me he's black."

"Didn't know. Is he hiring us to tail his round-heels wife?"

"Well . . . not yet, but I'm pretty sure he will."

"Oh, really?"

"Yeah, he wanted to check out a couple other P.I.s first, but he told me he was very impressed."

Pomerenke laughed. "I bet. One look at you in your zoot suit and he probably couldn't get out of there fast enough."

"No, no, no . . . I talked to him for twenty minutes or so."

"Yeah? What about?"

"He wanted to be sure we know what we're doing when we tail people. I told him about tailing that girl to Gresham a couple days ago."

"Gordo," Pomerenke said, his eyes boring into Millican's, "never *ever* talk about a case. To anyone. This business is like Fight Club—you keep your yapper shut about it."

"But I didn't reveal any names or anything that could identify the girl or the client."

Pomerenke stopped chewing his gum. "You talked about the client?"

"Just in general terms. Nothing specific, I swear."

"You better pray nothing comes of it. And in the future, Gordo, not a peep about our cases, active or inactive, or you'll be wearing that costume in the unemployment line."

"Understood."

"Good. Now, I need you to go get something from the office for me. In my desk, top drawer, is a vial of muscle relaxants. My back's killing me. Go."

"Sure thing, Neil." Millican reached for the fedora.

"And for God's sake, change out of that ridiculous outfit. Take that gun with you."

Millican got the gun from the drawer and slinked off.

Pomerenke sighed. If he didn't need the skinny bastard's computer and Internet expertise he'd have fired him on the spot for talking about a case. But for the time being he was stuck with him.

He got rid of the wad of gum and sat down in front of a monitor. The rooftop camera trained on the Transcend Foundation's entrance showed no activity. He closed his eyes and dozed for what seemed like only minutes. When he opened them again . . . on the monitor, a steady procession of vehicles were turning into the foundation's entrance.

"Jesus Christ," he said, fully awake.

Fortunately, the van's roof camera had recorded the first arrivals. But getting a drone in the air as soon as possible was a high priority. Cautiously, taking care not to aggravate his back, he rose to his feet.

Drone Two was fully charged, so he disconnected it from the charger. Now both drones were ready to fly. After popping a stick of gum in his mouth he picked up Drone One.

Twenty seconds after launch, the drone was airborne at an altitude of 500 feet, with a heading that would take it over the foundation's parking area. Five seconds later it arrived at the destination and hovered. Perhaps sixty vehicles, including several limos, were parked below, with late arrivals still straggling in. As for the passengers, judging by their clothes they weren't attending a formal event.

Pomerenke chewed his gum faster as he watched the visitors stream into a granite-slabbed building. No windows. That put a serious damper on surveillance.

He'd read an article predicting that camera drones the size of a fly—with audio capability—were on the horizon. No more sneaking into places to plant hidden cameras and microphones, something he'd done more than a few times. Unfortunately, not in the building below.

He maneuvered the craft directly over the structure and nearly swallowed his gum. The roof had three big skylights. Back in business. He landed the drone squarely on the middle skylight. Not bad, considering the short time he'd been flying the things.

From its perch the drone had a bird's-eye view of the auditorium's interior below. The gimbal-mounted camera had a 360-degree range of motion as well as pan and tilt. What's more, its lens had auto focus and telescopic capability, which would enable him to zoom in on the action. If he couldn't be a fly on the wall, this was the next best thing.

With any luck, the battery would have enough charge to observe the entire event. It shouldn't be a problem, since the camera and electronics consumed far less power than the four electric motors during flight.

Pomerenke started to unwrap a fresh stick of Juicy Fruit but changed his mind. Instead, he opened the half-size fridge and grabbed a Pabst Blue Ribbon. He didn't often indulge while on the job, but things were going so smoothly a celebration was in order.

From the back door, the secret knock. He went back and flipped the locking lever. Millican climbed in, wearing khakis and a white polo shirt.

"Happy now, Neil?"

Pomerenke grunted. "Got a job for you, Gordo. Come with me." He led Millican over to one of the monitors. "Something big's going on at the foundation. This is the video feed from the camera on the van's roof. Around sixty cars went in that entrance. Their license plates are clearly visible. I want you to jump on the computer and run every plate."

"Okay, but that'll take a while."

"What else you got to do?"

"I'm on it."

Pomerenke took a swig of beer and sat down in front of the drone's monitor. The event had yet to begin; people were still milling about. Some kind of conference, obviously, but no signs or banners were visible, so no telling exactly what was going on down there.

While panning the camera over the crowd, everyone well dressed and groomed, he saw the girl they'd been keeping an eye on, Andie McInnes, talking with an Asian woman. Too bad he couldn't read lips.

He continued panning, and spotted another familiar face. Not just familiar—famous. He zoomed in close to make sure. Jane Fonda, no doubt about it. He'd had a crush on her for a year after seeing *Barbarella*. Watching *The China Syndrome* on TV last week stirred echoes of that adolescent passion. And now here she was.

Hers wasn't the only famous face in the throng. George and Amal Clooney were chatting with . . . Oprah Winfrey? It sure as hell was, in the flesh. The ex-wife, she didn't miss an *Oprah* show in ten years of marriage.

Pomerenke leaned forward. "Holy mother of God," he said. "That's something you don't see every day."

Millican got up from his chair and stood behind his boss. "What is?"

Pomerenke pointed at the screen.

"Holy shit," Millican said. "Jeff-freakin'-Bezos."

The World's Richest Man was talking to Warren Buffet, not exactly a pauper himself. Their combined worth was greater than many countries' GNP. Shaking his head, Pomerenke resumed scanning the crowd.

"Wait ... go back ... hold it. See the black guy in the horn-rimmed glasses? That's Logan. That's who I talked to today."

"You making a bad joke?"

"I'm telling you, that's him."

Pomerenke followed Logan with the camera as he threaded his way through the crowd ... to Andie McInnes, who greeted him with a smile. It didn't take Pomerenke long to add it up. "Gordo," he said, "you are one gullible son of a bitch."

"What do you mean?"

"Logan's a fake name, I'd bet on it. That guy pumped you for information about this case. You were conned."

"Get out of town."

"Look closer. Recognize the girl he's talking to?"

Millican peered at the screen for several seconds and then groaned. "Goddamn. The guy sure seemed like the real deal."

"Gullible, like I said. Now go finish running those plates so I can send a report to the client."

Head hanging, Millican returned to his workstation.

Pomerenke sat back. How in hell had "Logan" zeroed in on them? After thinking about it a few minutes, he looked over at Millican with eyes narrowed. He'd begged and wheedled until Pomerenke let him tail McInnes. A bad decision. Because sure as hell, Millican screwed the pooch.

No need for the client to hear about the slip-up; they'd look like a couple of nincompoops. They *were* nincompoops, but the client didn't need to know that.

The client would get his money's worth, he'd see to that. A report on the conference, accompanied by video and a list of vehicle registrants, should make him happy as a clam.

As for Millican, he needed tightening up. The careless son of a bitch could have cost them a gig that paid five hundred a day, the fattest fee that Pomerenke Investigations had ever gotten.

To shell out a fee like that, the client must have money up the ying-yang. And the secrecy—no names, cash payments only, everything done by courier—it was like a C.I.A. operation.

But so what? He couldn't care less. Enough money can snuff out curiosity.

33

They had a competition to see who could spot the most celebrities, Andie's idea. So far she was ahead of Eli, four to two.

"Look, Eli," she said, pointing. "George Takei. I'm up by two now."

"Do politicians count? Because I see Senator Jeff Merkley and Representative Peter DeFazio over there."

"Well . . . I guess. Then we're even. For now."

Dr. Soong walked up to them. "Hey, you two. people are taking their seats."

They found three adjoining seats in the next-to-last row. Andie ended up in the middle, Ritter on her left, Dr. Soong on her right. A man and woman directly in front of them were arguing, not bothering to keep their voices down. Moving wasn't an option; all the other seats were taken.

"It's totally unacceptable," the woman said. "I'm going to mention it to them. Don't you think they need to know that a swarm of wasps or hornets is threatening their guests? If you'd gotten stung you would be in anaphylactic shock right now."

"I didn't get stung, so let's drop it," the man said. "I didn't forget my EpiPen on purpose, for God's sake."

The words *wasps*, *hornets*, and *stung* had gotten Andie's full attention. It seemed she wasn't the only one who'd heard the menacing buzzing outside.

She turned to Dr. Soong. "I think there's a problem you should aware of."

"Yes?" the doctor said.

"For the past few weeks I've been hearing hornets or wasps on the foundation's grounds. And not just a few scouts, either—an angry swarm. The couple sitting in front of us also heard them. The man's allergic to stings, and he forgot to bring his . . . Epi-something."

The doctor leaned forward and tapped the man on the shoulder. "Excuse me," she said. "I understand you forgot to bring your epinephrine. I'm Dr. Soong, the foundation's medical director. After the conference I'll get an EpiPen from my office and escort you to your car."

The woman answered for her companion. "Doctor, we would appreciate that so much. Thank you."

To Andie, Dr. Soong said, "I'll have the groundskeeper look into the problem."

"Hey," Eli said, "it's starting."

The director stepped up to the dais and looked out over the audience. Her bearing gave her tailored tan pantsuit the look of a uniform. She had short straight hair, worn parted. Her spit-shined shoes gleamed.

"Welcome, all of you, to the Transcend Foundation," the director said. "My name is Laura Gannon. Before I accepted the foundation's directorship I was a colonel in the United States Marines. Any jarheads here?"

About ten audience members raised their hands.

"*Semper fi.* I retired after eighteen years of service—" The line drew applause, which the director acknowledged with a nod. "I hadn't planned to retire that early but, after serving in Iraq and Afghanistan, riding a desk in Hawaii didn't seem like the best use of my ability and training. I stuck it out for a year and then I did what they were hoping I'd do. I resigned.

"Had it been possible for me to delay my transition for three more years, I would have made twenty. Alas, it was not possible. I'd delayed transition too long already. Two decades too long. But better late than never, as they say.

"At any rate, that's how I went from commanding a Marine battalion to directing a nonprofit foundation. Know what I found? They're not all that different. Both are engaged in war. On the battlefield of social justice, far-right conservatives— so-called social conservatives—are waging all-out war on transgender people. Perhaps you've noticed."

There were knowing nods in the audience.

"While it might seem like the current onslaught came out of nowhere, social conservatives have been planning a full-scale assault for years, blowback for the gains transgender people have made against bigotry and discrimination. Conservatives have always regarded rights as a zero sum game, as if respecting a minority group's rights somehow diminishes theirs. So they declared war on the transgender community.

"The conservatives' favorite weapons are bathroom laws, rushed through Republican state legislatures and signed into law by Republican governors, served up with a generous helping of propaganda. Speaking of which, here's a recent salvo from our adversaries." She gestured at the theater-size screen behind her.

Opening shot, a door marked "Women." Next shot, two bathroom stalls, doors closed. The camera slowly panned down. Below one door, a young girl's bare legs and Mary Janes. Below the other door, a man's hairy legs and boat-like high heels. Ominous narration: "Should a grown man pretending to be a woman be allowed to use the women's restroom? It's not only inappropriate, it's dangerous." The door of the man's stall slowly began to open. Fade to black.

Gannon turned to face the audience. "There you have it, people—a thirty-second salvo of misinformation and fearmongering. Crude, but effective.

"To return fire we hired the howitzer of advertising firms, Heron Bickle Associates in Los Angeles. We asked them to create a series of ads for us that would counter the conservatives' shameless propaganda. The first three ads they produced for us exceeded our expectations. Let's have a look at them."

Andie thought at first they'd replayed the previous ad by mistake. But the legs and feet under the stall doors were different: two women—one white, the other black. The narrator, either Morgan Freeman or a soundalike, spoke: "Painting discrimination as protecting women from predators in bathrooms is hardly a new story in this country. Segregationists in the South argued that white women in bathrooms and other public facilities would be in grave danger from black women, most of whom they said had venereal disease and carried straight razors."

The women exited the stalls, washed their hands, and left.

"It's no coincidence that many of the states enacting discriminatory bathroom laws against transgender people are the same states that enforced segregation by race in the first half of the twentieth century. Looks like they're up to their old tricks." Fade to black.

The audience applauded.

"Our next ad," Gannon said, "zeros in on the problem with the implementation of bathroom laws."

The ad opened with the camera following a woman into a public restroom. As she started toward a stall, a uniformed woman blocked her way. "Excuse me, ma'am."

"Yes?"

Closeup on an official-looking badge. "Gender check. Come with me, please." She indicated a curtained booth nearby.

"You've got to be kidding. Nobody's ever questioned my gender."

"I'm sorry, ma'am, but the law went into effect last week. And you're tall and kind of broad shouldered, to be frank."

"What? Could you be more insulting? Just how are you going to determine whether or not I'm eligible to use this facility?"

"By checking your identification. Your birth certificate, preferably."

"Yeah, like I carry my birth certificate around. Let me ask you this—what would you do if I couldn't produce satisfactory identification?"

"I'd have to perform a visual inspection."

"Oh, really? I suppose you'd take your baton, lift my skirt, and check out my privates?"

"Only if you didn't have proper documentation."

"Yeah, I know. A birth certificate."

"One piece of photo ID with appropriate gender marker is also acceptable."

"Tell you what—I'll just hold it. I'll find another bathroom, one that respects a citizen's privacy."

"That might be hard to do, ma'am. Every public bathroom in the state now has gender monitoring to make sure the law is enforced."

"Then I'll hold it until I get home. After that I'm going to email my congressmen and the governor. And I'll attach scans of my driver's license and birth certificate."

"The law's for your own protection, ma'am. If you got nothing to hide, you got nothing to worry about."

"Your creepy law is an invasion of privacy. So much for Republicans' small government. Goodbye."

"Have a good day, ma'am."

Fade to black.

Bullseye, dead center, judging by the enthusiasm in the applause.

She and Dr. Soong looked at each other and nodded.

"Our last ad," Gannon said, "although disturbing, might be the most effective of the three. See what you think."

It featured a pretty girl of fifteen or sixteen standing outside a door marked "Boys." She looked up and down the hallway and then took a deep breath and pushed the door open. Her footsteps echoed off the empty restroom's tile walls. Ignoring the line of porcelain urinals, she entered a stall and closed the door.

Jump cut. Sound of toilet flushing.

She emerged from the stall and hurried over to a sink, washed her hands, dried them off with a paper towel, and headed for the exit. As she reached for the handle, the door swung inward and four adolescent boys swaggered in.

"Well, well, well," the tallest one said. "What've we got here?" He moved toward her, flanked by his pals.

Backing away, she said, "They told me I had to use the boys' bathroom. It's the law, they said."

The boys exchanged looks and then continued toward her. "Freaks like you make me sick," the tall boy said and turned to his buddies. "Keep watch on the door."

Her eyes darting around, the girl said, "Please . . . just let me lea—"

The first blow knocked her down mid-word. The attackers proceeded to punch and kick her without letup.

As the camera pulled back from the mayhem, the narrator said, "No one has ever been assaulted in a public bathroom by a transgender person. But thousands of transgender people have been harassed, beaten, or killed in bathrooms. So social conservatives are right about one thing—bathrooms can be dangerous places. Especially if you're a transgender person."

Fade to black.

The applause lasted a full minute.

Dr. Soong leaned over. "Are you all right, Andie? You look like you've seen a ghost."

Andie moistened dry lips and swallowed. "Maybe I have." She took a deep breath. "A girl I used to hang out with got beaten to death in a bathroom in Estacada. A Shell station. The guy who did it got off on a temporary insanity plea, said he panicked when he found out she was transgender. The ad kind of freaked me out. I think lots of people'll be freaked out."

Gannon was talking: ". . . first three of a nine-ad series. They begin airing nationwide on Monday. Any questions?"

A woman raised her hand. "Will the transgender people in your ads all pass perfectly?"

"Excellent question. I'm going to preface my answer by stating our position regarding passing. Whether or not someone passes, they deserve to be shown the courtesy of having their gender acknowledged. It's about respect and common decency."

The audience applauded.

"The truth is, many cisgender people—nontrans people—sometimes do not 'pass.' Recently in a Walmart in Danbury, Connecticut a cisgender woman with short hair was accosted in the bathroom by another shopper who decided she was transgender. And in Frisco, Texas a man appointed himself bathroom sheriff and followed a cisgender woman into a bathroom at Baylor Medical Center and confronted her because he felt she looked masculine.

"Only one of the ads you watched, the last one, featured a transgender person, but upcoming ads will have transgender people in them, male and female. The question of whether they should pass sparked . . . spirited debate.

"We do not subscribe to the elitist notion that only people who pass well should represent the transgender community. However, we do need to counteract the impression, fostered by depictions in movies and on television and perpetuated by our adversaries, that transgender people are all freaks—men in dresses and women in men's clothes. Those crude stereotypes are about to be blown to smithereens. The ads are our heavy artillery.

"So the first fusillade will feature transgender people who are undetectable—unclockable, it's called—to make the point. But let me be clear. Our objective is acceptance and equality for everyone, whether they pass or not. In point of fact, not everyone *wants* to pass. Some reject the concept of passing as a type of oppression, and they have a valid point."

She paused a moment.

"I tend to get carried away talking about this stuff. But I've sounded off enough. Our first guest speaker this evening is acclaimed documentary filmmaker Melissa Beauchamp, whose latest film, *My Birth Mother Was an MtF*, won this year's Candescent Award at the Sundance Film Festival . . ."

Andie tossed her bag on the sofa, opened the refrigerator, and grabbed the lone can of ginger ale. Then she sat down at the dinette and picked up the journal.

Just got back from the conference. Where I spoke to Lady Gaga! I totally did! Our conversation was brief, but meaningful. I said to her, "I think the restrooms are over there."

And I crushed Eli at Spot the Celebrity, thirteen to seven.

Director Gannon kicked off the event with three very hip, very slick ads that the foundation produced. Blew me away. Blew everyone away. I'm guessing those ads cost a freakin' ton. Whatever they cost, the foundation can afford it. By the way, Gannon reminds me of my grandma in her appearance and manner. (I miss you, Grandma.)

The ads exposed the stupidity and outhouse-rat craziness of those bathroom laws popping up like snakes in Ireland. (Thanks for the simile, Dad). The ads totally eviscerated (love that word) those laws. The bigots are going to be squealing. It ought to be entertaining.

The last ad did a number on me. In it, a trans girl forced by a law to use boys' bathrooms is caught in one and savagely beaten by several boys. It was like I was watching Kari get beaten to death in that Estacada Shell station. I hope that ad shakes up a lot of people, makes them think. If it doesn't, then nothing will.

Then Gannon introduced the first speaker, Melissa Beauchamp. Her documentaries rock. She excoriated (another great word) movie and TV directors who exploit trans women in dramas and documentaries that include scenes showing them doing stereotypically female things, like applying lipstick and mascara, putting on on pantyhose (who wears pantyhose anymore?), applying nail polish, walking in high heels, hooking a bra . . .

Arrgghh! That's also a pet peeve of mine. The nitwits who make those things think such scenes are obligatory. Melissa Beauchamp is determined to set them straight.

A half-dozen other speakers followed her—a couple of heavy hitters in the trans community, one of the politicians who made Eli's celebrity list, and a lawyer from the Southern Poverty Law Center.

An odd thing—halfway through the SPLC lawyer's talk, a man in the back row leaped to his feet and began shouting bible verses at the top of his lungs.

People yelled at him to shut the hell up, me among them, but it didn't faze him. Then security pounced on him like pit bulls on a butt steak and escorted him out, still screaming. How did he crash the conference? That was the question on everyone's lips.

Please, God, deliver me from religious nuts.

Anyway, the conference was freakin' amazing. So amazing that I'm almost tempted to believe the Transcend Foundation is on the level.

Almost.

My street cynicism, which kept me alive for three years and I can't forget that, prevents me from buying it completely. It whispers, "Psst . . . Scientology has hosted some impressive events, too. So what?"

At this point I neither believe nor disbelieve that the Foundation's a cult. I'll wait and see what happens. Because that's what agnostics do.

34

No sooner had he gotten his hair fully lathered than the phone rang. He shut off the shower and groped for the phone on the counter, eyes shut tight against the shampoo. "Hello?" he said and somehow managed to enable speaker mode while functionally blind.

"Mr. Ritter? Nicole LeFleur, from the state forensic lab." As if she needed to identify herself, with that accent.

"Ms. LeFleur. What can I do for you?" He grabbed a damp washcloth and wiped stinging foam from his eyes.

"You said to call you if I learned anything about the missing LIMS records."

"Right, right. What did you find out?"

"It is somewhat technical. I had better explain it to you in person. Can we meet?"

"Sure. I can be over there in under an hour."

"There is work I must do at the lab this morning, but my lunch break is at noon. Would that be convenient for you?"

"Perfect. Shall I pick you up at the lab?"

"I would prefer to meet at CG's Deli. It is in a small plaza just north of Costco on Eighty-fourth, not far from the lab."

"Fine. See you there at noon."

After he disconnected, Ritter looked in the mirror.

And for God's sake, no nervous babbling this time. Sure, she's lovely, but so what? Keep your head on straight, eye on the ball.

It was 11:55 when he parked in front of CG's Deli. A white Fiat pulled up beside the Range Rover.

Nicole LeFleur emerged, wearing a teal jumpsuit tailored perfectly for her lithe body. "Hi," she said. "Have you been waiting long?"

"No, just got here," he said as he stepped out of his truck.

Inside the deli the spicy aroma of soups and hot sandwiches made his mouth water. He was six years old again, standing in his grandma's kitchen.

CG's was filling up fast with the lunchtime crowd from nearby businesses. He and Nicole stepped up to the counter and ordered subs, roast beef for him and turkey for her, and Cokes. She objected when he paid for her lunch, but he insisted that it was compensation for her sleuthing and she gave in. When it began to look as though they'd have to eat standing up, a table by the front window opened up. They pounced on it.

"Actually, Mr. Ritter," she said, unwrapping her sandwich, "it did not require a great deal of, as you put it, sleuthing."

He chewed and swallowed a bite of the sandwich. "Call me Eli."

"Very well. Then you must call me Nicole."

"Deal."

A large young black man appeared beside their table. Small, tight braids covered his scalp. His name badge indicated his name was Attila. "I'll take those trays," he said, "and give you some room."

"Thanks, Hun," Ritter said.

Attila didn't catch it, but Nicole made a sound halfway between a squeak and a snort. After they were alone again she said, "You must have a death wish. He is a wide receiver for the Portland State Vikings. This is his part-time job."

"I'm sure he's got a solid grasp of football. History, not so much. You a football fan?"

"Not me. I get bored watching pituitary cases giving each other concussions. I know he is a football player only because someone told me."

"So what floats your boat, Nicole?"

"Floats my . . . oh. Two things—Texas Hold'em and A.I."

"Poker and artificial intelligence?"

"Specifically, artificial neural nets. I am working on a new backpropagation algorithm that—Eli, you are smiling. This amuses you?"

"I won't deny it. But I'm also fascinated."

"Your turn. What . . . floats your boat?"

"Sailing, literally. I own a forty-foot ketch I keep moored at Tomahawk Bay Marina. I live aboard. So I'll see your backpropagation and raise you a mizzenmast."

That got a laugh from her. "I fold," she said.

Down to business. "What did you need to explain to me?"

She reached in her bag, took out a one-page printout, and smoothed it out on the table. "This is a listing of logins and logouts on the LIMS server for the four-day period beginning July fifteenth, the date the lab received the missing evidence. It is the *server* log, at the operating system level. It does not log LIMS database activity. That is completely separate."

"Does it show what users did after they logged in?"

"No. It just records who logged in or out, the date and time, and where they logged in from." She pointed to a couple lines of text circled in red. "Look at these two log entries."

The entries were cryptic. He looked up from the printout. "What do they mean?"

She pointed to the first entry. "At six-ten p.m. on Monday, July eighteenth, user Sepers logged in from an IT terminal. The other entry indicates he logged out at six-nineteen. He was logged in for nine minutes, total."

"I assume this user works in the IT division. Why is this particular login out of the ordinary?"

"Because it was the only time he had logged in to that server in over a year."

"Yes, I see. Nine minutes . . . is that long enough to for someone to delete the evidence records from LIMS' database and cover his tracks, all except for this?" He tapped the printout.

"It would be more than enough time."

"Sepers . . . his first name is Jason, right?"

She looked surprised. "Yes. Do you know him?"

"We've met. Is he a friend of yours?"

"No. He is only a coworker."

Ritter, a microexpression expert, caught the fleeting scowl that had accompanied her answer. Sepers shouldn't count Nicole among his fans. "Can you fill me in about him?"

"What do you want to know?"

"Your take on him, your opinion."

She shrugged. "Jason Sepers is a weasel."

"Why do you say that?"

"He has serious character flaws."

"Such as?"

"Such as his arrogance, his narcissism, his misogyny, and his sexism. Such as his delusion that he is God's gift to the IT division, despite the fact that three-quarters of the people in the division are better at their jobs. Worst of all, such as his inclination to take credit for others' work. Which he has done more than once." She tilted her head to one side. "Does that answer your question?

Awed by the lethal takedown, he only nodded.

She sipped the last of her drink and then set the cup next to her empty sandwich wrapper. "When Monsieur Weasel removed the two evidence records from the LIMS database he should have deleted these server log entries at the same time. He did not cover his tracks completely."

Ritter picked up the printout. "May I keep this?"

"Yes, that is your copy." She dipped into her bag again, took out a flash drive, and set it on the table. "This is also for you. It contains a digital copy of the entire log file."

"Nicole, I owe you big time."

"Do you think this information will help your case?"

"In conjunction with other evidence, it might."

Mainly, it confirmed his suspicion that the evidence's disappearance wasn't due to a bureaucratic snafu, it was deliberate. Kellenberger had directed his brother-in-law to delete the records, making it virtually impossible to locate the evidence in the lab. Kellenberger, it seemed, would stop at nothing to win the case, even risk disbarment. But why? In the scheme of things the case was small potatoes.

He watched Nicole apply Chapstick, glad he'd overcome his tendency to babble around her. No doubt about it, though, she was a striking young women, with a unique style. No makeup whatsoever. Vivid, dark eyes with long, thick lashes that needed no mascara. Hair that fell in soft waves below her shoulders. Minimal jewelry, only a pair of small diamond studs in her earlobes.

Also unique, her demeanor. She seemed unaware of her beauty. No guile or artifice or coyness about her, no flirty business with eyes and mouth. She regarded the world with a frank, unapologetic gaze and the hint of an ironic smile.

All very well, but the most appealing thing about her had nothing to do with her appearance or demeanor. She had caught his silly Attila the Hun reference, a sign she had a quick mind. Sussing out the login Sepers had carelessly left behind—so far the only positive development in the case—confirmed it.

"Eli, you have a faraway look."

"Huh? Oh, sorry. Just thinking about the case."

"When does the trial start?"

"Much too soon. September seventh."

"Do you really live aboard a sailboat?"

"For the past five years." He hesitated and then blurted it out: "Would you like to go sailing with me sometime?"

It clearly caught her off guard. "I have never been sailing."

"This is your chance."

She was silent for a heart-stopping five seconds before she said, "I would like that."

"Then we shall sail. When we both have a weekend free."

But with the trial starting and his case on life support, a free weekend could be weeks or even months away.

Never the luck.

35

They were gaining on her. She risked a quick look back at her pursuers. Some of them she recognized: Kellenberger, in the lead. Burleson, Pfaff, and Hinshaw, blood spurting from his neck. Madeleine Sanger, the woman who'd refused to wait on her at the DMV. Also giving chase, dour people holding transphobic signs and a rabid mob clutching rebar clubs.

And God, how they could run! They were going to catch her, sure as hell, if she didn't take evasive action. She ducked around a corner—and found herself back in that same Chinatown alley. Trapped again. Ghastly smiles on their faces, the horde reached for her . . .

She woke with a start and lay trembling in the predawn twilight, her heart pounding. After a while she lifted her head to look at the clock. Quarter to six. So much for her plan to sleep in a bit and make up for other nights, other nightmares.

She switched on the bedside light, reached for her journal, and began an entry.

Wednesday, August 17, 2016 5:45 a.m.

Another dawn. Every morning I ask myself the same question: Why am I sticking around here, when it looks worse for me each passing day? Like the mob in that nightmare, a horde of vicious people are out to get me. Out to destroy me, literally.

I'm now a target for every mouth-breathing bigot in the country. To them I'm a sinner, a pervert, mentally ill, subhuman, a worthless piece of crap who doesn't deserve to exist.

The sensible thing would be to skip town. Hitch my way to somewhere, the farther from Portland the better. Line up primo fake I.D. and start fresh, with a clean slate, where no one knows I'm trans except the people I tell.

Gone by dawn. It's sounding better and better.

Staying is risky. I'd be betting it all that Eli can get me a not-guilty verdict. And if he can't, because of the missing evidence or some unexpected development, I'll be getting room and board in a penitentiary for men. The street had its dangers, but in an all-male prison with psychos, rapists, and killers I'd be a rabbit among wolves.

Time to cut and run. It's self-preservation.

Except it would be a shitty thing to do to the foundation, which would lose the half-million bucks they put up for my bond. They're trusting me to stick around.

But for a multi-billion-dollar institution, that's small change. Surely my life is worth five hundred grand? As for violating their trust, like my bracelet says, *Non credere*. Trust no one. I'd lost sight of that. They'd lulled me into forgetting it.

I'm going to take a shower and then throw my stuff together. I want to be out of here before seven.

While shampooing her hair she realized she couldn't do it, couldn't just skip out. It came down to two things: trust and courage.

The foundation trusted her, to the tune of a half-mil, plus a lawyer, an apartment, and a job. She wanted to be worthy of that trust. Somewhere along the line she began to trust the foundation. Her buds on the street would laugh their asses off at that.

And running away would be a gutless thing to do. She'd been running for three years, cowering from threats, real and imagined. She was tired of running, tired of cowering.

When the trial began in September she'd march into the courtroom with her shoulders squared, her head held high. Hoping she wasn't being the prize sucker of all time.

Ritter needed a cup of coffee to kickstart the day. As usual, he bypassed the Talbot Building's vintage elevator and took the marble stairs up to the fifth-floor lounge. In the stairwell he ran into Garrett Millward—Longcypher, Cannady & Moore's other black lawyer—coming down the stairs. "Hey, Garrett," he said. "How are things in Intellectual Property?"

Millward shrugged. "Not exactly a hotbed of excitement, but it's steady. Got a minute, Eli?"

"Sure. What's up?"

Millward started to speak but hesitated, as though he were having second thoughts. "Listen," he said, "I may be out of line, but . . ." The words trailed off.

"Don't leave me hanging, Garrett. Spill it."

"Okay, but you didn't hear it from me."

"My lips are sealed."

"Okay, then. I was having lunch at Portland City Grill the other day when I heard familiar voices. Ethan Cannady and Vernon Trollinger were at the table behind mine. My back was to them and they didn't recognize me. All black people look alike. I could hear them clear as a bell. You, my friend and colleague, were the subject of their conversation."

"No kidding? What was the gist?"

"The Troll is doing his damnedest to get you fired."

"Yeah? I'm not surprised."

"Over lunch he asked for his father-in-law's backing to demand your resignation if you lose your current case."

"Is Cannady going to support him?"

"Sounded like it. He commented that it would be an ideal time to do it, given that Douglas Longcypher won't be back until September."

"A *fait accompli*." As though he weren't already under a ton of pressure to win the case, now his job was on the line. "Garrett, I appreciate the heads up."

"Good luck, Eli." Millward continued down the stairs.

Ritter hammered the stair railing. "Bastards," he said aloud, his words echoing in the stairwell. Then he massaged his hand.

He could give Doug a call, tell him what Trollinger and his father-in-law were cooking up in his absence, ask him to intercede. But he was on a long-delayed around-the-world jaunt. His postcard from Tuscany had arrived yesterday, and he seemed to be having the time of his life. Bothering him with office politics was out of the question.

In the lounge Ritter poured a cup of rich-smelling Kona. He took a sip, with no expectation that the taste would live up to the promise of its aroma. At least he could count on the caffeine.

Descending the stairs he realized there was one sure way to foil Trollinger's and Cannady's scheme—win the damn case.

36

Shortly after dawn, Andie donned sweat pants and a fleece hoodie and stepped out of the apartment. After warmup stretches, she spotted a gray cat stalking something under a nearby tree. Slinking along on its belly, the cat's yellow eyes were fixed on the prey with feline intensity.

She took a stealthy step closer to get a better look, but it spooked the cat. It darted under a bush thirty feet away. "Sorry," she called out to it.

She crept toward the spot that had interested the cat. The last thing she wanted to do was step on it, whatever it was. A field mouse, maybe.

But it wasn't a mouse—not unless it was a breed of mouse that had a beak. A naked baby bird the size of her thumb, its huge eyes still covered by a bluish membrane, wriggled in the grass.

She looked up. The nest was directly above, nestled in the fork of a branch. Using thumb and forefinger, she picked up the creature. It reacted by moving its marble-size head in a circle and opening its beak wide. Gaping, it was called. Cupping it in one hand, she stroked its tiny belly with the tip of her index finger. It reacted with more gaping.

"Sorry, Gapey, I'm fresh out of worms." For a second or two she considered digging one up to feed to the little guy. But then she'd have to kill the worm. She couldn't do it.

She stashed the hatchling in her hoodie's fleece-lined pocket and checked out the tree. The last time she'd climbed a tree was before she turned twelve. Pretransition . . .

Perched in the maple in the side yard of the house on 138th, she'd agonized over the possibility she wouldn't get to transition before puberty arrived. Several sixth-grade boys at North Powellhurst had gone through early puberty, resulting in deeper voices and facial hair growth. The thought of that happening to her made her shudder. She had to make her parents and the doctors see that it was a matter of life and death. Because if she had to go through male puberty, she might as well be dead. Then, a month after her twelfth birthday, she got to transition. And never climbed the maple again.

The tree Gapey had fallen from looked easy enough to climb. Taking care to protect the contents of her pocket, she grabbed a low limb and hoisted herself up. A third of the way there already. The next limb was within easy reach. Monkeys had nothing on her.

The nest was on a limb twelve feet above the ground. The tree had thoughtfully provided another limb, thick enough to support her weight, four feet below that. She climbed onto the lower limb and straightened up. The nest was eight feet away, out where the limb forked. As she inched toward it, a thin chorus of peeping became louder. In her pocket, Gapey answered with a solitary peep.

The nest, at chest height, contained Gapey's three siblings, all gaping. Where was Mama Bird with breakfast? Her babies were hungry, for crying out loud.

She took Gapey from her pocket. "It's a family reunion," she said and set him next to his siblings. He was smaller. Small enough to have fallen through a hole in the side of the nest, where twigs and stalks of grass had come unraveled.

"You're in luck," she said. "Nest repair's my specialty." It took her a few minutes to knit things back together and seal the breach. "Not perfect, but it'll do. Listen up, you guys—I want you to stay out of trouble, okay?"

The avian quartet answered with more sightless gaping.

Climbing down, she lost her footing on a limb and dropped the remaining six feet, jarring her teeth when she landed. Not the most graceful dismount. She walked over to the path and then looked back.

A lone robin was circling the tree. Mama Bird, probably. Sure enough, the bird flew into the tree and landed on a branch next to the nest, a fat worm in her beak.

"Listen here, Mama," she said, wagging her finger at the bird, "you need to make sure Gapey gets his share."

She zipped up the hoodie and set off down the path.

37

It was a 1930s-vintage two-story house, a Foursquare style common in older Portland neighborhoods. Steep-pitched roof, dormer, full-width porch, four columns supporting the porch's roof. Probably stylish in its day, but its day was long past. Now it was a dump—roof in dire need of repair, chalky white paint peeling in places, boarded-up windows, and a jungle of knee-high weeds in the front yard. Squatting silently in the dusk, the house somehow managed to retain echoes of its former dignity in spite of its dilapidated state.

Karen reached in through her cruiser's open window and grabbed her Mag-lite. Manheim and Phipps had called it in, but she couldn't see them. Illuminated by the flashlight's beam, the weeds on the left side had been trampled, forming a path that led around back. There, she found the pair of uniformed officers.

They said they had discovered the female victim when they were checking out the old place, making sure it hadn't become a den for local crackheads, who were drawn to abandoned houses like bats to caves.

An elm at least a hundred years old dominated the back yard. The perpetrators—several, by the look of the trampled grass—had tossed a rope over a thick tree limb, slipped the noose around the victim's neck, and hoisted her several feet off the ground.

The purplish color of the victim's hoodie matched her swollen face and tongue. She wore jeans and a white cotton knit top. A blue Nike running shoe lay upside down directly beneath her, no doubt kicked off during her violent death throes. Zip ties bound her wrists behind her, so tightly it looked as though she were wearing extra-large purple gloves. She had wet herself.

Hard to tell how old she was or what she had looked like before her executioners got hold of her. Karen turned to Manheim. "Have you found her purse or any I.D.?"

"Not so far. But the grass and weeds are tall enough back here to hide a Volkswagen."

A team from C.S.U. arrived to process the scene. They took extensive photographs of the body and collected samples from the rope and victim's clothing in hopes of getting some of the attackers' DNA.

Medical Examiner Jon Wu arrived next. He looked up at the victim and shook his head. "Let's get her down," he said.

Phipps unfastened the rope and eased her to the ground onto her back, fanning out her chestnut hair on the matted grass. Her eyes were swollen slits, open just enough to reveal the brown irises.

"Wrists," Wu said.

Phipps lifted her onto her side, and Manheim produced a Leatherman tool and snipped the zip tie. Then he loosened the noose and slipped it off over her head.

Someone had gone to a lot of trouble to construct a noose exactly like those used in official hangings. Making it on the spot would take too long, so the murder had been premeditated. They'd planned it.

Karen sent Manheim and Phipps off to canvass the neighborhood in case someone saw or heard something.

Wu checked over the body. "No bloating, so she's been dead less than three days." He grunted and pointed. "The top button of her jeans is unfastened. We might have a murder-rape case here, Woj. I won't know for sure until I get her to the lab, but I'm going to take a quick look now."

"I wouldn't be a bit surprised if they raped her, too," Karen said. "These animals are capable of anything."

Wu unzipped the jeans and worked them down over the victim's hips. After examining her for perhaps three seconds he straightened up and turned to Karen. "Forget the rape charge," he said. "What we got here is a hate crime."

She looked to see what he was talking about and then met his eyes. The victim was transgender, preop.

"Two possibilities," Wu said, refastening the victim's jeans, "this is a one-off . . . or they've started lynching transgender people."

"I vote for one-off, seeing as how your second possibility is unthinkable." As the segregated South had demonstrated.

"Hey," Wu said, "my guys finally made it here."

Two of them, with a stretcher and a body bag. They dropped the stretcher beside the body and bent to the task, their movements practiced and impersonal, as though they were setting tile. In minutes they had her zipped into the bag, lifted onto the stretcher, and toted off to the waiting van. Wu gave Karen a nod and followed after them.

She put on a fresh pair of latex gloves and then picked up the rope and began coiling it. Apart from the trampled grass under the tree, no sign remained that an act of unspeakable brutality had taken place there. They had wanted her to suffer, the twisted bastards. The term *hate crime* didn't cover it. Not something that vicious.

Back at the cruiser, she sealed the rope in an evidence bag and stowed it in the trunk. Then she waited for Manheim and Phipps to return, a ten-minute wait. "Any luck, guys?"

Manheim shook his head. "Nobody saw nothing, nobody heard nothing."

"I figured," she said.

"What now, Woj?"

"When you were knocking on doors did you happen to notice any dumpsters in the neighborhood?"

The duo exchanged glances. "I didn't notice any," they said, almost in unison.

"Just to be sure you didn't overlook one, what say we hop in our respective vehicles and look specifically for dumpsters within a three-block radius? Manny, you and Phipps check the east side, I'll take the west."

Halfway through her reconnaissance, Phipps radioed her. *"Woj, be advised we found a dumpster on Seventeenth."*

"On my way," she said.

She parked the maroon Chevy Caprice behind Manheim's and Phipps' unit. They were standing beside a blue dumpster.

"We figured you'd want to do the honors," Phipps said.

"You're a peach." Grunting with effort, she flipped open a heavy lid and switched on her flashlight.

She didn't see it at first, not until she looked closer at a bundle of rags in the far corner. The rags turned out to be a crumpled handbag made of tan coarse-weave fabric trimmed with fringe. After looking around for something to hook it with and finding nothing, she knew she'd have to climb in. "Hey, Manny . . . give me a spot, huh?"

The dumpster's interior contained mostly clean, dry cardboard and Styrofoam peanuts. Thank God for small favors. She handed the bag to Manheim and climbed out.

She began removing items from the bag and setting them on the cruiser's hood. Hairbrush. Makeup (mascara, eyeliner, eyeshadow, blush). A bottle of nail polish. Two nearly full prescription vials with the labels obscured. A blue vinyl wallet, no cash inside, only some discount coupons and an expired Washington state driver's license belonging to Corey Lane Ryan, address 1910 Richard St., Lacey, WA 98503, DOB 04-05-95, height 5' 7", weight 128 lbs., hair and eye color Brn, sex M. The individual in the photograph had an androgynous look.

At the bottom of the bag, the jackpot: a phone. A Yoshika. Not exactly a leading brand, but it could contain intel that would lead them to the sick assholes who murdered its owner.

At least it was something to go on.

38

On a tropical beach, shaded by palm trees, Boonstra lay supine on a chaise lounge while two giggling island girls clad in brief halters and sarongs attended to him. They rubbed suntan lotion on his shoulders and chest and belly, fetched him bourbon on the rocks, and lit his cigar. Not a phone in sight. Yet there was that annoying ringing . . .

He came to with a start and snatched up his desk phone. "Yeah, Boonstra here."

"Richard Ronson, Congressman . . . and Mr. Mullen?"

Short crackling burst of line noise. "I'm here, too."

"Gentlemen," Ronson said, "now that you've seen the investigator's report I sent you, I'm sure you have a better idea of what we're up against."

"I damn sure do," Boonstra said.

Crackle. "Yes, the report was quite informative."

"Question," Boonstra said. "How the deuce did your investigator record video from up above that get-together? We had us a crow's-nest view."

"A camera-equipped drone. Mr. Mullen generously underwrote the cost of a pair of them."

Crackle. "Money well spent."

"The investigator, how'd you hook up with him?"

"Google," Ronson said. "I searched for private investigators in Portland. His website was the most impressive."

"How about his office? Equally impressive?"

"I never saw it. Contact with him has only been by phone. Payment is delivered via courier, in cash. Tight security is of utmost importance, wouldn't you agree, gentlemen?"

"Yessiree, under the radar."

Crackle. "Very wise, Mr. Ronson."

"Anyways," Boonstra said, "the folks attending that shindig came from Hollywood, the Beltway, and parts unknown. Celebrities, politicians, the rich and powerful, flocking to a demonic liberal gala." The *demonic* was a nice touch.

Crackle. "Just think, one small, well-placed tactical nuke and—*kaboom!*—instant incineration in righteous hellfire."

Boonstra felt the hair rise on the back of his neck. But he guffawed as though Mullen had uncorked a knee slapper. "We'll nuke them with legislation instead."

"After reading the investigator's report and watching the video," Ronson said, "it's clear the Transcend Foundation is a more formidable adversary than I'd first thought. It would be a big mistake to underestimate the threat it poses."

Crackle. "Yes, Mr. Ronson, any and all threats to our goal of returning this country to traditional values must be taken seriously. But the enemies of decency do not have God on their side. God will make us mighty. Ephesians six-eleven says, 'I have put on the complete armor of God.' So let us gird our loins and do battle in the name of righteousness."

Boonstra shook his head, chuckling. The choice between God's help and Mullen's 54 billion helpers was a no-brainer. Money talked and bullshit walked, especially religious bullshit. But he'd best keep that bit of wisdom to himself.

"So, gentlemen," Ronson said, "what are we going to do about the Transcend Foundation? We need to come up with a strategy to neutralize them. Nonviolently, of course."

Boonstra cleared his throat. "What would you say to an investigation by a Congressional committee?"

"Would it be difficult to arrange?"

"Not at all, son. I can introduce a House resolution forming a select committee to investigate . . . whatever."

"Like Trey Gowdy's Select Committee On Benghazi?"

"Exactly."

"The ostensible reason for the investigation?"

"I'm sure I can come up with something plausible."

Crackle. "Give us an example."

"Well, just off the top of my head . . ." Actually, he'd been racking his noggin, thinking on it. "Many of the transgenders they supposedly help are underage. The select committee can investigate them for corrupting the morals of minors—or better yet, for brainwashing children."

"Brainwashing children . . . hey, that's a winner," Ronson said. "Mr. Mullen?"

Crackle. "I concur. Good thinking, Congressman."

Boonstra smiled to himself. "It'll put the Transcend Foundation on the defensive, and it might give us a peek behind the curtain. I'd give my eye teeth to know who's pulling the strings at that outfit."

"Also," Ronson said, "the hearings will garner a lot of press and draw attention to our cause."

"The press will lap it up, you can make book on that. I can almost see the headlines."

"Like 'Foundation Accused of Brainwashing Children'?"

Crackle. "Or 'House Committee Says Foundation Turns Kids Transgender'?"

"Gentlemen, I do believe you've got the idea."

"This conference call," Ronson said, "has brightened my day considerably."

Crackle. "Congressman, what's the status on the Protect Our Children bill? Last I heard, it was in committee."

"Scheduled to come to the Senate floor pretty soon. Unfortunately, a pain-in-the-ass senator from Washington state—McCoy's his name—has vowed to filibuster it."

Crackle. "Don't lose hope, Congressman. Perhaps God will change Senator McCoy's mind."

Boonstra chuckled. "Perhaps." And perhaps pigs will fly.

The call didn't last much longer, and that was a good thing. A little of that God crap went a long ways.

He picked up the phone again and buzzed his office manager. "Ronette, see if you can get hold of the Speaker."

"Speaker? What speaker is that?"

He looked at the ceiling and sighed. Ronette was a looker, but she didn't have to worry about missing any job offers from NASA. "The Speaker of the House of Representatives."

"Oh. Okay."

He trimmed a cigar while he waited.

She called him back in a few minutes. "His office said he's gone for the day."

Maybe it was just as well. Tomorrow he'd pay a visit to the Speaker in person and run the select committee by him.

He lit the cigar and sat back. Things were coming together,

39

Repeat a word enough times and it will lose its meaning, become simply a sound. The phenomenon even had a fancy name: semantic saturation.

Dead dead dead dead dead dead dead dead dead dead dead . . .

Trouble was, the effect didn't last long enough. All too soon a terrible finality again infiltrated the word.

Andie wadded the soggy Kleenex into a tight ball, trudged into the bathroom, and dropped it in the toilet. She caught sight of her reflection in the mirror over the basin. Her eyes and nose were an angry crimson, hair a freakin' fright wig. Still, she was alive, something that could not be said about Corey Ryan.

Corey had been her mentor when she first struck out on her own at fifteen. The older girl showed her how to survive on the streets—where to go, what to do, what *not* to do, and especially who to avoid. "A newbie like you, they'd eat you alive," she said. "Stay close, listen, and learn." Under her tutelage Andie caught on quickly.

And now Corey was dead, murdered by a mob driven by ignorance and hate—people who felt that someone like Corey did not deserve to live, and who without a doubt believed the monstrous act was completely justified. A chilling reminder that such twisted creatures existed in the world.

Not that she needed a reminder.

Corey was the third trans girl she'd known who had been murdered. As a demographic, transgender people had the mortality rate of Tutsis in Rwanda. Had it not been for the freakish outcome in the Chinatown alley, the statistics would have included her.

She needed to go for a run. Running was the best medicine for the kind of funk she was in. She tied her hair back and put on running clothes. Fortunately, it wouldn't be necessary to leave the foundation's grounds; a dozen asphalt paths criss-crossed the campus.

Thirteen minutes into the run, on the path between the auditorium and the groundskeeper's shed, she heard the swarm following her. She gritted her teeth and ran faster.

The shed's door was locked. She pounded on it. No response. The swarm sounded closer. As she was thinking about making a headlong dash to her apartment, the grounds-keeper appeared carrying a hedge trimmer.

"Mr. Nakamura," she called out.

"Yes?" A trans man, Nakamura had a baritone voice, a Vandyke beard, and a pretty good start on a receding hairline. Powerful stuff, testosterone. "Annie, right?"

"It's Andie, actually. Listen . . . do you hear that buzzing?"

Nakamura cocked his head to one side as he listened. "Yeah, I do. Wasps, maybe?"

"Or hornets. A swarm."

"Sounds like it's coming from . . ." He shielded his eyes with his hand and scanned the sky directly above. "But I don't see anything up there."

"Neither do I." But then she did see . . . something. "Wait, maybe I do."

"Your eyes must be sharper than mine."

Andie pointed directly above them. "Up there. Darn, now it's gone. Maybe my eyes were playing tricks on me."

"Wait a minute," Nakamura said. "I saw it . . . I see it." He turned to Andie, an enigmatic expression on his face. "And it sees us."

She spotted it again, a couple of hundred feet above them.

"Stay here," Nakamura said, "I'll be right back." He disappeared into the shed for a moment and returned holding a rifle with a scope. "Pellet gun," he said. "Legal to fire within city limits."

"You're going to shoot it down?"

"You bet, and we have every right to do it. It's trespassing in our airspace to spy on us, and it's creating a disturbance."

"Tell me about it. That thing has scared the bejeezus out of lots of people, including me."

"Stay there." Nakamura walked over to a rhododendron the size of a small tree and ducked beneath its foliage. From above, the bush concealed him totally, like a hunter's blind.

The pellet gun made a sort of *whuff* sound. The craft above seemed unaffected by the first shot.

A second shot also had no discernible effect.

The third shot did the trick. The drone began oscillating wildly and quickly lost altitude.

"I must have hit one of its propellers," Nakamura said, his voice breaking. "Made it unstable as hell."

"No kidding. I think it's going to crash."

"That was the idea, Annie."

"Andie."

The drone careened into the top of a light pole beside the path and dropped upside down, striking the asphalt propellers-first with a loud quack of protest, like a pissed-off duck.

Up close, the X-shaped drone had propellers—two intact, two damaged—at the tips of the arms and a camera slung underneath its middle. The craft's top half was brown and green camo, its underside the same shade of blue as the sky above.

"That's why we didn't spot it at first," Nakamura said. "It's practically invisible from the ground."

"I wonder who was flying it?"

"Good question. Expensive drones like this have a range of up to a mile. The operator could be anywhere around the perimeter of these grounds. Wherever he is, I bet he's not too happy. He's out a couple grand, at least."

Pomerenke glared at the monitor. "Screw you," he said to the on-screen SIGNAL LOST message.

Millican swiveled his chair to look at him. "Problem?"

Pomerenke sighed. "You might say that. I was flying Drone One, keeping tabs on the McInnes girl while she jogged. She stopped and talked to some guy, a Jap. Then she and the Jap looked up and pointed at the drone. I was just about to get it the hell out of there when the damn thing went bat-shit crazy on me. Complete loss of control. It crashed in what I'd call spectacular fashion. A three-thousand-dollar drone, gone."

"That seriously sucks. We still have Drone Two, though. And the drone that crashed can be replaced, right?

Pomerenke shot him a withering look. "You want to pay for it, Gordo?"

"Sure thing, boss, if you give me a big enough raise."

Pomerenke grunted. "These people were already aware they were under surveillance—thanks to your clumsy tailing technique and your loose lips—and now, to have *this* fiasco happen . . ." The embarrassing truth was, he'd delayed pulling the drone out of there while he popped a stick of gum in his stupid mouth. So when it came right down to it, he was almost as incompetent as Gordo. *Clowns. A pair of frickin' clowns.*

"What you gonna do, Neil?"

He leaned his chair back and looked at the ceiling. "I don't know yet. I need to give it some thought."

It was a catastrophe. A goddamn, big-titted catastrophe, and it could cost him the best-paying gig he'd ever had.

To hell with surveillance, he needed a drink.

40

The damaged drone squatted in the middle of the conference table, looking like a giant injured insect. Director Gannon stood at the head of the table eyeballing the thing, her lips tight. Of the dozen people around the table Ritter knew only six: Andie, Dr. Soong,, Detective Wojanowski Nakamura, IT Manager Krishnamurti, and his technician and wunderkind, Rix. The rest were foundation board members.

Andie leaned over to him. "What's the cop doing here? She's a homicide detective."

"The director invited her. She briefed the director earlier about Corey Ryan's murder."

Gannon cleared her throat. "First of all, I want to commend Mr. Nakamura for his outstanding marksmanship. I would've been proud to have him in my infantry."

Nakamura inclined his head in acknowledgment of the praise and the polite applause that followed.

Gannon looked at Wojanowski. "Detective, did we break any law by shooting it down?"

"Well," Wojanowski said, "technically, the police should handle such matters, but the drone would probably be long gone by the time officers got here. It was trespassing in your airspace, which extends five hundred feet above your property, and the noise it made was frightening people. I'd say you were within your rights."

"I'm guessing that's Pomerenke Investigations' drone," Ritter said, "and they're not likely to file a complaint. Which is too bad, actually."

"The gang that couldn't shoot straight," Gannon said.

"All the more reason to not make an issue out of this—" Ritter gestured at the drone. "—and their other surveillance activity. Their bumbling is to your advantage."

"Good point." Gannon turned to the IT manager. "Dr. Krishnamurti, you and Rix examined this piece of—this drone. What have you learned?"

A turbaned, bearded Sikh with a heavy accent, Krishna-murti said, "Quite a lot. This radio-controlled craft records everything it sees on one of these." He held up a micro SD card. "Rix, if you please."

The technician, who looked to be around six-three and a hundred and ten pounds, got up and switched off the over-head lights.

"This is aerial footage recorded by the drone's camera." Krishnamurti pressed a key on the laptop computer in front of him and the wall-mounted flat-screen TV came to life.

"Here we see the drone taking off beside a large white delivery van parked within sight of the foundation's front entrance on Covington Boulevard. The drone's four powerful motors enable it to gain altitude quite rapidly. And now we have an overhead view of the grounds from several hundred feet up. The administration building is directly ahead, and the auditorium is on the left.

"The drone performs a reconnaissance of the foundation's grounds, zooming in when it sees activity. The tennis courts and swimming pool seem to be of particular interest. Now it continues on . . . until it is directly above the living quarters. A person emerges from one of the apartments—"

"Hey," Andie said, "that's me."

"So the drone follows Miss McInnes as she runs on the paths. Nothing interesting happens for another ten minutes, so I will fast forward." Andie's running figure on the screen sped up comically, looking like a character in a silent movie.

"Here we are," Krishnamurti said. "Miss McInnes runs to the groundskeeper's shed and knocks on the door. The drone hovers over her in a stationary position, observing. Mr. Nakamura arrives, and he and Miss McInnes talk. Both appear to search the sky. Miss McInnes points directly at the drone. Mr. Nakamura disappears into the shed and returns twenty seconds later holding an object that cannot be identified from our vantage point. Then he moves out of camera view.

"Several seconds later chaos erupts, and we are privileged to see a sensational crash from an intimate perspective, culminating in the drone's transition to a nonfunctional state."

"Thank you, Dr. Krishnamurti," Gannon said. "Now, here's what bothers me, people—why didn't the drone immediately retreat after Ms. McInnes and Mr. Nakamura spotted it? Instead, it hung around. Any theories as to why?"

Wojanowski raised her hand. "Pomerenke or whoever was flying it didn't anticipate it would be shot down."

"Makes sense," Gannon said. "Mr. Nakamura was totally hidden by the rhododendron. No way the drone's pilot could see him shooting at it, so he was unaware of any danger."

"He might have assumed that altitude and camouflage paint gave it invisibility," Krishnamurti said.

"Or," Ritter said, "maybe he just wasn't paying attention. A distracted driver."

"Perhaps we will get an opportunity to ask him," Gannon said. "In the meantime, how long will it take you and Rix to get this drone operational, Dr. Krishnamurti?"

"Well, considering that it hit the asphalt when it crashed, the damage is surprisingly minimal. Luckily, it struck upside down, sparing the camera. If we replace the broken propellers, check all the connections and linkages, and obtain a transmitter with the proper frequency, it should be flyable. I'm sure Rix can rig up a monitor-receiver."

"What do you have in mind, Ms. Gannon?" Ritter asked.

She smiled. "It's only fitting that we watch the watchers with their very own drone."

That brought nods and smiles all around.

"If you'll recall," Wojanowski said, "our Mr. Kellenberger was asking around about the foundation. Maybe he hired Pomerenke. Is there any way we can find out for sure?"

Nakamura raised his hand. "We could send Pomerenke a ransom note asking for his client's identity in return for the drone."

"Except," Ritter said, "that would violate Oregon Revised Statute 164, which classifies extortion as a Class B felony."

Gannon laughed. "Gotta like the way Mr. Nakamura thinks, though. Adapt and improvise."

"The only legal way to force him to reveal the identity of his client is by court order," Ritter said. "I guess it could be Kellenberger—I wouldn't put it past him—but Pomerenke's sidekick said the investigation was open-ended and their client had 'money to burn,' which doesn't sound like Kellenberger."

"Maybe he found a sugar daddy to foot the bill," Gannon said.

Ritter shrugged. "I can buy Kellenberger wanting Pomerenke to keep tabs on Andie, but conducting surveillance on the foundation? It doesn't make sense."

But then, charging Andie with second-degree manslaughter didn't make a whole lot of sense, either.

41

Senator Jim McCoy's eyes snapped open at first light and he threw the covers back. After a visit to the bathroom he exercised, showered, shaved, dressed, and wolfed down a light breakfast, all of which took just over an hour.

The Protect Our Children Act, or SB1947, was slated to hit the Senate floor at ten. For the past six weeks, preparing for his avowed filibuster, McCoy had maintained a strict regimen of megavitamins, exercise, a high-protein diet, and sufficient sleep. It was how he used to train for marathons, back when he was a decade younger and had time to run marathons. Still, the regimen worked; he felt good. Better than he'd felt in years, in fact.

A filibuster was also a marathon, the verbal type. He'd sucked on eucalyptus and slippery elm lozenges, drank tea with honey and lemon, and did his level best to save his voice by talking only when necessary.

Shoes were of utmost importance, since he'd have to stand for the duration of the filibuster. Sitting down would yield the floor, and then the presiding officer would recognize another speaker. He was wearing his Skechers Air Cross Trainers (with cloud-like gel-infused memory foam insoles).

At eight he loaded a duffle bag with containers of water and milk from the refrigerator. They were allowed. Food was not, except for hard candy from the "Candy Desk."

The longest one-man filibuster on record was Senator Strom Thumond's 24-hour 18-minute filibuster of the Civil Rights Act in 1957. Amazing, considering bathroom breaks weren't allowed during filibusters. But Thurmond had a trick up his sleeve—he took a steam bath beforehand to dehydrate his body. McCoy had opted for a different approach to achieve the same objective—he used a diuretic.

He also had a backup. At a healthcare supply store he'd bought a high-capacity urine bag ("with anti-reflux valve"), which he taped to the inside of his right leg. It didn't show under his slacks. A condom-like sleeve fit snugly over his penis (although inserting a flaccid penis into the sleeve took some doing, with the help of a dab of Vaseline).

In short, he was well prepared for what promised to be a long, grueling ordeal, both mentally and physically.

The August sky darkened during the three-block walk from his apartment to the Metro's Spring Hill stop, but damned if he'd allow it to spoil his resolutely upbeat mood.

The Metro pulled in right on time. He boarded and took a seat by the window, right side. Just before departure a man wearing mirrored aviator glasses got on. McCoy felt an itch of recognition. He'd seen the guy recently. As to where and when, it would bug him until he nailed it down.

He dug out his tablet and checked his notes for the filibuster. They consisted of key points, concepts, ideas, notions, digressions, and bloviations. Filibuster rules decreed that speaking be continuous. If he couldn't come up with a more or less constant stream of words, the presiding officer would declare the filibuster over. So spew he would, with vigor.

He closed the notes and called up *The Washington Post*. On the front page, North Carolina's Governor Pat McCrory again defended HB2, his "bathroom law," its projected cost to North Carolina of five billion a year in lost federal funding and business revenue. McCrory stated, "The people of North Carolina are entitled to both privacy and equality." Equality? Republicans were oblivious to irony. And McCrory's discriminatory law would likely cost him reelection. Good riddance.

He got off at the Capitol South stop on Southeast First Street. The guy in the mirrored aviator glasses also disembarked, McCoy noticed. After he reached street level he walked north on First toward the Capitol Building. A quick glance showed Mirrored Glasses Guy twenty feet or so behind him, but he appeared to be texting on his phone as he walked along, seemingly paying no attention to anything else.

McCoy snapped his fingers when he made the connection. The day he gave a statement on the Capital Building's steps, that was the first time he saw the guy. And then he saw him again on the Metro. He probably also lived in Spring Hill and often rode the train. Mystery solved.

McCoy crossed Independence Avenue and proceeded west on the sidewalk along the south edge of the Capitol Building grounds. It began to sprinkle. Fortunately, his destination was less than a block away. He walked faster, head down.

A faded maroon utility van pulled to the curb just ahead. The side door slid open. McCoy turned his head to see what was going on, and out of the corner of his eye he saw that Mirrored Glasses Guy had closed the distance between them. And he was pointing some sort of—

McCoy felt a stab of pain on the left side of his neck. His fingers closed around a small cylindrical object. He yanked it out. It was a hypodermic dart about two inches long, a needle on one end and a bright pink ruff on the other. The reservoir was empty.

"What the hell is this?" he roared, but what came out was "Quad me erfin summa?" Street signs and light poles leaned in to listen. The rain cried as wind snickered through the trees. Somewhere a choir sang a minor chord.

Rough hands pushed and pulled at him, and then he was lying on the floor of the van, his cheek abraded by the carpet. The door closing reverberated for what seemed like an hour. The world shrank to a single dot of light that finally . . . winked . . . out.

Coppery smell. Road noise. Vibration. Male voices. Headache. Nausea. Those stimuli jarred him awake and into a Ripley's-record hangover.

He tried to lift a hand to his throbbing head and couldn't. His wrists were bound with a sturdy zip tie, he discovered, as were his ankles. A strip of duct tape covered his mouth.

He wormed his way into a position that enabled him to see the two men in front. The driver had close-cropped black hair and a four-day stubble. The passenger was Mirrored Glasses Guy, who was talking:

". . . turned out to be a clusterfuck like the one in Fallujah. I tried to warn them, but they wouldn't listen to me."

"The bastards deserved what they got," Mr. Driver said.

"You're wrong, mate. Nobody deserved that." The guy had an accent. Australian?

"Hey, Gergen," Mr. Driver said, "how long d'you think our guest'll be in la-la land?

Gergen, formerly known as Mirrored Glasses Guy, looked back at McCoy, who had quickly closed his eyes. "Unknown. It's new stuff. Fast acting, fast recovery, or so they said. He'll probably be coming around pretty soon. Yoo-hoo, Senator . . . you awake yet?"

By pretending to be unconscious, McCoy hoped to buy more time to size up the situation.

"Nope, he's still out cold," Gergen said. "Maybe he'll stay out until we get there."

Get where? McCoy pressed his chest against the van's floor, feeling for his cell phone in his suit coat's inside breast pocket. No such luck. They'd taken it and probably destroyed it. Too bad. Its signal could be triangulated after his staff reported him missing.

He wondered how long he'd been unconscious. For all he knew, he'd been out for hours or even days. The smoothness of the ride indicated they were on a freeway. An overhead sign flashed past the windshield: "Centreville 1 mi." So they were in Virginia, barreling west on Custis Memorial Parkway, about forty minutes from the center of D.C.

He'd been awake about ten minutes, so the dart's sedative had knocked him out for . . . say, half an hour. And left in its wake what felt like the aftermath of a three-day bender, although it seemed to be subsiding somewhat.

The possibility of abduction had never crossed his mind. Not even remotely. Now he wouldn't be able to deliver the filibuster. But then, that was the idea. Someone had hired the two goons to make sure he wouldn't. A brazen move, but not surprising. Nothing hard-right social conservatives did surprised him anymore. He clenched his jaw. He'd been so psyched for that filibuster.

A grim possibility crept into his mind. The duo up front might intend to kill him and bury his body in the woods. One less liberal in the Senate—that could well be their goal. Again, he wouldn't put it past them.

The van took the Centreville exit and drove for about five minutes. McCoy counted two right turns and three lefts before the van slowed and stopped, engine off. The side door slid open and Gergen stood grinning at him.

"Rise and shine, mate," Gergen said. "I'll show you to your new temporary accommodations."

McCoy couldn't decide whether *temporary* signified good news or bad. It could be taken either way.

Gergen snipped the zip tie around McCoy's ankles and helped him out of the van. He had trouble standing; Gergen steadied him and ripped the tape off his mouth. It stung.

They were in an industrial area, surrounded by rows of new-looking metal buildings. No signs on the buildings. No other visible human activity. But the sun's position indicated it was midmorning. Where the hell was everybody?

The building next to the van had a keypad on the wall. Mr. Driver punched some keys and the articulated aluminum door slithered up in eerie silence. Gergen gave McCoy a shove.

Inside, two Humvees the color of desert sand crouched side by side. "Hey, Hassler," Gergen said, "did you or did you not say this place would be empty?" He stood with arms folded, facing Hassler, formerly Mr. Driver.

"I'm as surprised as you," Hassler said. "They weren't here yesterday."

"I knew I should have blindfolded him." Gergen looked at McCoy. "Well, I'm sure the senator's seen a Humvee before—right, Senator?"

So they hadn't wanted him to see the Humvees. Or perhaps the black and white P/G logo on the Humvees' doors?

"Maybe that juice addled his brain," Hassler said.

"Politicians' brains are already addled, or they wouldn't be politicians."

Hassler pointed at a fenced-off area in the corner. "Parts room. Got a locking door. You can stash your boy in there."

"Outstanding." Gergen walked McCoy over and shoved him through the doorway. "At least you got a desk and chair, Senator," he said, locking the door.

McCoy dropped into the chair and surveyed his surroundings. Floor-to-ceiling cyclone fencing comprised the parts room's walls and door. Its furnishings were spartan: desk, chair, empty shelves, trash can, also empty. A folding cot and blanket. A push broom. The ceiling had a grate for heat and air conditioning. Unfortunately, it was a good twenty feet above the floor, and not a ladder in sight.

Gergen opened the door and tossed him the duffel. "You might as well have your water and milk, mate. We're fresh out of cookies, though."

After Gergen went away McCoy unzipped the bag. The tablet was missing. No surprise there; these were pros. No way they'd overlook something like that. Their bearing, the way they handled themselves, bespoke military, active or ex. The Humvees wouldn't look out of place in Afghanistan or Iraq. He wouldn't be surprised to learn they were equipped with armament.

"My watch says it's beer thirty," Hassler said. He opened a small refrigerator with a camo paint job, grabbed two cans of beer, and tossed one to Gergen.

Gergen thumbed it open and held it away, dodging the spray.

"Gergen, when are you going to get fed up with being a security guard on a boat and come back to the company? See some real action."

Gergen scowled. "It's not a goddamn boat, Hassler, it is a ship. And there's no shortage of real action. Last year two dozen Somali pirates tried to board us. They now reside at the bottom of the Arabian Sea. Most of the crew are ex-military—Navy Seals, Green Berets, Army Rangers, Israeli Commandos, even French Legionnaires. Mullen's Militia, all badasses. And the pay's outstanding. I make more in two weeks than I made in a month with the company. And sometimes I get to do special ops. Like this one."

"Relax, bro, just giving you shit. Seriously, if the gig doesn't work out, you always have a place in the company. Pinkler told me to tell you that."

"Thank him for me. I'll keep it in mind."

Pretending to doze from the aftereffects of the drug, McCoy filed away the conversation for future reference.

In the present, however, he was imprisoned in a cell that seemed escape proof, without any hope of rescue. Sure, his staff would report him missing to the police, but how could they possibly find him? As if that weren't depressing enough, the hateful bathroom bill, unimpeded by the filibuster, would undoubtedly sail though the Senate.

Tendrils of nausea announced its imminent return. He took several deep breaths and reached in the duffle for a bottle of water. He had to unclench his jaw to take a sip.

42

Outside the Capitol Building the Protect Our Children Act's supporters and protesters wielded their respective signs with stony-eyed defiance, chins jutting. Three incendiary confrontations had already erupted—taunts had led to shouting matches that escalated to shoving, slugging, kicking, biting, hair pulling, and wrestling on the concrete steps. Maintaining separation between the two factions kept the Capitol Police busy.

Visitors packed the Senate gallery, and a carnival atmosphere pervaded the chamber, abuzz with excitement ginned up by media flogging the story for the past week.

Three questions were on everyone's lips. What had happened to Senator McCoy and his promised filibuster? And in his absence why hadn't the bill been brought to the floor for a vote? Why in hell weren't the Republicans taking advantage of a golden opportunity?

Boonstra dropped onto a bench at the back of the chamber and yawned. He looked down at his watch. It was almost eleven-thirty, an hour and a half past the time the bill had been scheduled to come to the floor. He'd smoked two cigars since arriving at nine o'clock. One of the senators, a Democrat, walked by grinning at him like a possum eating a sweet potato. The goddamn Democrats were of course elated at the unexpected turn of events.

He badly wanted to go outside and smoke another cigar. Instead, he rose to his feet and set off to look for the majority whip, ask him what the hell was going on. He spotted him in front, talking with the majority leader. He slathered on some down-home affability and approached them. "Gentlemen," he said, "Don't mean to pester you . . . any chance of the bill making it to the floor today?"

"Sorry, Dale," the whip said, "but we're one vote short. The holdout is an independent named Krakenflosser, who almost always caucuses with us. Turns out his sister has a transgender kid. Sis made him change his vote."

"His mind's made up, I'm guessing."

"I would describe his position as inflexible, intractable, and adamantine."

"Damnation. I gather you're going to postpone the bill."

The majority leader spread his arms wide. "We need to nail down all the votes before we allow it to come to the floor."

Boonstra sighed. "Well, tomorrow's another day."

"Except we break for four days. Next session is Monday. Maybe we can give it another shot then."

"I swear, old son, I should run for the Senate. I could use the rest."

The majority leader rolled his eyes. "Yeah, we're getting a ton of rest over here."

"Any word on McCoy?"

"Haven't heard a thing."

"Maybe we're shut of him. Well, keep me posted."

Boonstra took the back route to his office to avoid encountering anyone who might want to talk to him. On the way he recalled what Mullen had said during the conference call: "Perhaps God will change Senator McCoy's mind." And perhaps He had. But Mullen failed to consider that God might also cap the votes.

The Lord giveth and the Lord taketh away.

It seemed the Almighty—that holy figment of Bronze Age goat herders' imagination—was a prankster.

43

Jury selection, known as *voir dire*, was likely to take up most of the day. Questioning two dozen prospective jurors about their backgrounds, interests, and potential biases was a time consuming but necessary process. A hostile jury could render impotent even the most competent defense.

He'd brought along a paralegal, a young woman named Phoebe Potterf, to take notes and assist. With her dark hair in a bun, Ann Taylor business suit, sensible shoes, and strand of pearls she seemed to be trying to project a dead-serious image. And succeeding.

"This is my first *voir dire*," she said, laying out her notepad and pens on the tabletop. "Mr. Trollinger said you would show me what to do."

Ritter frowned. He should have anticipated that the Troll would give him a paralegal without jury selection experience. "The proceeding's about to start, so here's the abridged version. Set up a seating chart. Write down the names of jurors as they're called and their occupations. Describe their physical appearance—how they're dressed, if they're skinny or overweight, hirsute or bald. Note anything out of the norm. Record all their answers. Use your intuition and initiative." He paused a beat. "Keep this in mind—I need as much information at my disposal as possible when I make my peremptory challenges."

"Got it," she said.

"And while you're gathering information, I'll be talking to prospective jurors."

"Understood."

He could only hope for the best. But Vernon Trollinger obviously wasn't content to sit back in the hope Ritter would lose the case. The Troll was taking an active role, trying to sabotage him. How perfectly goddamn delightful.

The courtroom door opened and people began filing in. A diverse-looking group, they could have been chosen at random from an airport terminal. Or a bar. Ritter was pleased to see Phoebe already making notes. Kellenberger took his place at the opposing counsel's table and nodded to Ritter.

"I'm up at bat," Ritter said and rose to his feet.

The proceeding broke for lunch after Ritter and Kellenberger both had a chance to interview the prospective jurors once. It was almost noon, so they'd been at it three solid hours. Only an hour or two to go. If they were lucky.

Ritter turned to Phoebe. "Where shall we have lunch?"

"I vote for someplace that has good salads."

So they drove to the Garden Bar on Southwest Market Street. She ordered a cobb, he the tuna. After they found a table and sat down, Phoebe slid her notepad across the table.

Ritter scanned the first page of notes, written with precise printing that bordered on calligraphy. But that wasn't what made them far and away the best *voir dire* notes he'd ever seen. He looked up at her. "I'm impressed."

She took a bite of her salad.

And to think he'd been worried. Notes for each potential juror were coherent, concise, informative. During the interviews he'd made a mental list of top choices. He quickly located them and with a pencil put a check beside each of their names.

"Those are your picks?" Phoebe said.

He chewed and swallowed. "They are."

"Want my opinion? I mean, I'm only a paralegal. But you did encourage me to use my intuition."

"I welcome your input."

She pointed to one of his choices—Monica Townsend, 48, single, bookkeeper.

"My first pick," he said.

"She's my first strike."

"In God's name why?"

"I noticed a paperback sticking out of her handbag—*Left Behind*, a Christian-themed novel about the Rapture. She's unlikely to be sympathetic to your transgender defendant."

He couldn't argue with that. "Okay, she's out."

"And I'd strike this guy." She pointed to William Gormley, 33, welder.

"He struck me as a decent chap."

"The man sitting next to him is his buddy." Gary Castleberry, 34, machinist. "He took off a 'Make America Great Again' hat when he walked into the courtroom."

"Say no more. Gormley's history."

She pointed. Gerald Mims, 41, shipping clerk. "When you were interviewing other people he sat with his arms folded and made a face like he smelled excrement every time you said 'transgender.'"

"I'm glad you caught that, because I sure didn't. Any other strikes from my picks?

"One more . . . this woman." Helen Piddler, 37, teacher. "I didn't care for her hunched-over posture, and she seemed anxious. Her eyes darted around like an animal in a trap."

Ritter sat back. "Well, that leaves us four jurors short. Any recommendations for their replacements?"

"Yes. The first one is this fellow." Ainsley Bloodwood, 54, motorcycle mechanic.

"Tell me you're kidding. A biker with a bushy beard, ponytail, and tattoos?"

"He has a tattoo on his arm—'*Ratio vincit omnia*.' It means 'Reason conquers all.' Mr. Bloodwood's a thinker."

Ritter put a check by the biker's name. "Next?"

"This gentleman. Russell Silverman, forty-five, works at a bicycle shop."

"Why do you like him?"

"He wears Birkenstocks. People who wear Birkenstocks are open to new things, new ways of thinking. I'm basing that on personal observation."

"Birkenstocks," he said shaking his head. "Okay, I defer to your judgment . . . again." Something told him he'd be nuts not to. He looked at his watch. "Hey, we need to get going. Quickly, who are your other two picks?"

She identified three, one extra: Rodney Mittlestaadt, 36, roofer; Virginia Cox, 55, waitress; and Salvatore Fortuna, 47, sign painter. She had convincing reasons for each.

On the drive back to the courthouse he looked over at her. "I want you to assist me with the trial. Interested?"

"I would like that very much."

"Good. I'll square it away with Trollinger." He couldn't wait to see the surprise on the Troll's fleshy face when he learned his sabotage had backfired.

Looking out the window, Phobe said, "Beautiful day."

He smiled at her. "It is indeed."

And if he could slip their juror picks past Kellenberger it would be even better.

44

McCoy was stretched out on the cot, staring sightlessly at the ceiling, when Gergen unlocked the door and said, "Toilet break, mate."

Not a minute too soon. He'd been on the verge of using the urine bag still strapped to his leg.

Gergen escorted him past the Humvees, past a workbench covered with tools, to the far corner of the building.

The small bathroom, illuminated by a bare incandescent bulb, had a concrete floor and raw sheetrock walls. Like the main building it had no windows. He emptied his bladder and washed his hands. No towels, so he dried his hands on his pants. No mirror over the basin, which was just as well.

Gergen followed him back to the improvised cell and locked the door.

"How long," McCoy said, "do you intend to keep me here?"

Gergen grinned. "Don't you worry about it mate. I'll make sure you got everything you need. Fact of the matter, I'm about to make a chow run. Hope you like fast food."

McCoy nodded. Giving him food, that was a hopeful sign.

Hassler tapped Gergen on the shoulder from behind. In one continuous motion Gergen wheeled, pulled out a Glock, and pointed it at Hassler's gut. "Bad idea to sneak up on me like that, mate. Liable to end up with an extra orifice or two." He put the pistol away.

Hassler's raspy laugh sounded like coughing. "Point taken, point taken. Listen, hows 'bout you run me home and then you can pick up the senator's eats on the way back?"

"Fair enough." Gergen turned to McCoy. "What's your pleasure, Arby's or Taco Bell?"

McCoy shrugged. "Arby's—a Market Fresh turkey sandwich and a large iced tea." As long as Gergen was asking.

Gergen grinned. "Know what, mate? You got it."

Hassler pressed the switch on the wall to raise the outer door. As soon as there was adequate clearance they ducked under it. Before the door closed, a grinning Gergen stuck his head underneath and said, "Don't go anywhere."

Very funny.

McCoy slumped against the door of his cage, leaned his head back, and closed his eyes. When he opened them again the grate in the ceiling came into view. He turned around and looked at the ceiling outside the enclosure. Three grates, plus the one in his cell. All unreachable without a ladder.

Or something to stand on.

Even if he could get up there somehow, removing the grate might require tools. And if he managed to remove it and climb up into the ducting, what then? He'd have a twenty-foot drop to the concrete floor from one of the other grated openings. Hard to run away on shattered ankles.

However . . . above one of the Humvees—almost directly over it, in fact—was a grate. A plan began to form. It hinged on a number of ifs, but it might work.

He studied the furnishings in the cage: metal desk, metal chair, canvas cot, empty wooden shelf unit, tall steel trash can, wooden push broom.

The desk was standard height, about thirty inches. But standing on end it would be five feet high. The shelf unit was six feet wide, four high, two deep. On its side it would be six feet high.

Stacking the shelf unit on the upended desk would provide a platform eleven feet high. He was five-ten, with a reach of, say, seven feet.

Still a couple feet short.

Anyway, how would he climb up on top of the shelves? He made some quick calculations. Then he picked up the trash can and turned it upside down. Three feet high and stable enough to stand on, it would do the trick.

Well and good, but there was that two-foot deficit to consider. He saw a way he could reduce it, by placing one of the desk drawers upside down on top of the shelf unit to gain a foot more height without sacrificing stability all that much.

No reason not to give it a shot. Wasn't it a prisoner's duty to try to escape?

He upended the desk and slid it directly under the grate. The shelf unit turned out to be heavier than he'd expected. Wrestling it onto the desk took every erg of energy he could summon, and afterward he leaned against the wall, breathing hard. Next, he set the inverted trash can on the desk. Finally, he located the release for the bottom desk drawer, the deepest one, and pulled it all the way out. Made of sturdy metal, it would easily bear his weight.

He grabbed the push broom and leaned it against the desk. He might be able to use it to bash in the grate, if it came to that.

He stared at the unwieldy structure and swallowed. High places made him nervous. But the choice was clear, either scale the tower or stay in the cage.

The chair provided a handy step up onto the desk. He reached down and hauled up the drawer and then lifted it above his head and jockeyed it on top of the shelf unit crosswise and upside down. Then he pulled up the broom and leaned it against the shelves.

The most intimidating part of the ascent lay before him. He was very glad he was wearing Skechers instead of his usual Florsheims.

Steadying himself with the shelves, he stepped up onto the trash can. After he straightened up, he made the mistake of looking down. His stomach lurched at the sudden wave of vertigo.

No turning back now, though. The top of the shelf unit hit him about hip level. He climbed onto the top surface. Before he stood, he reached down and pulled up the broom. Holding it horizontally, he rose to his feet with an inkling of how high-wire walkers must feel.

He gripped the broom handle near the brush and used the other end to probe the grate three feet above him.

"Well, I'll be damned," he said aloud.

Luck was on his side. The grate lifted without resistance. He gave it a good jab and knocked it almost completely out of the opening, easily shoved aside.

He stepped up onto the upturned drawer and the opening loomed tantalizingly near. Stretching to the limit, he reached for it and came up short about a foot. He'd jumped higher than that to reach the horizontal bar for chin-ups at the congressional gym.

But then, if he missed the horizontal bar at the gym, there wasn't much chance of ending up a quadriplegic.

He could clamber down and get a couple more drawers, but the remaining drawers were shallower than the one he stood on, and how stable would a whole stack of drawers be? Stability aside, the key issue was time. Gergen could walk in at any moment, and then he'd probably reach for his Glock.

McCoy hyperventilated several seconds and then leaped for all he was worth. It sent the drawer crashing to the floor, a ringing metallic cacophony that echoed throughout the cavernous building. By the time the din subsided he'd fought his way up through the opening. He crawled into the ducting and lay panting, waiting for his heart rate to return to a semblance of normalcy.

A minute later he lifted his head and took stock of the situation. The ducting was two feet in width but only about a foot high, too low for him to crawl on hands and knees. He rolled onto his stomach and started inching down the duct, using his hands, elbows, knees, and feet for locomotion. Progress was slow and he felt claustrophobic, but the glow from the grate about thirty feet ahead gave him incentive.

Halfway there his hand landed on something small, furry, and very dead. A rat. He grimaced at the putrid stench and continued on, ignoring the racket he was making, as though someone were attacking the ducting with a large Nerf bat.

He managed to reach the grate without encountering any other dead rats. Through the grate he could see, fourteen feet below, the sand-beige top of a Humvee. Hanging from the opening, he'd have a seven-foot drop. But the Humvee's metal top would surely flex a bit, so it wouldn't be like a drop to concrete.

Dicey, but doable.

He lifted the grate and shoved it into the ducting on the other side. The frame around the opening felt sturdy and had no sharp edges, one more lucky break in what had been a string of lucky breaks.

He took several deep breaths. After making sure he had a good grip on the frame, he swung his legs over the edge and dropped through the opening . . .

And became a human pendulum bob, hanging on with a death grip. He timed the swings and let go over the middle of the Humvee's top, landing dead center. He'd been mistaken about the metal flexing; it didn't give much at all. The landing jarred him from teeth to tailbone, but he was all in one piece, with no apparent injuries. His luck seemed to be holding.

He slid down the vehicle's slanted back, a playground slide built to mil spec. He started toward the wall switch to raise the big aluminum door and then halted. The plan had been to head off on foot, try to find a taxi. He turned around to face the Humvees.

He walked back to the Humvee he'd landed on, opened its door, and climbed into the driver's seat. The airplane-like cockpit had an assortment of gauges, levers, and knobs. He located the automatic transmission's shift lever on the massive center console between the driver's and passenger's seats. Brake and accelerator pedals, turn-signal lever, hand-brake—all in the expected locations.

Except he couldn't find the damn ignition.

Then he noticed a three-by-five card taped to the dash, to the left of the steering column:

DIESEL ENGINE STARTUP PROCEDURE

1. TURN SWITCH TO 'ON' POSITION UNTIL
ORANGE LIGHT COMES ON
2. WAIT FOR ORANGE LIGHT TO GO OUT BEFORE
CONTINUING
3. TURN LEVER TO RIGHT TO CRANK ENGINE

The switch and lever were near the card. Executing the three-step procedure rewarded him with the marbles-in-coffee-can clatter of the diesel engine. He checked the fuel level. A bit less than half a tank, more than enough. By the time he raised the outer door the Humvee should be warmed up and ready to roll. He started to get out to go press the wall switch but then he closed the Humvee's door.

It would be rude not to leave his hosts a lovely parting gift.

He popped the transmission into drive, released the hand brake, floored the accelerator. The Humvee leaped forward.

"Coming though," he yelled.

With a colossal boom no doubt heard all over Centreville, the Humvee tore through the big aluminum door as though it were made of paper-mâché.

He blared the horn for good measure. Shame he wouldn't get to see Gergen's and Hassler's faces when they saw what was left of their door. Or when they saw a Humvee was gone. Or when they saw the makeshift tower he'd built to reach the ceiling grate. *Kiss my ass, mates!*

Rolling down the street at thirty-five miles per hour, the Humvee seemed wide as a tank and gave a bone-jarring ride, due to its stiff suspension and rugged tires. But then, it was a military off-road vehicle, not a Bentley, and it beat walking all to hell.

The dash-mounted clock indicated 15:38, or 3:38 p.m. in civilian time. Roughly seven hours after Gergen and Hassler ambushed him on his way to the Senate to deliver an epic filibuster. The two goons made damn sure he wouldn't make it. But at whose behest?

Five minutes later he was steaming east toward D.C. on the Curtis Memorial Parkway at sixty miles per hour. At that comparatively sedate speed the low-geared Humvee seemed to be working hard. Sound deadening had not been a priority in its design. And his was the slowest vehicle on the Parkway. Everyone stared at the Humvee as they passed. Not the best choice of vehicle for anyone wanting to keep a low profile.

After half an hour's driving he crossed over the Potomac on the Theodore Roosevelt Memorial Bridge and exited the Parkway on Constitution Avenue. He stayed on Constitution past the Vietnam Veterans Memorial and the Smithsonian. At the National Gallery of Art he made a hard left onto Pennsylvania Avenue.

Three blocks further, on the right, loomed the J. Edgar Hoover Building. At the corner of Pennsylvania and 9th he hopped the curb and screeched to a stop in the middle of a small brick-paved courtyard in front of the FBI's building's entrance. After he killed the engine he sat there a moment wondering if the tinnitus would be permanent.

A knuckle rapped on his window. It belonged to a stocky man with a florid face, a crew cut, and a wrinkled gray suit. "Can't park here, pal," he said through the glass.

McCoy opened the door and dropped down onto the bricks. "I just did." Crew Cut started to say something, but McCoy cut him off. "Excuse me a minute," McCoy said, and started toward the entrance without looking back.

He told the woman at the reception desk inside he needed to speak to an FBI agent right away. Before she could ask him a series of time-wasting questions, he pulled out his wallet and showed her his identification.

It got action. "One moment, Senator," she said and picked up the phone.

As he waited on a nearby bench, his stomach protested with a series of feral growls. He should have stopped on the way for something to eat. The Humvee would have been a sensation in the Drive-Thru, especially if it took out a post or two on the way through.

"Senator McCoy? Special Agent Goodwillie." Crew Cut.

McCoy sighed and rose to his feet. "Sorry about the hasty parking job."

Goodwillie's face was impassive. "What can we do for you today, Senator?"

"Could we go somewhere more private? It'll take a while, what I have to tell you."

"Yeah, we can use an interview room just down the hall." On the way, Goodwillie pointed at his clothes. "Were you in a brawl or something?"

McCoy looked down. What had been his favorite suit was torn and dirty. He hadn't noticed. "It's in the or-something category."

"Okay, now you've woken my curiosity," Goodwillie said. He held the door open. "After you, Senator. We'll sit at the table and you can tell me the whole story."

So McCoy sat down and recounted the saga, beginning with the Metro ride that morning. While he talked, Goodwillie made notes, tip of his tongue at the corner of his mouth.

"Tell you what, Senator," Goodwillie said when McCoy finished, "after an ordeal like that, you should be able to park anywhere you damn well please."

"Thanks," McCoy said. "That's how I felt about it."

After knocking, a young man with spiky red hair stuck his head in. "You wanted to know who's the registered owner of that Humvee out there."

Goodwillie twisted around in his chair. "Yeah, who is it?"

"I ran the plate," the redhead said, "but also O'Connell recognized the P-slash-G logo on the doors."

"You going to tell me who owns it or make me guess?"

"A company called the Peregrine Group. They're government contractors. Mercenaries, like Blackwater."

"Never heard of them. I want a background report on that group. And on an employee named Hassler and a man named Pinkler, who's connected with the group somehow. Then see what you can dig up on a former employee named Gergen."

The redhead jotted down the names on a notepad. "On it," he said and closed the door.

Goodwillie turned back to McCoy.

McCoy sighed. "Too bad I didn't get the license number of the maroon van. I wasn't firing on all cylinders. Whatever was in that dart was damn powerful stuff."

"Listen, Senator ... what you managed to pull off is nothing short of miraculous. No shit, it's like something out of *Mission Impossible*. My hat's off to you."

"Thanks, but all I can think about right now is getting some food. I haven't eaten since six-thirty this morning."

"The cafeteria in this place is pretty decent. Let's go."

"You won't have to talk me into it, Special Agent."

In the FBI cafeteria he chose a turkey sandwich on sourdough—so he could stop thinking about the Market Fresh turkey he'd missed out on by escaping. Goodwillie got coffee. After they found a table McCoy pounced on the sandwich like a jungle cat on a rabbit. Nothing had ever tasted so good.

"So," he said between bites, "what now?"

Goodwillie added a generous dollop of creamer and four packets of sugar to his coffee, sipped it, added another packet of sugar. "Well," he said, "your abduction and unlawful imprisonment are felonies that crossed state lines, so the FBI has jurisdiction. We'll get arrest warrants for Gergen and Hassler, take them into custody. And I'm going to arrange for the Capitol Police to give you personal protection. Say—you got a gun by any chance?"

"Yes, I do. And a concealed-carry permit."

"Good. Make sure you carry it with you at all times."

He'd already decided to to do just that.

45

The captured drone Rix repaired was ready for its post-crash maiden voyage. The lanky technician made last-minute adjustments to the handheld transmitter and video monitor as Dr. Krishnamurti, Director Gannon, Dr. Soong, Detective Wojanowski, Nakamura, Ritter, and Andie looked on. The monitor was large enough that they'd all have a good view of everything the drone's camera saw.

"Dr. Krishnamurti," Gannon said, "what's to stop Pomerenke from taking over this thing if you fly it within range of his transmitter?"

"I had Rix change the frequency."

Rix turned around. "Okay, ready to launch."

"Go ahead," Gannon said.

The drone's propellers began to spin, humming softly while the craft was on the ground, increasing in intensity as it lifted off, finally producing the familiar swarm-of-hornets buzz when it gained altitude. It stopped climbing and hovered twenty feet above them.

"Look at the monitor," Nakamura said. On-screen, a view of the group from overhead. "We're seeing ourselves from above." He gave two thumbs up to the camera.

"Mr. Rix," Gannon said, "make it climb to five hundred feet and then do a reconnaissance of the perimeter."

"Aye aye, ma'am." Rix pushed the throttle control forward.

The craft shrank to a dot in the sky, barely visible, but still audible.

"Jesus. That thing is fast," Ritter said.

"Such performance is expensive," Krishnamurti said. "This drone was not purchased at Toys-R-Us."

On the monitor, the overhead view of the foundation's campus held everyone's attention. The detail was breath-taking.

"Superior optics," Krishnamurti said.

"Rix seems to have gotten the hang of flying it fairly quickly," Gannon said.

"It almost flies itself," Rix said. "It's a smart bird."

Nakamura said, "If you would, Rix, please fly over the rose garden. My grounds crew is supposed to be doing some clean-up there this afternoon."

Five seconds later the rose garden filled the screen. A half-dozen figures—tiny, but plainly visible—seemed to be engaged in various slow-motion tasks below.

"I think I need to get a drone," Nakamura said, "so I can keep tabs on goof-offs."

Ritter laughed. "Big Brother comes to groundskeeping."

"Now," Gannon said, "let's have a closer look at that large white van that's parked down the street from the entrance."

Andie turned to Nakamura. "It belongs to the P.I.s who've been spying on us."

"There it is," Ritter said, pointing.

Gannon moved in closer to the monitor. "Take us down to, say, a couple hundred feet, Rix."

Seconds later they were able to read the faded lettering on the side of the van. The lettering increased in size.

"That's through the zoom lens," Rix said. "Makes it seem like we're only twenty feet away. I can zoom even closer."

"Okay," Gannon said, "give us a closeup of the foundation entrance. That's it . . . perfect. Now pull back a bit."

Four vans, a pickup, and an SUV pulled over to the curb near the entrance. Men and women jumped out and grabbed signs from the back of the vehicles.

Gannon grunted. "What the hell are those people up to?"

Shouldering their signs as though they were rifles, the two dozen arrivals took up positions around the entrance.

"Zoom in on those signs, Rix."

Not counting duplicates, there were only six basic signs: "GOD HATES TRANNIES," "TRANNIES WILL BURN IN HELL," "TRANNY = ABOMINATION," "GENESIS 2:18-25," "TRANNIES ARE MINIONS OF SATAN," "TRANNIES DESERVE DEATH."

"Middleboro Baptist Church," Wojanowski said, "from Middleboro, Idaho. Religious fanatics."

"Those bastards picketed Corey Ryan's funeral last week."

"They have no shame. Last year they picketed the funerals of the five transgender sex workers murdered by serial killer Jimmy Chapman."

"I wonder who sicced them on us?"

"I have a suggestion," Nakamura said. "There's a stable a few miles up the road. We fill up some paper bags with horse manure, attach the bags to the drone, and . . . bombs away."

Gannon laughed. "You're talking my kind of lingo, but we will maintain a defensive posture for the time being."

Pomerenke was unwrapping a stick of Juicy Fruit when his phone rang. "Yeah?"

"Are the protesters there yet?" The reedy voice belonged to the client. Who didn't waste time on greetings.

Pomerenke sat up straighter. "Yes, sir. They got here ten minutes ago."

"I'll expect video later today."

"No problem. I'll have a flash drive for your courier."

The client hung up without saying goodbye, as usual.

The back door opened and Millican climbed in. "Neil, I heard loud buzzing outside, so I figured you'd deployed the drone. Guess I was hearing things."

"Probably bees," Pomerenke said and shoved the stick of gum in his mouth.

"Maybe so, but they sound exactly like a drone."

Pomerenke stroked his chin. "You don't suppose—Gordo go back out and see if you can still hear it."

Millican returned two minutes later. "Yeah, I could hear it, but just barely. Sounded like it was going away."

"Okay, never mind for now. I want you to load up a flash drive with the video of the protesters."

"I'm on it, Neil."

Pomerenke sat back and chewed his gum rapidly while the hunch materialized. He'd learned to listen to his hunches. This one told him the folks across the street had turned the tables on him. They were surveilling him with his own drone.

He spat out the gum, got a Pabst from the fridge, and drained half. The craving for a cigarette clawed at his insides.

46

Curled up on the sofa, toasty under a soft comforter, Andie watched a program on the National Geographic channel featuring a female bald eagle and her hatchlings. Using her talons, the mama eagle caught salmon in a nearby river and fed it to her brood, first tearing it into bite-sized chunks with her beak. Size difference aside, the similarity between the eaglets and Gapey and his siblings was unmistakable.

Exactly one week had gone by since she'd put him back in the nest. She wondered whether his mama had made sure the poor little runt got his share of food. Only one way to know for sure . . .

She threw off the comforter and slipped into her shoes. Hand on the doorknob, she hesitated and then went back and put on a hoodie. The pockets would free up her hands if she needed to carry something. A baby bird, for example.

"I'm coming, Gapey," she called out as she jogged toward the tree. Standing underneath its canopy, a disturbing possibility occurred to her. What if she got up there and found he'd died? She pushed the thought aside and reached for the lowest limb.

The climb was easier than before because she knew which limbs to use. She approached the nest with caution, hoping for the best but fearing the worst. Holding her breath, she peeked over the rim.

Gapey hadn't died. That was the good news. The bad news was he looked like he was about to. A membrane no longer covered his eyes and he'd grown some since she last saw him, but he was still much smaller than his siblings, about half their size.

"Poor little guy," she said, "your mama's been shorting you on food."

Gapey seemed too weak to gape. He couldn't fully open his little beak, but he tried. His brothers and sisters were gaping up a storm.

"Did you guys shove your little brother aside at dinner time?"

They looked at her and gaped.

"Poor little guy," she said again. He had no one. He was on his own. She could relate.

During her many forays to the public library, she hadn't delved into ornithology. Maybe the foundation's library had a bird book or two.

But he couldn't wait for her read up on birds. Something had to be done now.

She remembered the half-pound of raw ground round in her fridge. Seemed like it'd be nutritious and easy to swallow. "Hang in there, little guy. I'll be right back."

She descended the tree like a spider monkey and ran toward her apartment. At the path she stopped cold. Within the past hour or so, someone had stepped on a night crawler, crushing it. It was more-or-less intact but very dead.

A sandwich bag would've come in handy to put it in, but she didn't want to take the time to go get one. She scooped it up and ran back to the tree. Cupping the night crawler in her left hand, she climbed back up to the nest one-handed.

"Breakfast is served." Using her thumbnail as a blade, she sliced off a fat segment and held it out to him. It took him several seconds to open his beak wide enough to accept the morsel. Several more seconds went by until it disappeared down his gullet.

"How was that? Let's try another."

He downed another five segments in short order. With each morsel he seemed to gain more strength. Opening his beak wide was no longer a problem.

His siblings tried to get in on the action, but she brushed them back. "Listen, you guys . . . you haven't missed a single meal. Let your brother have some."

She fed him six more segments, and he showed no sign of getting full. Still, she didn't want him to founder, like an overfed horse.

"Tell you what," she said. "You digest your breakfast, and I'll be back with lunch in a couple of hours."

At lunchtime she gave him eight segments she'd cut up and pulverized, as recommended by *Wild Birds: Care and Feeding* by Beatrice Plinth-Garnell, which she'd found in the Foundation's library. They disappeared down the baby bird's craw.

"Okay, another couple of bites . . . there you go."

She wondered where he put it all. With his voracious appetite, he could probably polish off the rest of the night crawler. Just as she suspected, though, overfeeding was not recommended. So sayeth Beatrice.

"That'll have to hold you until dinner."

Dinner turned out to be a recap of lunch. He gobbled down everything and gaped for more. As her dad liked to put it, he "pounded" his food.

"C'mon now," she said, "you ate nearly half of that huge night crawler. Save some for tomorrow."

She hadn't planned it, but now she had a dependent, a scrawny baby bird with a bottomless stomach. If she didn't shoulder the responsibility, Gapey would be a goner.

"Don't worry, little guy, I've got your back. See you in the morning."

47

Breakfast conversation paused momentarily in the Capitol Hill Club dining room when Boonstra's cell phone rang. "It's been postponed again," the Senate majority whip said, adding some empty, keep-the-faith encouragement before he hung up. Boonstra pushed away his untouched sausage and eggs and threw his napkin on the table. He'd counted on the bill making it to the Senate floor that day, for the Monday morning session.

During the two-block walk to his office he unleashed a string of expletives that turned curious heads. If the bill were to sink into the congressional quicksand he'd have to kiss his dreams of higher office goodbye. It could even jeopardize his reelection chances. A snot-nosed Oklahoma state senator, Bud Scofflaw, had called him a do-nothing congressman, threatened to challenge him for his seat. He hadn't been primaried since his first term, eighteen years ago. Getting the goddamn bill passed into law would nip that kind of thinking in the bud and thrust him into the national spotlight.

On one of the paths that traversed the Capitol Building's parklike grounds he noticed a tall figure walking ahead of him. It was Krakenflosser, the stubborn holdout. Convenient as ants in a sink. Boonstra hailed him.

Krakenflosser stopped and waited. He had a long, thin face with a beak nose, graying black hair, eyes the color of ice.

"Senator," Boonstra said, his tone jovial. "Fancy running into you on this glorious day."

Krakenflosser gave him a curt nod. "Congressman."

"Talk to you while we walk?"

"What about?"

"Just a little friendly conversation, perhaps see if we can eat out of the same trough."

"You'll have to forgive me," Krakenflosser said. "I flunked Folksy Expressions one-oh-one."

Boonstra guffawed. "I just meant we maybe could help each other. You're running for reelection this November against a tough opponent, right?"

"So?"

"Well, I'm sure your superPAC welcomes big contributions, the kind that makes a campaign sit up and bark at the moon. Say, fifty thousand?" It would be pocket change for Mullen.

"In return for an aye vote on your bill, I suppose?"

"I think it'd be a fair exchange."

"Congressman, leaving aside the fact that it's bribery, my niece is in the sixth grade and transgender. The prospect of being forced to use the boys' restroom gives her nightmares. My sister would disown me."

"Seventy-five thousand."

Krakenflosser shook his head. "I usually caucus with your side and I like to do favors, but I have to refuse. I'm sorry."

"A hundred thousand."

"It's not a question of money. Blood's thicker than money."

Boonstra sighed. "Well, I had to give it a shot."

"Don't blame you a bit. See you around, Congressman."

A swing and a miss. But the game was far from over; Krakenflosser was only one player. What he'd do, he'd make a list of potential swing voters and pay each one a friendly visit. Sooner or later he'd hit a home run.

Speaking of which, he had tickets to the Nationals' next home game. He whistled "Take Me Out To the Ball Game" the rest of the way to his office.

48

McCoy was taking a nap when the text message arrived, levitating him off the sofa. He'd been on edge for the past week. The text was from Goodwillie. It said only "Call me." He punched in the number. When Goodwillie answered he said, "McCoy here. What's up?"

"Hi, Congressman. Thought you might want an update on our progress in nabbing Hassler and Gergen."

"I've been wondering how you're coming along with that."

"Hassler's in custody. Picked him up day before yesterday. He was uncooperative, lawyered up immediately. His attorney maintains he's innocent of all charges, that it was someone else's play. He didn't name Gergen, of course. Speaking of which, Gergen's still in the wind. Probably ran back to his ship, which by the way is owned by an eccentric billionaire named Omar Mullen, who made his fortune in pharmaceuticals. The ship's in international waters, which presents a problem. No extradition in nautical law. It also prevents the U.S. Navy from intercepting the vessel and arresting Gergen. But they can't stay out there forever. Sooner or later that ship has to come to port in a country that has reciprocal extradition, and then we'll snatch him up."

"What's the Peregrine Group's part in all this?

"They claim they had no knowledge of their facility being used for any unlawful activity and said Hassler went rogue."

"I'll bet they were thrilled about the damage to their door."

Goodwillie laughed. "That's my favorite part of your story. I can just see the Humvee tearing through that big door. You definitely made a statement."

"Oh, hey—Gergen had an accent I couldn't place. Sounded sort of like Australian, but not quite. New Zealand?"

"Gergen's originally from South Africa."

"Ah. Mystery solved."

"So how are you doing these days, Senator? You've been through an ordeal that would devastate most people."

"It left me a little jumpy. More than a little, actually. I'm a *lot* jumpy. Sudden noises startle me. And I hear things that aren't there." He held out his hand, fingers spread. It shook slightly. He made a fist.

"You'll get over it. It just takes time. Are you carrying your handgun?"

"Everywhere, sometimes even at home. And I got in some practice at the range last week. At night I sleep—if you could call it that—with it next to me on the bedside stand."

"Best security blanket you can have. And what about your police protection?"

"A plainclothes officer accompanies me whenever I'm out in public. I don't need him when I'm in my apartment, since I have the gun."

"I'd just as soon you had round-the-clock police protection until we round up Gergen, but it's your call."

"I'll be fine." He wished he was as confident as he sounded.

"You're taking time off from the Senate?"

"I haven't been back to my office or the Senate since I was a guest at the Peregrine Hotel. But I've been getting ready to put in an appearance on the Senate floor next Monday to filibuster a bill. Looking forward to it, in fact."

"Glad to hear it. Best thing for you—get back on the horse."

"Uh, right. You'll let me know if there are any further developments?"

"I will definitely keep you apprised. Take care, Senator."

A bit later, as he was fixing himself a tuna sandwich in the kitchen, McCoy heard a noise he couldn't identify. The Colt came out of the holster. The weight of the gun in his hand was reassuring.

He checked the living room.

Clear.

He sneaked across the carpet and put his ear to the door.

Nada.

He crept to the window overlooking the street and peeked out. Below, two workmen were loading a sofa into a truck.

Nothing like a little paranoia. He holstered the revolver. What was he doing, anyway, wearing it at home? It wasn't what he'd call comfortable. A corner of the grip poked the small of his back.

He reached around to take it off and then stopped. Gergen carried that big, heavy, square Glock all the time, probably even when he slept. The Colt was smaller and lighter, so what was he bitching about? It wouldn't hurt to wear it around a while and get used to it.

But it wasn't just the physical discomfort. When he carried the gun he felt . . . silly. Felt like an impostor. But then, he'd felt like an imposer when he first arrived in D.C. to serve his first term in the Senate. He'd just needed a little time to get used to it. Same deal with the gun, probably.

As for Gergen, he wouldn't dare come anywhere near this apartment, not with the FBI and police looking for him. Like Goodwillie said, he probably fled back to his ship. He'd have sanctuary there, at least for a while.

He finished making the sandwich and took a bite. Like chewing a mouthful of cotton. He shoved it into a sandwich bag for later and grabbed a Guinness instead.

Much better.

Then he put the gun and holster back in the drawer.

49

Andie stopped in at the 7-Eleven on Hawthorne to pick up a quart of milk. As she waited her turn to be rung up, she idly scanned the magazines and tabloids in a rack next to the counter. A headline on *Inside Scoop* caught her eye. She took one out of the rack and tossed it on the counter next to the milk, avoiding eye contact with the cashier. Back in her apartment, she put the milk in the refrigerator and opened the tabloid to the featured article.

Trannies Are Waging War On Normalcy

Trannies, or "transgenders" as they call themselves, seem to be everywhere these days. They rule the media—books, newspapers, magazines, radio, television, movies, the Internet—it's all but impossible to avoid them. One well-known tranny even has a television reality series.

But their media presence is only the beginning. Trannies will soon be allowed to serve openly in the military. Even more alarming, the Girl Scouts now welcome trannies, and the Boy Scouts are being pressured to accept them into their ranks, including serving as scout leaders.

If you have a child in school then you have a more immediate concern: Schools are required by law to allow students who feel they are the wrong gender to use restrooms that correspond to their chosen gender. In other words, if a boy says he's really a girl, he can freely use the girls' restrooms, showers, and changing facilities. He's also entitled to play on girls' sports teams.

Worried yet?

Dr. Mikhail Sonovavich of Johns Hopkins claims that transgenders are mentally ill. "They demand that society sanction their delusion," he said, "and so far society has accommodated them. But this is an all-out assault on reality. Transgenders, aided by political correctness, are waging war on normalcy, it's that simple."

It's sounding like normalcy will be forced to surrender, right?

Not so fast.

Backlash has been swift and terrible. On August 18 a Portland transgender, Corey Lane Ryan, 21, was found hanged from a tree behind an abandoned house in Portland, Oregon. On August 22 two transgenders (names and ages withheld) were lynched side by side from a bridge in Great Falls, Montana. On August 24 a tranny prostitute known locally as Kristal Parisienne, 27, was found hanged behind a bar in Tampa, Florida. A note was pinned to "her" dress that read, "this is just the begining [sic]." Police say they have no leads in any of the incidents.

Whether these four lynchings are a preview of more to come remains to be seen, but it's clear that some folks objected to having this unnatural lifestyle shoved down their throats. *Inside Scoop* will be covering this situation as it develops, so stay tuned.

Andie started to wad up the tabloid and then smoothed it out again. The director and Detective Wojanowski should maybe have a look at it. Not that it contained any clues about who killed Corey, but if it identified a trend then they definitely needed to be aware of that.

Inside Scoop's tacit approval of the lynchings could very well incite "copycat" violence. Did that fall under the First Amendment's freedom-of-the-press protections?

Still, the tabloid had one thing right—there was a war going on. But it was a war waged *against* trans people, not by them.

She made some tea and then flipped though the rest of the tabloid. The back pages were full of ads posted by people looking to hook up with like-minded people for sexual purposes. Many ads had an undercurrent of desperation and pathos. A few were unintentionally hilarious.

"Bi male seeking men or women into S&M, B&D, fisting, spanking, flogging, leather, latex, humiliation, submission, foot worship, anal toys, gangbanging, and golden showers. No weirdos, please."

That last line cracked her up. But it would take more than goofy ads to counteract the queasiness the article had left her with.

Four lynchings—so far. Trend or not, there were monsters out there who'd gleefully put a rope around her neck just because of who she was.

A shudder rattled every vertebra.

"Good morning, Gapey. Since we're out of night crawler, the breakfast special today is lean ground beef." She rolled up an M&M-size morsel and popped it into his open beak.

He pounded it.

"Glad you like it," she said. "Night crawlers are in short supply." Freshly dead ones were, anyway. She could probably dig up a live one, but killing it would be out of the question. Even worms had a right to live.

She'd been feeding him three times a day for a week now, and the change in him was astonishing. His growth rate was freakish. He hadn't caught up to his siblings in size, but he was gaining on them. And gray down covered his formerly naked body. Before long he'd have feathers.

"See you for dinner."

Pomerenke connected Drone #2 to the charger and then he stretched, his spine crackling like dry twigs. His back hadn't given him trouble for a couple of weeks, a blessing from on high. Since Millican wasn't around to bother him, he'd been thinking about taking an afternoon nap. A phone call from the client put the plan on hold.

"I want you to step up the surveillance," the client said in that strange reedy voice. "All comings and goings are to be videoed, no exceptions. McInnes is to be tailed whenever he leaves the premises alone, just in case he tries to make a run for it."

"I understand."

"Good." A click indicated disconnection.

Pomerenke grunted. What the hell was all that about? He was already videoing all arrivals and departures, and Millican usually tailed McInnes—taking care to hang back—when she left the premises by herself.

And apparently the client was under the impression that McInnes was male. Maybe he assumed that because of her first name: Andie and Andy sounded the same. That was probably it. But why would she "make a run for it"? She'd be a fool to leave that dream setup.

Bottom line, though, the client asked him to step up the investigation, and the client was always right. As long as that fat fee kept rolling in, he'd step it up to the goddamn summit of Mt. Hood.

50

Karen drove to work under a sky of indeterminate gray that matched her mood to a tee. She parked her car and trudged into the station house—dead woman walking. The phone on her desk rang the instant her butt made contact with the chair. She scowled and snatched it up.

The caller introduced himself as Mark Glickman, a lawyer with the Southern Poverty Law Center. Nothing southern about his accent, though; it was New York all the way.

Karen grabbed a pen and opened her notebook. "What can I do for you, Mr. Glickman?"

"I'm calling about Corey Ryan's murder. I understand you caught the case."

"That's right. What about it?"

"Do you have any leads yet?"

"Not really. They found some DNA on the rope, but CODIS came up empty."

"Too bad. You're of course aware of recent similar cases across the country?"

"Yeah, Great Falls and Tampa." She had Andie to thank for that information.

"So you haven't heard about the cases in Bismarck, North Dakota and Pocatello, Idaho and Midland, Texas?"

She snapped her pen in two. "No. I hadn't."

"Counting yours, we're looking at seven lynchings."

"Seven. Jesus."

"So far, that is. I've got a sick feeling the note pinned to the Tampa victim was right, that it's only the beginning."

"Do the police in the other cities have any leads?"

"They've got bupkus, same as you."

"That sick feeling of yours must be communicable."

"Detective, I can't believe all these lynchings are isolated events, despite the distances between them. They must have a connection in common."

"Makes sense, but what could it be?"

"That's what we need to find out. Think about it, and if you come up with anything, any leads turn up, please give me a call. My cell number is five five five, eight six seven five three oh nine."

The number sounded oddly familiar. She grabbed another pen and wrote it down. "Got it."

"Thank you for your time, Detective."

Her phone rang again just after she got back from lunch. It was the desk sergeant, who informed her that a young man wanted to talk to someone about the Ryan case.

She sat up straight. "I'll be right there."

He was skinny and young enough to have traces of acne. She took him to the squad room and indicated the chair beside her desk. He sat down and looked around at the room.

"You have information about the Ryan case, Mister . . .?"

"Kimmel. Fred Kimmel. They said on the TV that if anybody saw anything we should tell the police."

"You did exactly the right thing in coming forward, Fred, and we appreciate it. Now what did you see?"

"So I work at the Dominos on Division. I been riding my bicycle to work until I can afford to buy a car. I pass by that abandoned house on the way. Real early Wednesday morning —it was August seventeenth, the day before they found that body—I rode home from work after closing."

"What time does Dominos close?"

"Midnight on weekdays, but it maybe was as late as one-thirty when I rode home, because me and the guys messed around some after work, talking about cars and stuff."

"Okay. Go on."

"It's just that I never seen anything parked in front of that old house before, but that night there was a pickup and an SUV parked there."

Her ears stood up in tall points. "Can you describe these vehicles, Fred?"

"I'm kinda into cars and stuff, so yeah, I can tell you a little bit about them. The pickup, it was a Chevy and it was tan and sorta beat up. I don't know what year it was . . . maybe mid-nineties, somewhere around there. It had an empty gun rack in the back window. The other one was an older Bronco. It was red and the paint was real faded . . . what do they call it?"

"Oxidized?"

"Yeah, that's what it was. Real oxidized."

She wrote it down, with a quickening feeling in her gut. "Anything else you recall about the vehicles?"

"Well . . . they both had a sticker in the back window. A cartoon frog wearing what looked like a military helmet. And the pickup had one of those 'Make America Great Again' stickers on the back bumper. That's about it."

It was quite a bit, much more than she'd expected. She took down his contact information and closed her notebook. "Fred, you have sharp eyes. It helps us out more than I can tell you." She wanted to hug him.

Fred was beaming when he left.

After shaking her head at the wonder of it, she reached for the phone and punched in Glickman's number. When he answered she said, "Detective Wojanowski, Mr. Glickman."

"Well," he said after a thoughtful pause, "I didn't expect to hear from you so soon. Got something?"

"Possibly." She recounted Fred Kimmel's story.

After she finished, he said, "You know that connection we talked about? You just might have found it."

"I have? You lost me there."

"The stickers on the back windows, the helmeted frog. His name is Pepe. He's a symbol of the alt-right, a militant confederation of white nationalists, xenophobes, homophobes, racists, and bigots of every stripe. Looks like they've added transphobes to their roster."

"So you think they're responsible for all the lynchings?"

"Yes, I do, Detective. It explains how six disparate crimes were coordinated. They have an extensive communications network—printed literature, emailed newsletters, and websites. All oozing with anti-trans rhetoric, I'd bet on it."

"Inciting the troops to lynch transgender people? Sick, but the pieces fit."

"This is big—a nationwide conspiracy to commit murder. It will certainly need a federal task force. I'm going to go talk to the FBI."

"In the meantime, we'll keep an eye out for those vehicles and their owners."

"Good luck on that, Detective. Let's keep in touch."

"Definitely."

After hanging up, Karen leaned back in the chair and marveled at the unexpected revelation. Militant transphobes represented by a cartoon frog named Pepe were lynching trans people all across the country.

Christ Almighty.

She stood and put on her jacket. Gannon needed to know about this.

51

Cameras weren't permitted in the courtroom, a boon to the sketch artist hunching over a work-in-progress in the spectators' gallery. Ritter had seen him before and suspected he doubled as a police artist. It would explain why the people in his sketches all looked like crooks.

Andie would probably get the same treatment. But sitting at counsel's table with a fresh haircut, light makeup, blouse and skirt, cardigan sweater—tasteful rather than trendy attire, as per counsel's advice—she could be Jennifer Lawrence's square younger sister. Fitting, given the distinct possibility of the trial devolving into *The Hunger Games*.

The pretrial news coverage in the preceding weeks had been almost nonstop. For the most part, the media had been respectful—using female pronouns, not sensationalizing the transgender aspect of the case. The exception: *Inside Scoop*, Portland's infamous tabloid, which gleefully portrayed Andie as a "murderous tranny" intent on perverting all that was good and decent in American society. Ritter didn't have to advise her to avoid newspapers, television, and radio. Security provided by the Transcend Foundation kept reporters and paparazzi at bay.

Judge Bondurant got introductions, charges, and other trial preliminaries out of the way and then turned to Kellenberger. "Is the prosecution ready to present its opening statement?"

"Yes, Your Honor." Kellenberger stood and faced the jury. "Good morning, ladies and gentlemen. My name is Bret Kellenberger. It is my honor to represent the people of the state of Oregon as the prosecutor in this case. And I promise you this—I will move heaven and earth to make sure that the people's confidence in me is not misplaced."

Ritter snorted. Kellenberger seldom passed up an opportunity for Trumpian self-aggrandizement, delivered in the dulcet tones of someone imagining himself an orator.

"I will show conclusively that Defendant Andrea McInnes shot and killed Howard Hinshaw. Without provocation. Two witnesses, friends of the victim, will testify to that.

"Mr. Ritter might argue that Ms. McInnes acted in self-defense . . . but the witnesses tell a different story. They were accompanying Mr. Hinshaw to the Greyhound bus depot, minding their own business, when Ms. McInnes, who seemed unhinged, accosted the three of them on Fourth Avenue and forced them into an alley at gunpoint, whereupon Ms. McInnes fatally shot Mr. Hinshaw and would have shot the witnesses as well had they not fled for their lives."

Ritter wondered how long Kellenberger would pause for effect. *Two . . . three . . . four . . .*

"So, ladies and gentlemen of the jury, at the conclusion of this case I am going to ask you for a verdict of guilty. Thank you." He nodded to the judge and sat down.

"Mr. Ritter?" Bondurant said.

"Your Honor," Ritter said as he rose to his feet, "I opt to defer my opening statement until after Mr. Kellenberger rests his case." He sat down again.

Andie leaned over. "How come?"

"More effective that way."

"Please proceed, Mr. Kellenberger."

"Thank you, Your Honor. I call Dr. Stanley Merkin."

Ritter raised an eyebrow. Calling an expert witness right out of the gate? An expert on what? It would be handy to know beforehand. Too bad the discovery process in Oregon couldn't compel expert witnesses to give depositions.

Merkin turned out to be a bald-with-beard type, fiftyish, with wire rim glasses. After he was sworn in he took his place on the stand and repositioned his glasses on the bridge of his nose with thumb and index finger.

"Dr. Merkin," Kellenberger said, "what is your professional background and area of expertise?"

Merkin cleared his throat. "I have a Ph.D. in psychology and counseling from Liberty University. Currently I'm the chairman of the Family Morality Council's gender research program, a position I've held for five years."

Phoebe slid her thin laptop in front of Ritter. "The guy's a crackpot," she said. "Have a look."

Ritter scanned some of the scathing articles she'd found on Merkin, and "crackpot" was only one of the terms used to describe him; others were "wackjob," "quack," and "kook." He slid the laptop back to her. "Thanks, Phoebe." Cross-examination was going be interesting.

"Based on your experience, Dr. Merkin," Kellenberger said, "how would you say transgender individuals' mental health compares with the general population's?"

Ritter jumped up. "Objection, relevance."

"I'll allow some leeway," Bondurant said. "Do not abuse it, Mr. Kellenberger. The witness may answer the question."

Merkin adjusted his glasses. "Speaking in general terms, transgenders tend to have—"

Ritter was on his feet again. "Objection. The transgender community considers 'transgenders,' instead of 'transgender people,' a slur."

"Sustained," Bondurant said. "In this proceeding *transgender* shall be used as an adjective only. You may continue, Dr. Merkin."

"I was about to answer that transgender *people* have many more emotional and psychological problems than the general population."

"Oh? What kinds of problems?"

"Aggression, poor impulse control, delusional thinking, drug addiction, self-mutilation, suicidal tendencies . . ."

"Do these problems manifest in antisocial behavior?"

"They do indeed. Prostitution, theft, assault—" He looked directly at Andie. "—even murder."

"Thank you, Dr. Merkin. No further questions."

Ritter got up and walked over to a spot directly in front of the witness. "Dr. Merkin, are you an APA member?"

A microexpression of annoyance flitted across Merkin's face. "No, I am not."

Ritter turned to face the jury. "APA, which stands for American Psychological Association, is the leading scientific and professional organization for psychologists in the United States. Its counterpart in the medical profession is the AMA, the American Medical Association. Virtually all doctors are AMA members. Reputable psychologists are APA members."

Merkin flushed. Easily baited—good to know.

"Objection," Kellenberger said, "Mr. Ritter is trying to impune Dr. Merkin's reputation with disrespectful innuendo."

"You're walking a thin line, Mr. Ritter," Bondurant said.

"Dr. Merkin, have you written any articles that were published in psychology journals?"

Merkin smiled. "As a matter of fact, an article of mine was just published in *Fresh Perspectives*."

"I'm not familiar with that one. Is it a psychology journal?"

"I would call it a science journal that reports on matters related to psychology and other scientific matters."

Phoebe caught Ritter's eye. "Excuse me a moment," he said and went over to her.

"Look at this," she said, pointing to her laptop's screen. "*Fresh Perspectives* is an online monthly publication that disseminates conspiracy theories, crackpot ideas, anti-science rants—climate change and evolution denial, things like that. Here's Merkin's article. It's about something called Reclamation, which purports to cure transgender people of being transgender."

"Great work, Phoebe." He turned back to the witness. "Dr. Merkin, please summarize for us the *Fresh Perspectives* article you mentioned."

Kellenberger sprang to his feet. "Objection, Your Honor. Mr. Ritter is straying far afield."

"Mr. Ritter," Bondurant said, "is this line of questioning relevant to your cross-examination?"

"Goes to witness credibility, Your Honor."

"Objection overruled. Witness may answer the question."

"The article examines the psychology of gender identity, based on studies I've conducted and on extensive observation over thousands of hours of counseling."

"You don't say." Ritter moved a step closer to Merkin, who'd pointedly refused to make eye contact with him. "Dr. Merkin, what can you tell us about . . . Reclamation?"

Now Merkin made eye contact. "Reclamation is a program I developed to treat gender identity issues."

"By 'treat,' do you mean *cure* gender identity issues?"

Merkin's glasses magnified his hostile glare.

"Otherwise known as 'conversion therapy'?"

"I prefer the term '*reparative* therapy.'"

Phobe signaled him and held out a sheet of paper. He took it, scanned it. It was a list she'd dashed off by hand.

He turned to Merkin. "Conversion therapy—or reparative therapy, whatever you want to call it—has been condemned as pseudoscience by the Surgeon General, American Medical Association, American Psychiatric Association, American Psychological Association, American Association for Marriage and Family Therapy, American Counseling Association, National Association of Social Workers, American Academy of Pediatrics, National Association of School Psychologists, and American Academy of Physician Assistants. In other words, it has a huge credibility problem."

"Objection," Kellenberger said. "Mr. Ritter is badgering this witness instead of cross-examining him."

"Sustained," Bondurant said.

"No further questions." He'd unmasked Merkin as a fraud, with his prescient new assistant's invaluable help. He sat down. "Phoebe," he said with his marginally passable Bogey, "I think this is the beginning of a beautiful friendship."

52

The courtroom, with its center aisle and rows of benches like pews, reminded Andie of a church filled to capacity with devout parishioners attending the day's service. Behind the bench-cum-pulpit the robed pastor presided over his flock, gavel in hand. She took out a notepad and jotted down the metaphor for her journal.

Sitting at counsel's table between Phoebe and Eli, nervous electricity coursed up and down her spine. She felt a hand on her arm. Phoebe looked concerned; she had no doubt noticed the fidgeting.

It began when Pfaff testified. Under direct examination he'd recited the same story he told during the preliminary hearing. It had been rough, enduring the jury's scalding stares while he regurgitated those horrible lies. Eli's cross-examination had been an abbreviated version of the preliminary hearing's cross. He'd interrogated Pfaff about the distance between the three friends and her (eight feet), whether any of them had touched her (no way), whether they and she had remained standing (yeah, except Hinshaw, when he bent over to pick up the rebar and she shot him). The business about 4chan.org and how they had known she was transgender was even more embarrassing than at the prelim.

Eli leaned over to her. "You doing okay?"

"I've been better," she said.

"Hang in there. Let's see what Gary Burleson has to say."

Burleson came forward and was sworn in. He had close-set eyes and small ears that stuck out. Like Pfaff, he'd been given a makeover, including haircut and clothes. As with Pfaff, they couldn't do anything about his insolent expression.

Under direct examination by Kellenberger, Burleson's testimony about the events of that night mirrored Pfaff's. In fact, the two accounts were identical in choice of words and phrases. And both witnesses' deliveries had a flavor of front-of-the-class recitations.

"Your witness," Kellenberger said and sat down.

Eli rose to his feet. "Mr. Burleson, in your deposition you stated that none of you at any time physically touched Ms. McInnes. Is that still your testimony?"

"Yes. We didn't come anywhere near ... her. She was pointing a gun at us."

"So you and Mr. Pfaff did not restrain Ms. McInnes by holding her arms and Mr. Hinshaw did not physically touch her or her clothing?"

"That's right."

"Estimate the distance you and Mr. Hinshaw and Mr. Pfaff were standing from Ms. McInnes, if you would."

"Maybe ... eight feet or so."

"Eight feet. None of you came any closer at any time?"

"No. We were afraid she'd shoot us."

"Did Ms. McInnes remain standing the whole time?"

"Yes."

"So she shot Mr. Hinshaw from a standing position?"

"Yes."

"I want you to describe for me again Mr. Hinshaw's actions in the moments before Ms. McInnes shot him."

"Well, like I said, we were standing there and then Howie saw that piece of iron on the ground between his feet, so he bent over and picked it up, and she shot him before he could even straighten up."

"Help me to understand—he was still bent over when she shot him?"

"Yes, he was."

"Mr. Burleson, I'd like you to step down here in the well and give us a brief demonstration ."

Burleson shrugged and got to his feet. He left the stand and sauntered over to where Eli stood.

"Now I want you to demonstrate as closely as you can Mr. Hinshaw's posture when he was shot."

Burleson crouched. "About like this."

"Hold that position, please." Eli took a clear protractor from an inside pocket of his coat and measured the angle. "According to this instrument, the plane of Mr. Burleson's back is almost precisely forty-five degrees from vertical." He turned to the judge.

"The court accepts your measurement," Bondurant said.

"Thank you, Your Honor." Eli put the protractor back in his pocket. "Mr. Burleson, you may stand upright."

Burleson straightened up.

"No further questions." Eli returned to counsel's table and took his seat.

Bondurant looked at Kellenberger. "Redirect?"

"No, Your Honor," he said. "The prosecution rests."

"Very well, the witness is excused."

Looking sour, Burleson left the witness box.

Eli stood. "Move to dismiss for lack of evidence."

"Motion denied," Bondurant said.

Eli sat down and looked at Andie. "Just a formality."

Bondurant looked at this watch. "Court is adjourned until two o'clock, at which time the defense can present its case."

Back in the courtroom after lunch she felt much better. Phobe suggested that her attack of heebie-jeebies had been caused by hypoglycemia, from having skipped breakfast., Other than a few residual flutters in her gut, she felt fine. Fuller, for sure.

"Court is now in session," Bondurant said. "Mr. Ritter, call your first witness."

Eli stood. "I call Doctor Jon Wu to the stand."

Wu came forward and was sworn in.

"Doctor, please tell the court your official title and length of employment."

"For the past nine years I've been chief medical examiner for Multnomah County."

"Thank you. Did you perform an examination on Howard Hinshaw to determine cause of death?"

"I did."

"And what was your finding?"

"The cause of death was loss of blood due to a partial severing of the left carotid artery by a projectile, consistent with a twenty-two caliber bullet. Death was quick."

"Did you calculate the angle of entry of the fatal bullet?"

"Yes. The bullet was fired from a position approximately forty degrees from horizontal. It entered the neck two centimeters above the left carotid's maxillary branch and just grazed the left underside of the occipital as it exited in the rear."

"What conclusion can you draw from that regarding the position of the shooter relative to the deceased?"

"The obvious conclusion is that the shooter was below the other person, shooting at an upward angle."

"An upward angle. If the shooter was lying on the ground on her back and the deceased was standing, would it satisfy that condition?"

"Yes, it would, perfectly."

"Can you think of any other possibility, one perhaps not so obvious?"

Wu's eyebrows knitted. "Well ... if the deceased was standing on an elevated platform, the angle of entry might be similar."

The jury seemed to be paying rapt attention.

"Let me ask you this. If the deceased was bending over forward, having picked up an object from the ground, and the shooter was standing eight feet away, is there any possible way for the angle of entry to be the same?"

"In my opinion that would be physically impossible."

"Why?"

"The angle of entry would be downward, not upward."

"Interesting. Did Mr. Hinshaw have any other injuries?"

"A minor one. His thumbnail, right hand. Like he'd jabbed something under there. I found blood—his blood—under the nail and on the tip of the thumb."

"Thank you, Doctor. No further questions." Eli returned to counsel's table and sat down.

Kellenberger half rose. "No questions."

Bondurant excused the witness.

Phoebe leaned in. "Good job."

"Thanks," Eli said. "I just hope it convinced the jury."

"It's almost three o'clock," Bondurant said. "I'm going to adjourn early today so I can attend an important function. Court will reconvene tomorrow morning at ten o'clock sharp." He rapped his gavel.

"I get a reprieve," Andie said. "I hope I'm in better shape to testify tomorrow."

"Get plenty of sleep tonight," Eli said.

Phobe patted her shoulder. "And eat some breakfast in the morning."

Easier said than done. Especially the sleep part.

Sure enough, sleep proved elusive. She switched on the light, propped up the pillows, and started to reach for *Heart of Darkness* but picked up the journal instead to make a quick entry.

Wednesday, September 7, 2016 11:52 p.m.

I have to testify tomorrow. I'm scared shitless. I'm afraid I'll royally screw up, despite Eli's and Phoebe's reassurances that I'll do fine. It's that asshole Kellenberger, who'll be doing his level best to trip me up. I get the feeling he'd ask for the death penalty if he could. I need to get a grip. I can do this. I hope.

53

On the drive to the courthouse, what had begun as a light summer rain turned into a sudden deluge that bounced off the streets and sidewalks. The windshield wipers flung the water off in gray sheets. A stray dog, its fur drenched, slinked across the street in front of them, requiring Eli to slam on the brakes to miss it.

"Poor thing," Phoebe said from the back seat. "I hope he finds some place that's warm and dry."

Andie, in the passenger seat in front, nodded agreement. She felt a connection to the animal. Once when she'd had no place to stay she'd been caught in a torrential downpour and had huddled, wet and shivering, under a bridge until it passed. Not one of her most pleasant memories.

They parked in the SmartPark garage on Southwest 4th and walked the block and a half to the courthouse. When they got there they found reporters swarming outside the courtroom. They spotted Andie and began shouting questions at her. She ignored them. Eli and Phoebe, blocking like linebackers, rushed her past the scrimmage and through the double doors.

The courtroom was close to standing room only, every eye seeming to bore into her. She took a deep breath. Looking straight ahead, flanked by Eli and Phoebe, she hurried up the aisle to counsel's table and then sat down and exhaled.

Bondurant called the proceeding to order. "Mr. Ritter, you may continue.

Eli touched her arm. "Just relax, you'll do fine." He stood. "I call to the stand Andrea McInnes."

Andie swallowed and got to her feet. This was it, make or break.

"Raise your right hand," the bailiff said. "Do you promise to tell the truth, the whole truth, and nothing but the truth so help you God?"

"I do," Andie said. She sat down in the witness chair and folded her hands in her lap to keep them from shaking.

Eli winked at her. "Ms. McInnes, please state your full *legal* name and your age."

"Andrea Lynne McInnes." She couldn't keep the quaver out of her voice. "I'm eighteen."

"Are you employed?"

"I work for a local foundation. In the personnel department." Her voice seemed to be growing stronger.

"Now," Eli said, "I'm going to ask you a somewhat delicate question."

She braced herself. *Here it comes . . .*

"Are you a transgender woman?"

Even though she'd been expecting the question, it didn't make it any easier. "Yes."

"At what age did you transition?"

"I was twelve years old."

"With your parents' full knowledge and approval?"

"Yes."

"Do you take female hormones?"

"Yes, I do."

"And you attended school as a girl?"

"Yes, until I was fifteen. That's when my parents were killed in an auto accident. Then I dropped out of school."

"So you've been on your own for the last three years?"

"Yes."

"During that time how did you get by? Where did you get money to eat and buy clothes?"

"I had fifteen hundred dollars from selling my parent's other car and from a yard sale. After that was gone I worked wherever I could—cleaning houses, babysitting, dog walking, washing dishes at restaurants, working at fast food places. I usually bought my clothes at used clothing stores and Goodwill, Saint Vincent de Paul, places like that."

"Where did you live?"

"I stayed with friends. Slept on a lot of sofas and even on the floor sometimes. I stayed at the Union Gospel Mission a couple of times."

"Where did you spend your free time?"

"At the library, usually. I like to read."

Eli looked at the jury and then back at her and winked again. "Now ... let's talk about the evening of July fourteenth. Why were you in Chinatown at ten o'clock at night?"

"I was walking down West Burnside, headed for the MAX station at Fifth and Couch so I could catch the train over to Eighty-second. I have a friend who lives on Siskiyou Street. She said I could stay with her for a while."

"You were walking down Burnside. What happened next?"

"I became aware of three men about a half-block behind me when one of them called out to me."

"What did he say to you?"

"He said, 'Hey, baby, come here,' or something like that."

"Did you recognize any of them?"

"Yes. The one with the shaved head. I remembered him from David Douglas High. I couldn't recall his name at the time, but it turned out to be Howard Hinshaw."

"Please continue," Eli said.

"All three of them started hooting and catcalling, telling me to be friendly, that they just wanted to talk to me. But I knew from the way they were acting that they had other things on their mind, and I was really scared. I'd intended to go down Burnside to Fifth, but I turned the corner when I got to the Chinatown sign on Fourth and ran as fast as I could. But it wasn't fast enough. They caught me and shoved me into that alley."

"You're referring to the alley off Fourth Avenue between the Shanghai Trading Company and Chinatown Kites and Fireworks?"

"Yes."

"What happened then?"

"They pushed me to the ground on my back and two of them held me down by my arms while Hinshaw unfastened my jeans and pulled them down." She tried to swallow. Her mouth and throat were bone dry. "Do you think I could have a drink of water?"

"Certainly." He walked over to counsel's table. Phoebe filled a glass from a pitcher of water and handed it to him. He brought it to Andie.

She drank half of it and set the glass on the floor, in case she needed it again. "Thank you."

"They had you pinned on the ground and Mr. Hinshaw had pulled down your jeans. And underwear?"

"Yes."

"So your genitals were completely exposed."

She looked down at the floor. "Yes."

"And you are preoperative? You have not had reassignment surgery?"

"No. Not yet."

That caused a commotion in the courtroom.

"Order." Bondurant pounded with his gavel. "I won't tolerate outbursts."

"Okay," Eli said, "what was their reaction?"

"They were surprised . . . and then very angry. Hinshaw picked up an iron bar and started toward me with it raised. He said something like, 'This is one he-she who'll never trick anyone again.' His eyes were crazy, and his two buddies were egging him on, saying, 'Do it! Do it!' I was scared out of my wits. I knew I was going to die, that he was going to beat me to death with that rusty iron bar."

A man in the gallery said, "Jesus," earning him a glare from Bondurant. There were gasps from the jury, and two of the woman jurors' hands flew to their mouths.

Eli got the rebar from the court clerk. "Andie, do you recognize this?"

She shuddered. "Yes, it looks like the same one he had."

He turned to the jury. "Mr. Hinshaw's DNA was found on one end of this rebar." He handed it back to the court clerk and picked up another item. "What happened then, Andie?"

"I remembered the gun in my bag. My friend Kayla gave it to me, made me take it, even though I didn't want to. I'd never even held a gun before, but she made such a big deal about it that I took it just to shut her up."

Eli held up the pistol. "This is the gun that police seized in the alley. It's an American Arms twenty-two caliber automatic. The magazine holds seven rounds. One round had been fired. Did you know that it had been reported stolen?"

"No way. And I'll bet neither did Kayla or her boyfriend. He'd bought it from a guy he knew."

Eli gave the weapon back to the court clerk. "So Mr. Hinshaw was coming toward you with the rebar raised and you remembered you had the gun in your bag. Please go on."

"I reached in my bag and found the gun. I thought maybe I could scare him, so I pointed it over his head—I *thought* it was over his head—and pulled the trigger."

"At what point did you realize that he had been shot?"

"I guess it was when I saw all the blood. There was a lot of it. He sat down on the ground with his hand at his throat. And his eyes, it was like they turned into a doll's eyes. The two other guys ran away then. I just stood there looking at him. Then I threw up. It felt ... unreal, like a dream. I couldn't believe what had happened, that I had—I just wanted to scare him and run away. I didn't mean to kill him." She lost it then and buried her face in her hands. Eli held out a box of tissues and she took a few and wiped her eyes and blew her nose. "I just wanted to scare him," she said again, her voice quavering.

It felt as though her heart was trying to jump out of her chest. Fortunately, she was too young to have a heart attack. Unless she was one of the rare exceptions. Given her luck lately, she'd be nuts to rule it out.

"No further questions," Eli said.

Kellenberger rose and walked over to stand in front of her. He didn't say anything for several seconds, just stared at her. When it began to get creepy he said, "Ms. McInnes, have you ever been under the care of a psychologist?"

She blew her nose again and said, "Yes, when I was eleven. It was required before I could transition. Standard procedure."

Kellenberger's eyes bored into her. "Are you aware that the incidence of mental illness in the transgender population is alarmingly high? That's according to several prominent psychologists."

"Objection!" Eli was on his feet. "Assumes facts not in evidence."

"Sustained," Bondurant said.

Kellenberger shrugged and then smiled. "Ms. McInnes, two witnesses have testified that you were acting like a crazy person, yelling at them and waving your gun around." He turned to the jury. "So who do we believe—two eyewitnesses, one of whom is the son of a Multnomah county commissioner, or a homeless person who killed a man with a stolen handgun?"

"Objection. Mr. Kellenberger is delivering his closing statement instead of cross-examining the witness."

"Sustained. Mr. Kellenberger, do you have any relevant questions to ask this witness?"

"Yes, I do, Your Honor."

Bondurant glanced at the wall clock. "Since it's getting close to noon we're going to adjourn now for lunch. We will reconvene at two o'clock, after which time you may continue your cross-examination, Mr. Kellenberger."

Eli stretched and then smiled at her and Phoebe. "Who's up for some Thai food?"

54

Over her plate of pad Thai at Bangkok Palace on Taylor, Andie basked in Eli's and Phoebe's effusive praise for her testimony.

"I know it was rough," Eli said. "But you came though like a champ. You were perfect. Flawless."

Phoebe nodded. "I paid close attention to the jury's reaction. They looked sympathetic."

"Kellenberger seemed rattled. The first part of his cross didn't make a whole lot of sense. It was aimless spewing and insinuation."

"Yeah," Andie said, "but maybe he'll make up for it this afternoon. I can't say I'm looking forward to it."

"What could he have up his sleeve, other than more of the same? Don't let him get to you and you'll be fine."

"He's right, Andie. You'll do great," Phoebe said.

Eli pushed his empty plate aside. "You know, missing evidence be damned, I'm feeling good about how things are shaping up. I think we've got this."

Andie wouldn't let herself believe it. Three years of hard knocks had taught her that optimism nearly always led to disappointment. Cynicism was safer.

Eli signed the check and smiled at them. "Shall we?"

Back in the courtroom Kellenberger was nowhere to be seen. Bondurant sat at the bench glowering, looking like someone you do not want to piss off.

Five minutes later Kellenberger rushed into the courtroom and down the aisle. "Sorry I'm late, Your Honor," he said, out of breath. "Traffic."

Bondurant answered with a grunt and then said, "If you're ready to resume your cross, Mr. Kellenberger, Ms. McInnes may take the stand again."

"Your Honor, I have no more questions for Ms. McInnes."

Relief washed over her. Whatever Kellenberger's reason for not continuing his cross-examination of her, she wasn't going to complain.

"Instead," Kellenberger said, "if it please the court, I would like to call a rebuttal witness."

Caterpillar eyebrow raised, Bondurant said, "Proceed."

"I call Kayla Giles to the stand."

Andie blinked. Why her friend would be testifying for the prosecution she hadn't the slightest clue. She shrugged in response to the quizzical look on Eli's face.

Kayla Giles was a tall girl with straight brown hair that fell past her shoulder blades. She didn't look at Andie while she was sworn in or after she sat down in the witness chair.

"Ms. Giles," Kellenberger said, "are you acquainted with the defendant, Andrea McInnes?"

"Yes," she said.

"How long have you known her?"

"About two years."

Kellenberger went over to the court clerk, got the tagged pistol, and showed it to her. "Did you loan Ms. McInnes this weapon?"

"No," Kayla said.

When Andie found her voice she said, "She's lying, Eli. I don't know why, but she's lying."

"Examine it closely, Ms. Giles," Kellenberger said. "Have you ever seen it before?"

"Never."

"Ms. McInnes testified that your boyfriend gave you this gun and you loaned it to her on July fourteenth."

"That's not true."

"Then why would she testify to that effect?"

Kayla shrugged. "I don't know. Maybe she thought you wouldn't check."

"Do you know where she obtained the gun?"

"No idea. But it wasn't from me."

"Thank you, Ms. Giles. Your witness."

"No questions," Eli said.

"The witness is excused," Bondurant said.

Kayla left the stand and kept on walking, up the aisle and out through the courtroom door, never having once made eye contact with Andie.

Bondurant said, "Court is adjourned until Monday at ten o'clock, at which time the prosecution and defense can present closing arguments." He rapped his gavel.

On the drive to her apartment, Eli was silent. That was fine with her. She didn't feel much like talking anyway. He had already assured her he had absolutely no doubt that Kayla had lied about the gun.

As she opened the door to get out he said, "Kayla's boyfriend—what's his name?"

"Kyle Brenner. No, Brennan. Kyle Brennan."

He jotted it down in a leather-bound notebook. "Try to get some rest over the weekend, okay?"

"I'll try."

But she had a bad feeling about the trial, about her future. The missing evidence was upsetting enough, and then to have a supposed friend turn on her . . .

Get some rest over the weekend.

Having a prison sentence hanging over her head like the sword of Damocles wasn't exactly conducive to rest. But she had *Heart of Darkness* and of course her journal.

Friday, September 9, 9:40 p.m.

Kayla Giles threw me to the wolves today. She testified that she hadn't given me the gun, claimed she'd never even seen the gun before. I thought she was going to deny knowing me. I've known Kayla for two years. I would have sworn she was my friend. Some friend.

But here's the good news: I testified without melting down! It was tough, but I made it through in one piece, despite Kellenberger's assholery. I just kept my cool and fielded his questions the way Eli coached me.

Afterward, Eli said he was very proud of me, and Phoebe—super-smart, mega-competent, tragically unhip Phoebe—said I could not have done better. She's sweet.

So despite Kayla's betrayal, I'm pumped.

It's the weekend, thank God. My plan is to get plenty of rest so I'll be fresh as a proverbial daisy on Monday when the trial resumes. I have a feeling the Zen routines for calming the mind will get a workout.

Right now I'm going for a run. Maybe the exercise will help me sleep.

55

The call came over the radio when Karen was on the way to August Moon on Clay to pick up some Chinese takeout to bring back to the station house.

"Faded red Ford Bronco with frog sticker in back window spotted moving east on Hawthorne, just crossing Third now." It was Gunderson, a veteran patrol officer. *"Oregon plate Ocean George Sam eight six two. Registered owner Delbert Louis Pike, age thirty-two, address one seven four eight Stark Street. Requesting backup."*

Karen snatched the mic. "Copy. Three X-ray Ten en route. Let's go over to Tac two." She changed the radio's channel, switched on her unmarked unit's lights, pulled a U-turn, and stepped on it. Luckily, traffic was light. She crossed over the Hawthorne Bridge and soon passed Third Avenue. "What's the Bronco's twenty now?"

"Just approaching Thirteenth, Woj."

"Probably heading home, so he'll make a left pretty soon to cut over to Stark. Hang back, Gunny. We don't want a high-speed chase." She switched off her unit's lights.

"Copy that."

"And good eye, spotting the suspect vehicle."

"Sullivan deserves the credit. It was his sharp eyes." Sullivan was Gunderson's partner. *"Suspect turning left on Seventeenth."*

"I'm a block behind you. Proceed through the intersection and I'll pick up the tail. You approach from the east on Stark."

"Ten-four."

Gunderson went straight and she turned left on 17th, at McMenamins Barley Mill Pub. The Bronco was a block ahead, just crossing Madison. Not likely he'd make the unmarked unit from that far away. The Caprice needed a wash, which made it look more like a civilian car.

"You guys need any help? We're on Stark at Fourth, proceeding east." It was Simmelink and Evans.

She keyed the mic. "Sure. Lights if you have to, but no siren. We don't want to spook the suspect."

"Can we join the party, too?" Manheim and Phipps. *"We're on Sandy, coming up on Twentieth."*

"Hey, the more the merrier." When it came to backup, it was true.

Given the other units' positions she'd probably be first on the scene. They wouldn't be far behind, though.

The cross streets flew by: Main, Salmon, Taylor. Colonel Sommers Park on the right, then Belmont, Alder, Morrison, Alder, Washington. Finally, Stark.

She hung a right on Stark. The Bronco was pulling into a driveway a block ahead. She eased the Caprice to the curb in front of the house next door and got out, revolver drawn.

A sizable laurel bush concealed all but the back two feet of the Bronco, so the suspect couldn't see her approach. She crept up behind the laurel and took a quick peek around it.

The suspect was still sitting behind the wheel. He seemed to be reading or examining something. She had intended to wait for backup to arrive, but it was a perfect opportunity to catch him by surprise. Known on the job as "cowboy stuff." *Yippee-ki-yay, motherflippers!*

Crouching below window level, she sneaked around the back of the Bronco and along its left side until she reached the open driver's window and then she yelled, "Delbert Pike! Keep your hands where I can see them! You so much as twitch and I'll shoot you dead on the spot!" She meant every word.

Pike looked at the cocked .38 and slowly raised his hands.

His eyes were pale blue, his lips thin. He was wearing a camouflage shirt and a red "Make America Great Again" cap.

Several units screeched to a stop in front, but her eyes never left Pike. She heard the patrolmen approaching on foot. "All right now," she said, "I want you to stick both hands out of the window—slowly—and open the door using the outside door handle. Do it!"

Pike did as he was told.

"Now get out slowly and get on the ground, on your face. Do it!"

Pike complied without a word. His camouflage pants were tucked into black combat boots, spit-shined to a high luster.

She glanced at the six uniformed officers. They were all standing there, gaping at her like a flock of blackbirds. "Would one of you gentlemen mind cuffing the suspect?"

"You sure you don't want to do that, too, Woj?" Manheim said. "You've done everything else."

Simmelink did the honors. Then he and Evans each took an arm and lifted Pike to his feet, walked him to their unit, and stuffed him in the back.

"Hey," Sullivan said, "look what I found." He was holding a large revolver. "Smith and Wesson forty-four magnum. It was under the seat. Thinks he's Dirty Harry." He leaned across the seat, checked the glove compartment, and came out with a .357 and a large combat knife. "This guy's armed to the teeth. No telling what he has inside the house."

"I'm going to go get a search warrant and we'll find out. You boys secure these premises until I get back."

Karen took a look through the one-way window. Delbert Pike was sitting at the table with his hands folded in front of him, staring at her as though he could see her. She opened the door and walked in.

She pulled out the chair across from him and sat down. She indicated his shackled wrists. "Comfortable?"

No answer, just a stare.

"And the ankles? Sometimes people complain they're too tight."

He answered with a snort.

"Mr. Pike, you're up shit creek without a paddle. Searching your house turned up some interesting things."

"Fuck you."

"*Very* interesting things. For example, in your basement we found some rope identical to the kind used in a murder committed not far from your house."

"So what?"

"And in your computer's browser we found a bookmarked site that shows how to make a noose."

"Is that illegal?"

"No, but lynching people is. You lynched a transgender girl named Corey Ryan with a noose you made."

He gave her a thin-lipped sneer. "You can't prove that."

"When they match your DNA to the sample they got from the noose, *that* will prove it."

"Kiss my ass."

"Too bad Oregon doesn't hang people anymore, Pike. You could have experienced what Corey Ryan went through."

"Ryan was a tranny, you said? Whoever hanged the freak should get a medal."

"Yeah? You have a thing about transgender people, don't you? In addition to all the bookmarked hate sites, you had a bunch of printed literature that calls for killing them. Funny thing—you also had a stack of tranny porn magazines. Your alt-right buddies know you're into that kind of stuff?"

"Eat shit and die. It was . . . research."

"It's very common, you know—a guy can't reconcile his sexual interest with some other part of his life, so he kills the object of his desire. It fits. Pike—I think you're conflicted."

"Says you, and you ain't anybody."

She smiled. "I'm the cop who took you down."

He sat back. "Just wait until our guy's in the White House. Things are going to be different. It'll be open season on those tranny freaks. Queers, spics, ragheads, and niggers, too."

"That so? In the meantime, we're going to round up the sick bastards who helped you murder Corey Ryan. The list of contacts we found on your phone should help a lot on that score. The text messages will also be very helpful."

His lips curled into a sneer. "You're a stupid cuck."

"Cuck? I guess that's supposed to be an insult." She pushed her chair back and stood. At the door she turned and smiled at him. "Nice talking to you."

She was writing the arrest report when Brownie stopped by her desk. "Eichler wants to see you, Woj."

She got up, stretched, and headed for Eichler's office. Dollars to donuts, he was going to give her hell for taking Pike down without waiting for backup. He looked up when she came in.

"What's up, L.T.?"

"First, good job bagging Pike. You took the initiative, and it paid off. The guys were quite impressed. They can't stop talking about it."

It was a day for surprises. "Hey, thanks."

"Second, I got a call from the FBI. A couple of their agents are on their way over. Looks like the feds are going to be calling the shots on this investigation."

"Damn. I expected it, though. Ryan's lynching has been connected to a nationwide conspiracy. But still."

"I know how you feel. It was a good bust and you wanted to see it all the way through."

"Oh well." There was nothing else to say.

"I watched you interview Pike. Those alt-right assholes are an unhinged bunch."

"He and his pals want to make America great again, L.T."

"Don't get me started. By the way, looks like you won't be getting rid of me after all. Bonnie's sister's coming up here and moving in with us instead."

"How can we miss you, L.T., when you won't go away?" But it was the best news she'd heard lately.

56

The infamous "bathroom bill," SB1947, was scheduled to come to the Senate floor early on that overcast Monday morning, early being 9 a.m. EST. The Republican leadership obviously thought they'd sewn up enough votes for it to pass with a veto-proof majority. McCoy was hoping his filibuster would change that state of affairs.

During the walk from his apartment to the Metro station, on the train ride into Capitol Hill, and during the walk to the Capitol Building he had new bodyguard, a bulldog-jawed plainclothes officer named Griffin, assigned by the Capitol Hill Police to accompany him when he was out in public. Griffin took his job seriously, although he wasn't much of a conversationalist.

When McCoy and his taciturn companion stepped onto the Capitol Building's parklike grounds it was 8:15, comfortably early. He saw the crowd of protesters in front of the steps from a block away. "I want to check this out," he said. "We've got time."

The protesters were carrying signs that had religious proverb-like messages, among them: "THE FRUIT OF WICKEDNESS IS SIN," "TURN FROM SIN OR FORFEIT SALVATION," "SINNERS REPENT," "THE WAGES OF SIN IS DEATH."

"Shouldn't that be *are* death?" McCoy said.

Griffin shrugged.

"I'm detecting a theme here," McCoy said. "Do they seem to you a trifle obsessed with sin?"

Griffin only grunted.

"Ah well, I guess everyone needs a hobby."

They heard him from a hundred feet away. A large man with a white beard and angry black eyebrows was holding forth on the bottom steps of the U.S. Capitol. If he'd had a robe and staff, instead of a short-sleeve plaid shirt and khakis, he could've passed for Moses. Sermon On the Steps. He pointed at someone in the crowd and, in a klaxon voice that carried across the plaza, said, "Sinner! Ye shall never know the Kingdom of Heaven."

"I seen him before," Griffin said. "Calls himself Jeremiah. Bills himself as a prophet." For Griffin, it was a talking streak.

A woman in front said, "So just because I'm trans I'm going to hell, is that what you're saying?"

The sign wielders jeered her. "That's right," one shouted.

Jeremiah spread his arms, hands palm-down as if calming the sea, and the jeers died down. "I speak God's words. Your body is a temple that you have defiled. You have sinned."

"Bullshit," the woman said. "What I have done has been absolutely *vital* to my health and happiness. *Vital.*"

"A vital sin is a sin nevertheless."

"Says you."

"Says God."

"Look, Jeremiah, or whatever you call yourself, I've got better things to do than argue with a kook who thinks he's God's mouthpiece. I believe that God loves and accepts me—vital sins and all." The jeers started again as she stamped off.

"Well," McCoy said to Griffin, "there you have it."

"I'll feel a lot better after I get you inside the building, Senator." And that was the longest sentence he'd uttered yet.

At 8:50 McCoy made a last-minute trip to the john. It was the last chance he'd get to use an actual restroom until after the filibuster was over. But that didn't worry him. He had the bag.

Scores of faces turned toward him when he entered the chamber—Democrats smiled, Republicans wore sucking-on-lemon expressions. He greeted his colleagues as he made his way down the aisle and over to his desk, third row back on the right.

The Senate majority leader called the session to order and presented SB1947 for a vote.

McCoy stood and addressed the presiding officer, the Senate president *pro tempore:* "Mr. President?"

The presiding officer gave him a nod and said, "The Chair recognizes the senator from the state of Washington."

Notes at hand, duffle bag stocked with water and milk, Skechers on his feet, urine bag securely strapped to his leg, McCoy took a deep breath and began what he hoped would be an epic filibuster.

57

Over the weekend Ritter turned up two very interesting facts. First fact: On August 16th Kyle Brennan, Kayla Giles' boyfriend, had been arrested and charged with a DUII, after blowing 1.8 on a breathalyzer test. It was his third offense, so he'd been facing a hefty fine and possible jail time. Second fact: On September 9th all charges were dropped.

It didn't take a genius to make the connection. Kayla testified for the prosecution and denied lending Andie the gun in return for having the DUII charges against her boyfriend dropped. *Quid pro quo.*

Hard to believe that Kellenberger would pull something so ham-handed. Then again, he'd had his brother-in-law delete the LIMS records to hide evidence, pretty ham-handed in its own right. Obviously he was willing to do anything to win the case, as though he had some sort of personal stake in it. Whatever it was, it undoubtedly involved career advancement. Ambition, unencumbered by ethics.

Ritter frowned. If he could get Kayla back on the stand, he could undo the considerable damage her perjurious testimony had done. Only one problem—she and her boyfriend happened to be *in absentia.* As in, left town. "Decided to take a vacay," she'd told a neighbor. Until after the trial, no doubt.

It wouldn't surprise him if Kellenberger had furnished the couple with airline tickets to Cabo San Lucas.

His best bet was to request a stay of proceeding until Kayla turned up again. But could he convince Bondurant that a stay was justified? It was worth a try.

Today was Monday. The trial would resume at ten o'clock. That gave him an hour and a half to collect Andie at the foundation, drive to the courthouse, and make the appeal to Bondurant in chambers before court.

He needed to get on the stick.

"I see your point," Bondurant said, "but I'm not going to hold up this proceeding by issuing a stay based only on conjecture. Our docket is clogged enough as it is."

And that was that.

Ritter left chambers with ice in his veins and joined Andie and Phoebe in the courtroom. Their faces asked the question for them. He shook his head. "He didn't buy it."

Phoebe winced. "So what now?"

"That's a good question."

"Eli," Andie said in a small voice. She looked scared.

With good reason. Her life, the next six years of it, was hanging in the balance. The truth was, the cards had been stacked against her from the beginning, in a case that, arguably, should never have gone to trial. Evidence tampering, perjured testimony, character assassination—all had been thrown at her by a predatory prosecutor who so far had operated with impunity.

But the trial wasn't over yet. An audacious idea took shape. He turned to Andie and Phoebe. "I'm going to try a long shot." Nothing could make matters any worse.

Bondurant called the court to order and asked Ritter and Kellenberger if they were ready to begin closing arguments.

Ritter stood. "Excuse me, Your Honor, but the defense has not yet rested its case."

It caught Bondurant by surprise, judging by his expression. "My apology, Counselor. Just trying to keep things moving along. Please proceed."

"May it please the court, I call to the stand . . . Assistant District Attorney Breton Kellenberger."

The courtroom erupted. Bondurant pounded with his gavel. "Order," he said. "Order!"

Kellenberger was on his feet with an objection.

"Your Honor," Ritter said, "may we approach?"

"Please do."

A red-faced Kellenberger strode up to the bench. "This is nothing but a delaying tactic by the defense," he said. "It's a transparent attempt to muddy the waters."

Bondurant looked at Ritter, one bushy eyebrow raised.

"Your Honor, I am calling Mr. Kellenberger to be a witness strictly in his capacity as assistant district attorney, given the fact that Kayla Giles is unavailable to recant her perjured testimony."

"Perjured testimony my eye," Kellenberger said. "This is just grandstanding. It's a total waste of the court's time."

Ritter couldn't resist. "It's perfectly understandable that Mr. Kellenberger would think I'm grandstanding, given his own considerable performance experience."

"Your Honor," Kellenberger said, "this is an outrage and I refuse—"

Bondurant held up his hand for silence. "It's an unusual request, Mr. Ritter. But then, the circumstances of this case are unusual." Decisive nod. "I'm going to allow it."

"Your Honor—"

"I've made my ruling, Mr. Kellenberger." To the courtroom he said, "Assistant District Attorney Kellenberger will now come forth and be sworn in as a witness."

It was a long shot for sure, but Ritter couldn't think of any other way to cast doubt on Giles' testimony.

Stone-faced, Kellenberger walked over to the bailiff and raised his right hand. After repeating the oath he dropped into the witness chair and fixed Ritter with a frosty stare.

Ritter said, "On August sixteenth Kayla Giles' boyfriend, Kyle Brennan, was charged with driving under the influence and resisting arrest. It was his third DUII arrest.

"On September ninth, the same day Ms. Giles testified, the district attorney dropped all charges." He paused to let it sink in. "As a result, Mr. Brennan was spared from having to pay a fine or serve a jail sentence.

"I would ask Ms. Giles about it, but she seems to have left town suddenly, so instead I will ask you this question. Did you drop the DUII and resisting charges that were pending against Mr. Brennan in return for Ms. Giles' testimony that she did not lend to Ms. McInnes the gun that was used to kill Mr. Hinshaw?"

A flush spread across Kellenberger's cheeks. "Certainly not," he said. "That's ridiculous."

"Then why were the charges dropped?"

"I—it was determined that the breathalyzer and field sobriety tests were not conducted properly."

"Determined by whom?"

"By the office of the district attorney."

"Can you say specifically who in the district attorney's office made that determination?"

Kellenberger half-smiled. "That is a confidential departmental matter. It requires a warrant."

"I thought you'd say that. No further questions." Ritter wished he had time to get that warrant and nail Kellenberger's hide to the wall, but it would have to wait.

Bondurant looked over at Kellenberger's assistant, a pale, balding young man named Ross. "Cross-examine, Mr. Ross?"

The assistant looked to his boss, who gave an almost imperceptible shake of his head. "No questions," he said.

Back at counsel's table Andie and Phoebe wanted to know if he thought the gambit had worked well enough to swing the pendulum in their favor.

He shrugged. "Remains to be seen."

"Tick-tock, Mr. Ritter," Bondurant said. "Please continue."

Ritter got up, resigned to the inevitable: resting his case. His fleeting hope was that his closing argument would offset the lack of evidence and other shortcomings of the defense's case. But the knot in his gut quelled any optimism.

Out of the corner of his eye he caught a flash of movement from the spectators' gallery. It turned out to be Nicole, sitting in the front row, waving to get his attention. Beside her sat Don Hunsaker from the forensics lab. Ritter thought at first they'd come just to watch, but then Nicole made a talking gesture with her hand and pointed to Hunsaker. The look on her face said it was important.

"Your Honor," he said, "I request a ten-minute recess."

"Granted," Bondurant said.

He led the pair out into the hall. "What's up?"

"I found it," Hunsaker said. "The missing evidence."

"I'll be damned."

"I tried to call you but got your voicemail, so Nicole and I drove over."

"You did the right thing. Have you tested it yet?"

Hunsaker shook his head. "I wanted to talk to you first. The evidence is still sealed in bags with their initialed seals unbroken."

"Doc, you are the cavalry, riding to the rescue in the nick of time," Ritter said. "The bad guys had us surrounded."

"I forgot my bugle, but glad to help."

Ritter turned to Nicole.

"I tagged along just to say hi," she said.

"I'm glad you did. Now . . . Don, how long will it take you to go process that evidence, including travel time?"

"Traffic is light this time of day, so . . . say, a half-hour to get there, an hour for testing, a half-hour back. "

"It'll be close. Let's go back in. I need to talk to the judge, apprise him of this development."

All eyes were on them when they walked in. The curiosity on people's faces was palpable, Kellenberger's especially.

"Approach, Your Honor?" he said.

Kellenberger hustled up to the bench.

Bondurant leaned forward. "What's going on, Mr. Ritter?"

"I was just informed that the forensics lab in Clackamas has located the missing evidence. I would very much like to present it today."

"Objection," Kellenberger said. "Broken chain of custody."

"Except," Ritter said, "the chain of custody was never broken. It was in the lab's possession the entire time, stored in their evidence room. They just couldn't locate it until today. The bags are still intact, their seals unbroken."

Kellenberger shook his head. "Be that as it may, the evidence was missing and therefore out of the lab's control for many weeks. I move to exclude on that basis."

"Your Honor," Ritter said, "Dr. Hunsaker is willing testify as to the integrity of the evidence and its handling. He says he can go back to the lab, conduct the DNA tests, and be back with the results within two hours."

Bondurant pulled at one side of his walrus mustache. "Mr. Kellenberger," he finally said, "your motion to exclude the evidence is denied. Mr. Ritter, go tell Dr. Hunsaker to get cracking." And to the courtroom he said, "It's eleven-fifteen. Court will adjourn early for lunch and reconvene at two o'clock sharp." He rose to his feet and headed straight for his chambers.

Ritter had been holding his breath. He let it out and went back to Hunsaker. "Green light, Doc. You have until two to do the tests and get back here. And I hope to hell you find something on those clothes. Otherwise, Andie's toast." And so was he. Trollinger and Cannady would see to that.

"Okay," Hunsaker said. "I should be back long before two, assuming I don't run up against any difficulties."

"I will stay here if that is all right," Nicole said. "I can do nothing to help Don."

Ritter smiled at her. "Then you can go to lunch with us."

Hunsaker didn't make it back until three minutes before two —too late to confer with him, since Bondurant was getting ready to call the court back into session.

Ritter ran his fingers through his hair, wondering if it had turned white waiting for Hunsaker's return. But he'd made it back in time, that was the important thing.

Adding to Ritter's tension, Hunsaker made no attempt to communicate nonverbally—no thumbs up, no circle with forefinger and thumb, no big smile. He found a seat and sat down, his expression opaque. But then, he'd brought the two evidence bags with him, surely a good sign?

Putting a witness on the stand without knowing exactly what he or she was going to say was asking for trouble, ordinarily, but this trial was anything but ordinary. Ritter said, "I call Dr. Don Hunsaker to the stand."

Hunsaker came forward and was sworn in by the bailiff. He sat down and placed the evidence bags on his lap.

"Dr. Hunsaker," Ritter said, "please tell the court where you work, your title, your job duties.

"I work at the Portland Metropolitan Forensic Laboratory in Clackamas, where I have been a senior lab director for the past eleven years, in charge of DNA processing."

"Those two bags, what are their contents?"

"A women's jeans and underwear."

"Remove the items from the bags, if you would."

Hunsaker did, and put them in Ritter's outstretched hand.

Ritter said, "These are the jeans and underwear that Ms. McInnes was wearing the night of August fourteenth. May it please the court, I ask that they be marked Defense Exhibits D and E."

He gave the clothes to the clerk, who recorded and tagged them. Then Ritter returned them to Hunsaker so he could refer to them during his testimony.

"Dr. Hunsaker, have these two items of clothing been tested for the presence of DNA?"

"Yes. I conducted the testing personally."

"What were the results?"

"I found two separate deposits of DNA from an individual other than the defendant." He held up the jeans and pointed to the zipper. "I found a smear of blood on the end of the brass zipper tab." He held up the underwear next. "And this item has a spot of blood on the waistband . . . here, on the left side."

"Did you identify the individual whose blood it was?"

"Yes, I did. The blood was Howard Hinshaw's."

Bondurant's gavel pounded like a pile driver until the clamor in the courtroom settled down.

"The coroner's report," Ritter said, "noted a lesion under Mr. Hinshaw's right thumbnail. It had been bleeding."

"He could have jammed the zipper tab under his nail, which would explain the blood I found in the two locations."

"Objection, speculation," Kellenberger said.

Bondurant said, "Sustained."

"No further questions." Ritter took his seat to watch.

Kellenberger stood. "Dr. Hunsaker, the evidence you tested had been missing until today. Your lab couldn't find it for almost two months. Tell me, how can you *lose* evidence?"

"When the lab takes delivery of evidence to be tested, the information is entered into a specialized database, LIMS, which keeps track of its location in evidence storage. The technician remembered receiving the jeans and underwear from a police officer and then creating two LIMS entries. However, the entries were subsequently deleted."

"By whom?"

"That's being investigated. The culprit forgot to cover his tracks completely, as it turned out."

Kellenberger's mouth dropped open. "Probably a hacker wannabe with too much time on his hands." He said it casually. "Or have you ruled that out?"

"I'd rather not say anything more until all the facts are in."

Kellenberger stared at him for what seemed an awkward pause and then said, "No further questions."

Bondurant excused the witness.

Hunsaker stepped down from the witness box and cast a sidelong glance at Kellenberger.

Ritter chuckled. He'd struggled keep a straight face during Kellenberger's cross-examination. Especially when he tried to put Hunsaker on the defensive about losing the evidence, and Hunsaker countered with a jab about the culprit failing to cover his tracks. Game, set, match.

Ritter took a deep breath and exhaled. The tension that had gripped him since the trial began seemed to ease up a bit. Hunsaker's testimony had been the final, crucial element of the defense's case. "The defense rests," he said.

A grunt from Bondurant conveyed his approval. "The court will now hear closing arguments."

Kellenberger got up, walked over to a spot six feet in front of the jury box, and adopted a pose he'd no doubt practiced in front of a mirror. "Ladies and gentlemen," he said, "thank you for serving on the jury for this unusual case, unusual because of the defendant's . . . lifestyle choice.

"The facts of the case are unambiguous and undeniable. One, on July fourteenth Andrea McInnes, a young homeless transgender, shot and killed Howard Hinshaw. Two, the revolver *she* used to kill him was stolen. Three, the person *she* claimed had given her the gun denied in her testimony any knowledge of said gun. Four, mysterious evidence that had been lost for months suddenly turned up today. Not last week, not last month—today. Coincidence or carefully staged? You tell me.

"Facts are facts, no matter how the defense tries to spin them. And one fact that's guaranteed spinproof is this—the defendant was the only person in the alley that evening who was carrying a firearm—a stolen one—while Mr. Hinshaw, Mr. Burleson, and Mr. Pfaff were all unarmed. That, ladies and gentlemen, says it all.

"Two witnesses, Gary Burleson and Norman Pfaff, testified that the defendant acted irrationally—'like a crazy person,' they said—screaming at them and waving the gun around. Dr. Merkin and other psychologists contend, based on their research, that many transgenders are mentally unstable, so the witnesses' testimony is entirely consistent with these experts' opinions.

"I'll leave you with this thought. When you're in the jury room deliberating, don't let yourself be swayed by social pressure or political correctness. If justice is to be served, you have only one course of action—a verdict of guilty. Thank you."

A closing statement comprised of equal parts insinuation and transphobia. But then, Kellenberger's case was paper-thin, resting on testimony from a crackpot, a perjurer, and two dubious eyewitnesses.

Ritter got to his feet. His close would be considerably more substantial. He'd given it a lot of thought. It was his favorite part of the process, laying everything out just so.

"Ladies and gentlemen," he said, making eye contact with the jury, "I'll add my thanks for your invaluable service."

The jury acknowledged him with smiles and nods.

"First off, I agree with Mr. Kellenberger. Yes, this is an unusual case. Yes, mostly because Ms. McInnes is transgender. Had she not been, there's a good chance this case wouldn't have come to trial at all. It's a classic case of self defense, and the evidence proves it beyond a shadow of a doubt. Let's examine the key points in the case.

"The prosecution's witnesses, Mr. Burleson and Mr. Pfaff, testified that neither they nor Mr. Hinshaw had any physical contact with Ms. McInnes. At no time, they said, did they come any closer to her than eight feet. And yet, Mr. Hinshaw's blood was found on Ms. McInnes' jeans and underwear. How did it get there? If you believe their story then the blood must have miraculously materialized on her clothes from eight feet away. But here's an explanation that does not involve the supernatural. It came from Mr. Hinshaw's bleeding thumbnail when he pulled down her jeans and underwear, as she testified he did. So which explanation seems more likely?

"Mr. Burleson and Mr. Pfaff also testified that Ms. McInnes was standing when she shot Mr. Hinshaw. He was bent over forward, they said, having just picked up the rebar from the ground. And yet, the coroner testified that the bullet entered Mr. Hinshaw's throat at a forty-degree upward angle."

He nodded to Phoebe, who brought him the easel and artwork he'd had prepared. It took them thirty seconds to set everything up. He thanked her and turned back to the jury. "I have some visual aids to help picture the scene."

"The first drawing shows Ms. McInnes standing with the gun, and Mr. Hinshaw is bent over forward, as per the witnesses' testimony. The red dotted line is the bullet's trajectory. Note that the angle of entry is downward, not upward.

"Now . . . in the second drawing Ms. McInnes is lying on her back when she fires the gun, while Mr. Hinshaw is advancing toward her with the rebar raised to strike her. Note that the bullet's angle of entry is precisely forty degrees.

"Once again, two possibilities—either the bullet violated the laws of physics . . . or it happened just the way Ms. McInnes described." He left the second drawing up for them to study. "Again, which explanation seems more likely?"

"On the subject of Mr. Burleson's and Mr. Pfaff's testimonies, did you happen to notice how similar they were? Actually, *similar* is the wrong word; *identical* would be more accurate. You know," he said in a confidential tone, "it's almost as though they worked out the story together."

Several jurors laughed.

"Mr. Kellenberger made much of the fact that Ms. McInnes had a stolen firearm with her. She hadn't wanted to take it, but her very good friend Kayla Giles insisted. On the stand Ms. Giles denied it. Then she and her boyfriend, Kyle Brennan, blew town. Come to find out, Mr. Brennan's pending DUII charge, his third, was dropped the same day his girlfriend testified. Imagine that. Ms. McInnes hadn't wanted to take the gun along with her—but had she not, she likely would be dead now. Beyond a shadow of a doubt, having the gun with her saved her life.

"The three men shoved Ms. McInnes in the alley with the intention of raping her. Two of them held her down while Mr. Hinshaw pulled down her jeans and underwear. And then they discovered she was a preoperative transgender woman. They were furious. Mr. Hinshaw picked up the piece of rebar and, blood lust in his eyes, came toward her. She realized he was going to bludgeon her to death. She remembered the gun in her bag and, intending to only scare him by shooting over his head, she pulled the trigger.

"Ms. McInnes believes in the sanctity of life. She told me she wouldn't even kill an insect. When she finds one indoors she catches it and releases it unharmed outside. To have caused the death of another human being, even accidentally, weighs heavily on her.

"But the simple fact is, if she hadn't shot Mr. Hinshaw he'd surely have killed her. That is the essence of self defense. Accordingly, only one verdict will serve justice—not guilty. Thank you, ladies and gentlemen."

Taking his seat at counsel's table, he winked at Andie. He had connected with the jurors, hit all the points he'd wanted to, and showed her in a sympathetic light. He'd take it.

"Eli, that was amazing," Phoebe said. "It was your jury all the way."

"I hope you're right." But he knew she was. Those jurors had been eating out of his hand.

Andie said, "So what happens now?"

As though in answer to her question, Bondurant said, "Ladies and gentlemen of the jury, it is your responsibility to decide this case based on the evidence you've seen and heard. To guide you in your deliberations I will now provide instructions for you to follow."

He outlined the relevant issues in the case, interpreted the governing laws, explained the standard of proof they should apply ("beyond a reasonable doubt"), and instructed them in what they should consider and disregard in reaching a verdict. He was excruciatingly thorough. It took him thirty tedious minutes, after which he at last adjourned the proceeding.

"There you have it," Ritter said, smiling at Andie. "Next time you're in this courtroom it will be to hear the verdict."

"I'm looking forward to it," she said. "I want to get back to my life."

"Can't blame you there. But right now, unless you want to stick around for some reason, I suggest we leave."

"The sooner the better."

She felt a tap on her knee. "Pretty quiet over there, Andie." He grinned at her. "You haven't said three words since we left the courthouse. You okay?"

"Fine. Trying to get my mind around the fact that this nightmare will be over soon. I've been thinking about all the things I want to do. Like get a car. Last week I stopped in at the Fiat dealership. They offered to let me test drive one, but I was too chicken. Fiats are crazy-cute and they get hella good gas mileage."

"You met someone today who drives a Fiat. She had lunch with us. Nicole."

"Really? Wish I'd known that."

"I'm sure she'll be glad to tell you all about it, especially its performance data, technical specifications, and engineering details."

She stayed quiet until they came to a stop in the parking lot near her apartment complex and he put it in park. She had to tell him. "Eli, I haven't said anything, but I want you to know how grateful I am. Given what could have happened to me in prison, you probably saved my life."

"Wait until the trial is completely over, then thank me."

"Spoken like a cautious lawyer," she said and reached for the door handle.

On the short walk to her apartment she hummed a tune, "Little GTO." She didn't know any songs about Fiats. Maybe she'd write one.

58

The heat wave swept across the Atlantic seaboard, scorching D.C.'s denizens like ants under a magnifying glass. Streets floated in the distance, shimmering with an illusion of wetness. Dogs and cats gave the searing concrete a wide berth, seeking refuge in the shade under trees and bushes. Humans were not as sensible.

Boonstra mopped his brow with a damp handkerchief. He hated Indian summer.

The building's air conditioning had been off for the past three hours. "We're working on it, Senator," the Capitol Building's maintenance office told him when he had called personally. "We're sorry for the inconvenience."

Inconvenience? It couldn't have come at a worse time. He had to stay there and meet with a Chamber of Commerce delegation from Tulsa, and then with his reelection campaign's fundraising chairman. If not for those things he'd be out of there like a striped-ass ape.

Ronette poked her head in the door. "I'm back from lunch, Senator. Do you need anyth—excuse me, my phone's ringing." She closed the door. Ten seconds later she buzzed him. "Mr. Kellenberger's on the line one."

He picked up. "How y'all doing, Bret?"

"I'm fine, but I can't say the same for the McInnes trial. That's why I'm calling."

"Tell me you're just funnin' me, old son."

"I wish I could. The prosecution's case is toes up."

Boonstra groaned. Why today of all days? "Goddamn it, Bret, did you or did you not assure me that you had everything under control?"

"I did, yes, but . . ."

"So what went haywire?"

"Well, the coroner's findings blew my two key witnesses out of the water, so their testimony probably won't stand up. And I had to rush another witness out of town before she got slapped with a perjury charge. Worst of all, the forensic lab found McInnes' missing clothes, and of course they had DNA evidence on them. Exonerating evidence."

"So what are the chances you'll win the case in spite of the hitches?

"About as much chance as a tanning salon in Compton."

"Mind, that's what everyone said about our orange-hued Republican nominee before he beat out sixteen primary opponents to win the nomination."

"Yeah, but that was a fluke. He doesn't have a snowball's chance in the general."

"Maybe not, but I wouldn't bet against him."

"Anyway, the analogy doesn't hold up. The jury's not a bunch of gullible, pissed-off simpletons. They started deliberating yesterday. I can't sleep, knowing that they're probably going to find McInnes not guilty."

"You're taking this trial a mite personal. I wanted you to win it, sure, but the goddamn world won't end if you don't."

"For me it might, if some of the things I've done should come to light. I stuck my neck out, way out, to tip the scales."

"How? No, don't tell me. The less I know the better."

"Plausible deniability. But any way you slice it, I'm fucked."

"Hang in there, son."

"Yeah, sure. Sorry to spoil your day with bad news. I'll talk to you later."

After he hung up the phone Boonstra mopped his forehead and sighed.

Sorry to spoil your day with bad news.

Yeah, right. The day had already been thoroughly spoiled before Kellenberger called. Despite the majority whip's convincing assurances, SB1947 came up four votes short of a veto-proof supermajority. That polecat McCoy and his 18-hour filibuster must have changed their minds. So his Protect Our Children bill was effectively dead. Ditto his plan to use the crusade against transgenders as a stepping stone to political glory. No guesting on Fox News for him.

Most worrisome of all, the prospect of holding on to his seat was in doubt. The latest polls had Crenshaw, his Democrat opponent, leading by eight to ten points. In previous years he'd enjoyed consistent double-digit leads over Democrat challengers. He'd needed that bill signed into law, needed it bad, to give his flagging campaign a shot in the arm.

More immediately, he dreaded telling Joylene that her boy's murderer got off scot-free. At least he could postpone that until after the jury returned their verdict.

He rummaged around in a desk drawer until he found the jar of antacids, shook out four of the tablets and gulped them down with a water chaser. Hopefully, they'd kick in quick and douse the four-alarm raging in his belly.

He leaned back in his chair and closed his eyes. Everything seemed to be turning to shit. He couldn't swear it was the worst day of his life, but it surely was in the running.

His phone buzzed.

"The Chamber delegation just arrived," Ronette said.

"Be right out."

When he opened the door to greet his visitors his pasted-on smile felt almost genuine.

59

McCoy killed some time by watching CNN while he waited for Griffin to arrive to escort him to Safeway to pick up some groceries. The Orange One was bloviating about how much more he knew about ISIS than the generals. Laughable, except a depressingly large segment of the population, discontented and gullible, would swallow it hook, line, and proverbial sinker. That was scary.

When he heard the soft knock at his door he switched off the TV and grabbed his jacket. He unlocked the door and pulled it open as he said, "Griff, I also need to stop by Walgreen's for some—"

A dark figure rushed him, knocking him back into the apartment. He landed on his backside, hard.

"Sorry about that, mate." Gergen, dressed in black from head to toe, stood grinning down at him. "I couldn't wait for you to invite me in."

McCoy got to his feet. "I can't say I'm glad to see you."

"Is that any way to greet your old mate, Senator? After all we've been through together?"

"What do you want?"

"Right to the point. Everybody and his brother's looking for me out there. This is the one place they wouldn't think to look. So I'll be your houseguest for a while, just until things cool down a bit. And I appreciate your hospitality, Senator."

Griffin was a no-show, which wasn't like him. The most likely explanation was that he'd seen Gergen, knew he was in the apartment. So McCoy had to be prepared for whatever happened next. In the meantime, it wouldn't hurt to engage Gergen in conversation to occupy his attention. "I can't fault your logic. They'd never look for you here."

"Pretty cute trick you pulled, mate, busting out of there the way you did. When Hassler saw his door I thought he was going to cry."

McCoy couldn't resist. "You should've heard the sound it made when that Humvee burst through it. It sounded like a huge metal drum tuned low. They probably heard it all over Centreville."

Laughing, Gergen slapped his knee. "Senator, you're in the wrong line of work. You got the mentality of a soldier of fortune."

"I guess that's a compliment."

"The platform you jerry-rigged to get to that vent—I don't think I would've climbed on top of that. It took balls."

"Or desperation."

"There's that. I been there enough times."

"Let me ask you this," McCoy said. "Why did Mullen want you to do it?"

Gergen shrugged. "Beats me, mate. I was paid to carry it out, not ask why. But as one soldier of fortune to another, I'll tell you this. He's a religious bloke. Everything he does, it's foremost in the mix."

"Well, no hard feelings, Gergen. You were just doing your job." Very sincere. McCoy almost believed it himself.

"Thanks, mate. In different circumstances we'd go to the pub, down a pint or two."

McCoy pointed. "There's the bar. It's fairly well stocked. Myself, I usually have a Guinness Stout or gin and tonic. How about I get us something to drink? Might as well relax, since nobody knows you're here."

"Well now, since you mentioned Guinness, I wouldn't mind one at all."

"Coming right up." McCoy ambled to the bar, studiously relaxed. He grabbed two dark bottles from the half-height refrigerator and brought one to Gergen. "Here you go."

Gergen opened it and took a long pull. "That hits the spot, mate."

"Tell me, living and working on a ship, is that a good gig?"

"Never a dull moment."

"Yeah? Pretty exciting is it?"

"It can be. Once, when we were in the Indian Ocean, some Somali pirates tried to board us, but they got a rude awak—"

The knock at the door shut him up fast.

McCoy shrugged. "I'm not expecting anyone."

Gergen had the Glock in hand. "C'mon." He herded McCoy to the door. "Ask who it is."

"Who's there?" McCoy called though the door.

"Esther Coan," a female voice said. "The manager."

"What do you need?"

"Your signature. You forgot to sign your rent check. The bank rejected it."

"Could you come back another time, Mrs. Coan?"

"The mister and I are about to take off for Hyannis Port for two weeks. I need to deposit the check before we go."

McCoy looked at Gergen and spread his hands wide.

"You need a peephole so's you can see who's out there, mate. Go ahead and open the door, just wide enough for her to hand it to you."

McCoy opened the door four inches and reached through the opening for the check.

Three things happened simultaneously: Something hit the door with tremendous force, knocking it wide open. Someone seized his wrist and yanked him out into the hall. An object flew through the doorway into the apartment.

A blinding flash and deafening bang followed.

A nine-man SWAT team swarmed into the apartment, which was filled with smoke from the flash-bang. Standing in the midst of it, Gergen dropped his pistol and raised his hands, his face expressionless, his eyes downcast.

They led him out, wrists cuffed behind his back. As he passed by, he gave McCoy a conspiratorial wink. McCoy watched until he was out of sight. Inexplicably, he felt sorry for the guy. Stockholm Syndrome? He'd always dismissed as nonsense the notion of hostages forming an attachment to their captors. But now . . .

Mrs. Coan stood to one side, captivated by the drama, her drawn-on eyebrows at high mast.

"You should be in Hollywood," McCoy told her. "I've never heard lines delivered more convincingly."

She beamed. "And only one take."

Griffin appeared. "You all right, Senator? I saw Gergen force his way into your apartment and called in SWAT."

"Good thinking. They kicked ass."

Goodwillie joined them. "Well, Senator, looks like you're home free."

"Unless Mullen sends someone else after me."

"He's unlikely to do that. He's on the run now. The Pharma Queen's somewhere in the Mediterranean."

McCoy turned to Griffin and shook his hand. "You're the man of the hour, Griff. Hell, man of the year."

Griffin gave a noncommittal grunt.

McCoy remembered the Colt, in the desk drawer. "Funny, I never once considered going for my gun."

"Just as well," Goodwillie said. "With a pro like Gergen, it might've got you killed."

"Still going grocery shopping?" Griffin actually smiled, the grimace of a pit bull eating peanut butter.

"Not today," McCoy said.

He wanted only to finish the Guinness and perhaps down one or two more. That's what soldiers of fortune did to unwind between missions.

60

The trial had attracted nationwide coverage. The court-room gallery was standing room only, due in large part to the battalion of journalists jockeying for room, including several well-known media personalities.

Andie ignored them. The acquittal would extinguish their interest in a hurry, and then she'd have a chance at a normal life: work at the foundation, take classes at Portland State, finish writing *Inside Game*, and adopt a loving dog, one with a fuzzy little face like Buddy's.

More immediately, she needed wheels. She reached in her bag and took out a dog-eared brochure with a red Fiat 500 on the cover.

Phoebe leaned over and shoulder-surfed as Andie turned the pages. "They're so cute," she said. "Have you decided on a color?"

"I'm torn," Andie said. "Keeping a low profile is important to me, so I should probably steer clear of red, but . . . I'm loving the red one. The one that screams, 'Hey! Look at me!'"

"Maybe that's not a bad thing. Maybe people would be too busy admiring the car to notice the driver."

"Keep talking, Phoebe, your logic is resonating."

"All rise!" the bailiff said, his unamplified voice as loud as a bullhorn. "Court is now in session, the Honorable Judge Thomas Bondurant presiding."

Robe flowing behind him, Bondurant took the bench. "Be seated," he said. A hundred people sitting down at the same time made a collective *whumph*. He turned to the jury. "Mr. Foreman, please rise."

A tall man with close-cropped white hair stood, his face like granite.

"Has the jury reached a verdict?"

"We have, Your Honor."

"The defendant will rise and face the jury."

Andie did.

"In the matter before this court, in which the defendant, Andrea Lynne McInnes, has been charged with manslaughter in the second degree, how do you find?"

This was it, a welcome end to three months of anxiety and sleepless nights.

"We find the defendant . . . guilty."

Andie started to mouth a heartfelt thank you to the jury when the word *guilty* belatedly sank in.

Her legs buckled.

Eli caught her and eased her into the chair. Someone shoved something that smelled like ammonia under her nose. She waved it away. Pandemonium had erupted in the courtroom. Bondurant's gavel pounded, but the uproar didn't die down. If anything, it became louder.

Phoebe touched her shoulder. "Are you okay, Andie?"

In no sense of the word was she okay. She was as far from okay as it was possible to get. She looked down at the silver bracelet, at the inscription. The inscription she'd disregarded. Instead of skipping town, she'd trusted Eli and the Foundation to get her out of this mess. What a fool.

And by the way, God, why hast Thou forsaken me?

"I'm sorry, Andie," Eli said. "We'll appeal, of course."

Swell—except she had no reason to think an appeal would turn out any different. And in the meantime, she'd have to go to prison. Unless . . .

"Eli, is there any possibility of remaining free on bond pending appeal?"

"Judge Bondurant might grant that request, yes."

If he did, she'd have another chance—the last one she was likely to get—to disappear. And she wouldn't blow it. Better a hunted felon than a dead or maimed convict.

Wherever she ended up, she must never, ever forget how totally the game was rigged against trans people. Maybe she should have the sentiment engraved on another bracelet to remind her.

61

Bondurant glared at a group of noisy spectators until they shut up. Then he said, "At this point in a proceeding I usually commend the jury for its work. I can't do that today, unfortunately, because the jury's finding is unacceptable. The weight of the evidence was insufficient to support the verdict, woefully so. Accordingly, I'm going to set aside the guilty verdict and enter a judgment of acquittal. This proceeding is adjourned. *Sine die.*" A single rap of the gavel punctuated his final words.

Mouth agape, Andie turned to Eli. "I don't understand. What just happened?"

Eli was smiling. "The judge vacated the verdict. He entered a judgment of acquittal, just as though the jury had found you not guilty."

"He can do that?" She hadn't seen it on *Law & Order*.

"He can and did."

"Then what's the point of having a jury?"

"A judge will set aside a verdict only if the jury has royally screwed up, as was definitely the case in this trial. They disregarded conclusive evidence exonerating you. Bondurant stepped in to prevent an egregious miscarriage of justice, a classic railroad job. He's a good judge."

"I'm not complaining. But . . . what's to stop Kellenberger from trying me again?"

"ORS one thirty-one, the statute against double jeopardy. You can't be tried twice on the same charge. You're a free woman, Andie, in the eyes of the law as innocent as a newborn babe."

"Congratulations," Phoebe said.

"Of course," Eli said, "Kellenberger has the right to appeal the ruling, but I don't think he will. He'd be crazy to. Besides, he'll probably have his hands full attending to other matters. Such as trying to avoid going to jail."

She glanced at Kellenberger. Urbandictionary.com could use his face to illustrate the definition of *bummed out*.

In all the excitement the Fiat brochure had fallen on the floor. She picked it up and made a decision.

It had to be the red one.

62

On the last day of September, Andie drove west into the waning sun on Sunset Highway, en route to Thomason's Fiat on Southwest Canyon Road. But she couldn't shake the feeling that she was being followed. She took the Canyon Road exit and then pulled over and let a half-dozen cars go by. The eerie feeling returned after she started moving again.

The dealership was only a few miles farther.

On a long, straight stretch an older tan pickup passed her and pulled into the lane ahead of her. The gun rack in its back window held two AR-15s, like the one Kayla's boyfriend owned. The window had a sticker, a frog wearing a helmet.

A shiny black SUV passed her and pulled up even with the tan pickup, matching its speed.

The man driving the pickup lifted a walkie-talkie to his mouth. The two vehicles slowed in unison.

She had no choice but to apply the brakes. Were they just a couple of jerks, or what?

The pickup and SUV continued to slow down.

When their speed dropped under thirty, she said, "Screw this," and tried to pass the pickup on the shoulder.

The pickup moved over, cutting her off.

In the rear view mirror, a car approached from behind, a welcome sight. When the SUV moved over to let it through, she'd be right on the car's tail.

But the car didn't try to pass her. It came up directly behind her, almost touching her back bumper, effectively boxing her in.

It felt as though icy needles were prickling every pore in her body, the same sensation she'd felt in the alley. Once would have been enough.

The three-vehicle pincers brought her to a complete stop.

She locked the doors. A lot of good that would do. They'd just shatter a window with a tire iron.

God help me, I wish I had one of those AR-15s in my hands right now. Fear swept away the pang of guilt.

Four men piled out of the three vehicles, two from the car. All wore camo shirts and pants, black combat boots, and red "Make America Great Again" caps that topped white-sidewall haircuts.

They didn't need to break a window. One of them slipped a Slim-Jim down her side window and unlocked the door.

They pulled her out and dragged her over to the SUV. Her rag-doll lack of cooperation had no effect. They zip tied her wrists behind her back. Then they stuffed her in the back seat, zip tied her ankles, and slammed the door.

The driver got behind the wheel and then turned around and inspected her for several seconds as though he were examining a prize. "Comfortable?" he asked, grinning. He had an underslung jaw.

With the zip tie cutting into her wrists, "comfortable" was not the word she'd choose to describe how she felt. She wriggled into a sitting position—a challenge, with her arms behind her—so she could see better. A tree-shaped deodorizer dangled from the rear view mirror. It must have been brand new; the scent of pine was so heavy it almost gagged her.

She looked out the side window. One of the men got in the foundation's Prius and drove off. Tires squealing, the SUV took off after it. The pickup and car followed them.

Minutes later the Fiat dealership flashed by on the left. Sitting in the front row, gleaming under the lights, a red Fiat. Possibly the very one she would have picked.

Her chances of seeing the car again faded with each passing mile. But she had a more pressing concern: staying alive. And that would entail getting away from these camo-clad assholes.

The sun had set by the time they reached Beaverton. The caravan, white Prius in the lead, slowed to thirty-five. They weren't going to take any chances on being stopped.

The traffic light up ahead turned yellow. She edged over to the door and leaned her back against it. If she contorted a bit, the handle was within reach. Assuming she could feel it— her hands were numb from the tight zip tie—she could open the door. Then she could tumble out onto the asphalt and yell for help. People were all around, in vehicles and on foot. Surely someone would see or hear her and come to her aid. It was her best chance to get away. It might be her last.

The SUV stopped at the red light. She groped for the handle, located it, and gave it a good yank. To her surprise, the door wouldn't open, no matter how hard she pulled at the handle.

Damn.

The driver laughed, a braying sound, his eyes in the rear-view mirror. He'd observed her futile struggle. "Child-proof doors and windows," he said. "But nice try." Then he opened the center console, took something out, and showed it to her. "Fifty-thousand-volt taser. Hurts like hell, and I speak from first-hand experience. 'Nuff said?"

So she sat back and waited.

They passed though town. Strip malls gave way to groves of trees. The driver raised a walkie-talkie to his mouth. "Jesus Christ, how far is this 'perfect spot,' Vogel?"

"*Keep your shirt on. We're just about there,*" came the reply.

Ten minutes later the caravan pulled up next to a wooded area. Her driver got out, came around, and opened her door. Then he pulled her out and slung her over his shoulder like a sack of wheat. She'd been hoping he'd cut the zip tie around her ankles. She might've gotten a chance to make a run for it. Even Usain Bolt wouldn't have been able to catch her.

Carrying military lanterns, the group entered the woods and tramped through brush and trees until they reached a clearing. The one carrying her dumped her on the dry, hard ground. Then he massaged his shoulder.

One of the others laughed. "What's the matter, Taggart—too heavy for you?"

Taggart flipped him off. "Screw you, Vogel."

"Knock it off, you guys."

"Yes, sir, Mr. Ayers, sir," Vogel said. "Anyway, this is the place. That's the tree I had in mind." He pointed to a large elm.

Ayers seemed to be the leader. "It'll do. McNutt, do you have the rope Pike gave you before they snatched him?"

"Right here." McNutt tossed the coil over one of the tree's lower limbs. It uncoiled in a spiral dance that became a noose swinging slowly back and forth.

Ayers, McNutt, Vogel, and Taggart. She memorized the names on the infinitesimally tiny chance she made it out alive.

"Stand the tranny up," Ayers said.

Vogel grabbed her under the armpits from behind and lifted her to her feet. McNutt slipped the noose over her head and pulled it snug around her throat.

The four men formed a semicircle with her in the center.

"This tribunal is now in session," Ayers said. "Since the liberal court system failed to mete out justice, it is up to us to correct matters. Our verdict is guilty. The sentence is execution by hanging, to be carried out immediately."

It had been building in her since they dragged her out of the car. Not fear nor panic nor sorrow—an icy anger, mixed with a strange calm.

"Does the condemned have any last words?"

"Damn right I do," she said. She looked at each one in turn. "Look at you. What a pack of screwups. All dressed up like badasses in camo and combat boots, but then you spoil the effect with those silly Trump caps." She laughed at them. "All that's missing is the propellers."

Taggart started toward her, hand raised to backhand her, but Ayers stopped him.

"Boys playing soldier, pretending you're brave warriors. Pathetic. Have any of you seen actual combat? My dad did two tours in Afghanistan. *He* was a soldier. *He* was a brave warrior. He would've kicked all your wimp asses." They were going to lynch her no matter what she said, so might as well tear them a new one.

She saw red faces and bulging jaw muscles, but she wasn't done yet. "You're hoping I'll cry and beg for my life? Go to hell. I'm just sorry I have to die at the hands of a bunch of beanie-wearing dickweeds like you. It's embarrassing."

"You finished?" Ayers said. "Vogel, cut that zip tie." He pointed to her ankles. "I want to see this tranny dance in the air, like the other one did."

Vogel kneeled down and snipped the zip tie and then her legs were free. When he stood, she hauled off and kicked him squarely in the testicles, hard enough to lift him off his feet. He bent over, coughing.

The back of Taggart's hand cracked across her mouth. It stung like hell, but she laughed anyway. "Dude, you slap like a girl."

Taggart lunged toward her, his face contorted with fury, but Ayers blocked him again. "Let's get on with it," he said and nodded to McNutt.

McNutt took up the slack and pulled.

The noose tightened, constricting her throat. She stood on tiptoe to lessen the pressure.

"Bit of a problem here," McNutt said. "There's not enough rope to tie around the tree trunk."

She laughed. "Like I said, a pack of screwups."

"Goddamn it," Ayers said. "Vogel, get over there and help McNutt with that rope."

Pulling together, Vogel and McNutt lifted her three feet off the ground. She tensed her neck and shoulder muscles to delay the inevitable.

Our Father who art in heaven, hallowed be thy name. Thy kingdom come, thy will be done on earth as it is in heaven. Give us this day our daily bread, and forgive us our trespasses as we for—

"Drop that rope." The sound of a shotgun being racked followed the command. The gruff voice had come from the darkness outside the circle of light cast by the lanterns. It spoke again. "I want to see hands in the air."

The rope slackened and her feet landed on the ground. The noose was still tight, but she could breathe okay.

"Better do as he says." A different voice in the darkness, it had come from the other side of the light circle. "We got you completely surrounded."

"Who's there?" Ayers said. "Show yourselves."

"If I don't see four pairs of hands in the air in two seconds," the gruff voice said, "I'm going to start blasting."

Her captors raised their hands.

Off in the distance, faint sirens grew louder with each passing second.

"This shotgun's got a hair trigger, so just stand there nice and quiet until I say different."

Sirens descended on the area from both directions. Lights emerged from the woods into the clearing. Sheriff's deputies, perhaps a dozen of them.

She stood and watched, enjoying the oh-shit expressions on her former captors' faces.

"Over here, Sergeant." The gruff voice belonged to a burly man with jowls and a receding hairline. He held the shotgun with one hand while he popped a stick of gum in his mouth.

"Pomerenke?" A tall black deputy with sergeant's stripes walked over to him. "You called it in?"

Pomerenke gestured with the shotgun barrel. "These four skells were lynching that girl. I stopped them." He took out his wallet. "Here's my P.I. identification."

While the sergeant checked out his ID, deputies photographed the scene, including shots of her standing with her hands tied behind her back and the noose around her neck.

"Hello?" she said. "A little help here?" A deputy loosened the noose and slipped it off. He snipped the zip tie around her wrists. A deep mauve color suffused her swollen hands. They tingled, not totally numb. Surely that was a good sign?

"Are you okay, Miss McInnes?" Pomerenke carried the shotgun in the crook of his arm like a duck hunter.

"Yes, thanks to you."

"I saw those three vehicles follow you when you left, so my associate and I jumped in his car and took off after you. I was watching though binoculars when they stopped you and yanked you out of your car. By that time I had already phoned the sheriff."

A skinny guy walked up, packing a gun the size of a cannon in a shoulder holster. "We did it, Neil. We got the drop on those dirtbags."

"Miss McInnes, this is Mr. Millican, my associate."

"Mr. Millican," she said, "thank you so much."

More sirens arrived.

A woman emerged from the woods and had to stand aside to let a procession of deputies pass with the handcuffed prisoners. She walked over to Andie. "Are you all right, hon?"

"I'm fine, Detective Wojanowski. Isn't this way out of your jurisdiction?"

"The sheriff's office knows I'm the lead on the Casey Ryan lynching, so they called me. Listen, I'm going to go talk to the sergeant for a minute."

Massaging her hands, Andie went over to Pomerenke and Millican. "I can't thank you enough. If not for you two I'd be dead, no doubt about it."

Millican did something strange with his upper lip, as though trying to dislodge a seed from between his front teeth. "All in a day's work for a P.I."

Pomerenke scowled. "Shut up, Gordo. You're welcome, ma'am." He shoved a fresh stick of gum in his mouth. Juicy Fruit flavored the air. "But no way would we have made it in time if you hadn't sounded off to those skells. While we were coming through the woods I was praying you'd keep talking."

"They didn't much like what I had to say, but I was past the point of caring."

"I'd sure like to have seen their faces. Anyway, it saved your life."

"Do they belong to some kind of goofy militia?"

"Yeah. They're a loose-knit bunch of hard-right assholes—pardon my French, Miss McInnes."

"No problem." She'd spoken that kind of French for years.

Two men wearing vests with FBI stenciled on the front and back came out of the woods. One of them picked up a stick and used it to scrape something off the sole of his shoe.

"Feds," Wojanowski said, inclining her head toward them. "They elbowed us aside when we nabbed Delbert Pike. The Washington County Sheriff has got Pike's four buddies in custody now. But not for long."

"Too bad," Pomerenke said. "It was a good bust."

Wojanowski turned to him. "Mr. Pomerenke, you are a hero. I salute you."

His smile exposed nicotine-stained teeth. "Thank you."

Millican nudged him with an elbow.

Pomerenke sighed. "And Mr. Millican deserves a share of the credit."

"Thank you, Neil," Millican said, "but I don't care about getting credit. Just knowing that I helped someone is reward enough."

Pomerenke glared at him for several seconds and then turned back to Wojanowski. "Detective, I know you're aware that we've been surveilling the Transcend Foundation. I feel kind of awkward, under the circumstances."

"No need. If you hadn't been watching, Andie would be swinging from that tree. You were just doing what your client wanted done. Hope you're getting a fat fee."

He smiled again.

She turned to Andie. "What do you say we get out of here? The sergeant said you can give your statement tomorrow."

"I'm ready to go," Andie said. "Totally, completely ready."

On the ride home, one thought kept nagging at her. The strange, cool anger she'd felt—it might have come directly from God. From the Almighty, the Lord, the Creator Himself.

Not long ago she would've laughed at that. But now she couldn't rule it out.

Because something miraculous had happened back in that clearing. She'd been angry plenty of times, but never like that —cold, calm, without fear, without the slightest concern for consequences.

Yea, though I walk though the Valley of Death, I shall fear no evil, for Thou art with me.

Twice now—three times, counting the trial—she'd escaped certain doom. Vegas oddsmakers lay thousand-to-one odds against a streak of luck like that.

So what was she supposed to do now, walk the earth wearing sackcloth and ashes?

Tooling down the road in a red Fiat, wearing a big grin— that was more her style.

God would know that.

And He'd approve, she was sure of it.

63

Seventeen-knot October winds whipped up more chop than Ritter had wanted to see on the Columbia River. It put the kibosh on smooth sailing. And if the darkening clouds made good on their threat, they might have to make a run for the home berth back at Tomahawk Bay Marina. The winds had an upside, though—Aquamancer's jib was sufficient to move them along at a good clip.

Nicole didn't seem to mind, or even notice, the sailboat's washboard ride. She was busy speed-reading Aquamancer's instrument manuals, her expression intent.

When she first came aboard she inspected the craft from stem to stern—literally—quizzing him about the operation of the autopilot, heading sensor, and wind gauge, peppering him with questions about transducers, anemometers, and gyro-controlled fluxgates. Questions for which he could not produce satisfactory answers. He'd handed her the stack of manuals and told her, "Knock yourself out."

Her expression had been that of a child reaching for an ice cream cone.

With her hair tied back and her face in profile, Nicole looked more like an Egyptian princess on a Nile barge than a technonerd extraordinaire. And to think he'd been tongue-tied around her.

She closed the manual and looked up. "Fascinating."

"It certainly is." He didn't mean the manual.

She caught it. "Is my interest in such things off-putting?"

"No. Awe-inspiring and maybe a bit intimidating, but not off-putting."

"It has made men run away for the hills."

"Some men are threatened by women who aren't simpering airheads. To hell with 'em. What do you say we let the autopilot steer the boat while we whip up some lunch?"

"I say *oui*."

He led the way below, to the galley. They made small talk while they assembled two roast beef sandwiches, a cooperative effort. Technonerd lingo spoken with a French accent had a certain charm, things like "Zee hot mustaird exceeds comfort parameters of my gastronomic subsystem." (It's too hot.)

The wind hadn't slacked off, so they ate in the nook next to the galley.

"How is Andie," she asked between bites, "now that the trial is behind her?"

"Enjoying her job screening applicants at the Transcend Foundation. She just started the fall term at Portland State. Oh—and she bought a new car and adopted a shelter dog. What about you? Anything interesting going on in your slice of the space-time continuum?"

"Mad props for that. Here is something that is interesting. Jason Sepers cornered me in the lunch room the other day and acted super-ultra-mega friendly, trying to sound me out. I played dumb."

"He's worried. He should be. Tampering with evidence and obstruction of justice carry jail time."

"You must serve the time if you perform the crime?"

"Right. Seper's brother-in-law, Kellenberger, will face both charges, plus suborning perjury. He's looking at disbarment and a prison sentence. O how the mighty have fallen."

"Two Samuel one twenty-five."

"Are you religious, Nicole?"

"I have read the bible, both testaments. Ancient tribal storytelling. So the brothers-in-law have been charged?"

"Charges are imminent. Judge Bondurant has ordered the D.A. to impanel a grand jury to probe the matter. I predict indictments will be forthcoming."

"I very much like that German word *schadenfreude*. Taking pleasure in an adversary's troubles."

It perfectly described his feeling about Vernon Trollinger. The Troll's face probably fell like a soufflé when Strother Moore demanded his resignation. He had alienated people right and left at the firm, but when he pissed off Moore, a founding partner, that was the final curtain. Even being Cannady's son-in-law couldn't save his ass.

He collected the plates, washed them, stowed them back in the cupboard. Ship's rule: No dirty dishes in the sink or on the counter.

"When you said you lived on a sailboat, I thought you were a crazy person. But it is very nice, and remarkably roomy."

"My dad designed it to be beamy, twelve feet in width. Most sailboats this length are barely ten. He didn't have time to enjoy it, though. Bladder cancer got him a year after he finished building it, a ten-year labor of love."

"I am sorry. By trade he was a boatbuilder?"

"Nope, a janitor. But sailing was his passion." He peered though a porthole. "Look at that. The sun's out."

They went topside. Not only was the sun shining, the wind had diminished considerably. The river's surface was smooth and the hovering mist had dissipated, revealing the tree-lined shores on the Washington side a mile and a half away. A decent October afternoon, after an uninspiring morning.

"Look over there," she said, pointing. "Another sailboat."

"A sloop. Maybe forty foot, under full sail. As we will be soon." He unfastened the mainsail and mizzen and handed her the smaller sail's halyard. "This line raises the mizzen. Care to do the honors?"

She answered with a determined pull on the line. Wind began filling the sail before she had it fully raised. "Eli," she said, "I have successfully deployed the mizzing thing. What do I do with this rope?"

He took the line from her and secured it to a cleat. Then he raised the mainsail.

"Hey," she said, "that gave us much more speed."

Wind was blowing from due west at nine knots. He gave in to the urge to show off and put Aquamancer though its paces: close haul, beam reach, broad reach, and running downwind. The equivalent of cutting cookies in a parking lot. Perhaps he should have done some handstands while he was at it.

But the adolescent display had the desired effect. "It is almost like flying," she said, clearly enjoying the sensation. "Can we overtake that sloop?"

He shook his head. "Not likely."

"Why? He has only two sails while we have three. Does that not give us a propulsion advantage?"

"No, because his two sails have about the same area as our three. And the sloop has a racing hull. A wide beam is a disadvantage when it comes to speed."

"That is logical."

They were about four miles from the marina. Time to head back. After setting the rigging for downwind running and engaging the autopilot, he went back and sat beside her. From time to time he stole glances at her regal profile.

She caught him looking. "You are doing it again."

"What's that?"

"The way you look at me sometimes, it is how the bloodhound looks at the moon."

"Is it that obvious?"

She gave him side eye.

"Want to hear something funny? When I first met you I was so tongue-tied I could only jabber."

"Tourette's, I assumed. So what has untied your tongue?"

"Not sure." Tourette's? She knew how to draw blood.

"Let us make certain that it stays unbound."

He searched her face. "What do you mean?"

She leaned over and kissed him lightly and briefly on the lips. Then she sat back and rested her head on his shoulder. He put his arm around her. Neither of them spoke for a time.

A half-mile from the marina he got up—reluctantly—and downhauled the mizzen and mainsail, fastened them to their booms, and secured all lines, leaving only the jib for motive power. Five minutes later he took down the jib and started Aquamancer's small diesel engine.

In the marina's waterway they motored past a formation of boats in their covered slips until they came to F-18, Aquamancer's home berth. He eased it into the slip and shut off the engine. Then he hopped onto the dock and fastened the bow and stern lines. For good measure he used a spring line. Extending the gangplank came last.

He hopped back on the boat and grinned at her. "So now you've been sailing. What do you think?"

"I think I am hooked, Eli."

"Me, too." He wasn't referring to sailing.

"It is getting late," she said. "I should be going."

He leaned over and kissed her, not lightly, not briefly.

She smiled at him after they separated. "Thank you for a lovely afternoon, Eli." Then she started down the gangplank. On the dock she turned and waved.

He watched her until she was out of sight and then went below and exchanged his windbreaker for a sweater. His lips still tingled from the kiss.

After pouring a glass of Merlot and cutting a slice of sharp cheddar, he went topside to double-check the lines.

She was standing silently at the foot of the gangplank, her lovely brow furrowed.

He called out, "Did you leave something behind?"

She walked up the gangplank to him. "In a manner of speaking," she said and presented her mouth to be kissed.

She didn't have to twist his arm.

64

The parking area was only partly full, a relief. She chose a space as far from the entrance as possible. Avoiding dings meant not parking next to other cars. The thought of some careless dillweed dooring her brand-new baby made her wince.

"C'mon, Leto," she said, snapping the lead on his harness. She opened the door and got out. Leto hopped out after her. The cherry-red Fiat gleamed in the afternoon sun. She whisked a speck off its headlamp and then stood back and admired her Italian beauty before proceeding across the Historic Columbia River Highway at the crosswalk. On the other side she took a selfie in front of the sign.

MULTNOMAH
FALLS
COLUMBIA RIVER GORGE
NATIONAL SCENIC AREA

On the right was the Multnomah Falls Lodge, built of stone. Opened in 1925, according to the plaque in front. Gift shop and restaurant seemed to be doing a brisk business. Maybe later Leto could guard the car while she grabbed a quick bite in the restaurant. First, though, they had a waterfall to see.

At the start of the trail to the falls, another sign: "DOGS MUST REMAIN ON LEASH AT ALL TIMES."

No problem there. The retractable lead gave Leto twenty-six feet of tether, not that he ran very far or fast with those stubby legs of his.

They set off for the falls, Leto in the lead. He ran from scent to scent beside the trail, his long nose twitching nonstop. So many smells, so little time. He expressed his joy with a doggie grin.

A middle-aged couple came walking down the trail toward them. Andie reeled Leto in.

"Such a cutie!" the woman said. "What breed is he?"

"A long-haired dachshund."

"Love his fuzzy face. How old is he?"

"About two." At least, that's what the shelter told her.

"So sweet." The woman bent down, reaching out and cooing at him.

Leto growled and showed her his fangs.

She jumped back as though from a rattlesnake.

"I'm so sorry," Andie said, too late to warn the woman not to try to pet him. "He's a bit cranky."

"I'll say." She and her companion moved on.

Andie looked down at Leto. "That's no way to win friends and influence people."

He resumed sniffing things alongside the trail.

Crankiness was a significant improvement over his disposition at the shelter. He'd been in the last pen in the last row. There, he'd sat trembling, hiding his head in the corner, doing his best to disappear.

"A stray," the shelter worker said. "He's been abused. Any attempt to touch him sets off hysterical crying and frantic attempts to get away."

"I want to adopt him," Andie said.

"Are you sure?" The shelter worker's eyes widened.

"Positive. He's going home with me."

And so he did, in a molded plastic crate, burrowed under a flannel blanket.

In the apartment she left the crate's door open but made no attempt to coax him out. She diced some leftover steak and put it in a bowl, filled another bowl with water, and put them outside the door.

Two hours later he was eating out of her hand. He even let her attach a leash to his collar. He'd stopped trembling.

"C'mon, sweetie, let's go outside so you can get busy."

Fighting the leash at first, he relented and saluted a dwarf Alberta spruce.

Back inside, she ignored him. She wrote in her journal, did a school assignment, and cooked dinner. He hunkered down in the crate, slinking out once for water. Later she enticed him out with pieces of chicken breast. Before she went to bed she took him outside again.

In the morning he poked his head out of the crate while she was fixing his breakfast.

"I dub thee Leto," she said as she set his food down. "What do you think of your new name?"

He was too busy scarfing to answer.

After breakfast Leto explored the apartment, sniffing every nook and cranny.

Two weeks later he was sleeping with her in bed at night, burrowed under the bedspread, snuggled up next to her. She took him for walks around the foundation grounds and rides in the car when she went to the store.

But he was always on guard, as though he expected her to flip out at any moment and start beating him.

It was a trust issue.

Even now he kept a suspicious eye on her. She sat down on a stone bench beside the trail and he hopped up and sat beside her. He permitted her to pet him. Progress.

"You and me, we were two strays alone in the world," she told him, stroking his soft brown fur. "Now we're packmates. Whatever happens, we've got each other."

He scratched his ear, mouth stretched with effort.

She stood. "C'mon, Leto, let's go see the tallest waterfall in Oregon."

A gray squirrel darted across the trail ahead of them and Leto went after it, barking as he ran. Not the kind of loud, shrill bark that sets teeth on edge and makes enemies of neighbors, it had a hoarse, chiding quality. He lectured the squirrel and then waddled back to her.

"Good work," she said. "Now let's move on."

She could feel it before it came into view; the roar shook the ground. The sight of it justified the sound. The waterfall was six hundred twenty feet of cascading awesomeness, a megafalls consisting of two tiers—the tall upper falls fell into a large, deep pool that flowed out into lower falls. A concrete footbridge traversed the falls a hundred feet above the dark pool.

Standing in the center of the bridge, she looked over the railing, and a rush of vertigo made her recoil. A fall from that height would be fatal. She touched the silver crucifix hanging around her neck, a celebratory gift to herself.

A robin swooped down over the water, reminding her of Gapey. Almost fully grown now, he paid her regular visits, usually when she went for a run. She always praised him extravagantly, complimenting his shiny gray plumage and fiery reddish-orange breast, and he would preen for her.

Leto pawed her leg. The bridge didn't interest him.

The bracelet caught her eye. *Non credere.* She unclasped it and bounced it in her hand a few times. Then she wound up as though throwing a baseball and hurled it as hard as she could. It sailed out in a long arc and disappeared into the pool below, hardly disturbing the surface.

She bent down to hug her sweet dog.

Leto growled and bared his teeth at her. The trust issue again.

"That's okay," she said. "You'll get over it."

THE END

Also by T.J. McCandless

DEEP STEALTH

A young woman is carjacked in a downtown Portland parking lot. The thief bashes her on the head, hard enough to put her in a coma for a month and disconnect her memories, leaving only vague impressions. The doctors say her memory loss is probably temporary. In which case, she has nothing to worry about.

Nothing except a serial killer, a religious fanatic who mutilates his victims. When she learns why he's stalking her, it leads to a startling revelation: The amnesia is a blessing, not a curse.

A fast-paced thriller that will challenge preconceptions.

About the Author

T.J. McCandless is currently touring the country in a motor coach, accompanied by an obstreperous terrier. When not writing spine-tingling thrillers, McCandless enjoys exploring places that are off the beaten path, always on the lookout for intriguing locales for future novels.

Before you go . . .

If you enjoyed *Vital Sins*, please let your friends know about it though Facebook, Twitter, or by making good, old-fashioned chin music. And if you're so inclined, T.J. would be honored if you would leave a review. Here's a link to the book's Amazon page:

https://www.amazon.com/dp/0986395730/